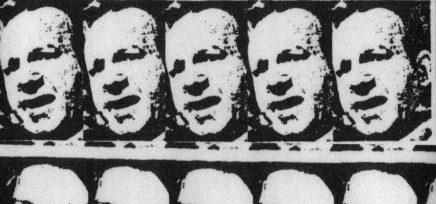

MW01001981

JACK RUBY & THE ORIGINS OF THE AVANT-GARDE IN DALLAS

& Other Stories

ROBERT TRAMMELL

DEEP VELLUM PUBLISHING
Dallas, Texas

Deep Vellum is a 501c3 nonprofit literary arts organization
founded in 2013 with the mission to bring
the world into conversation through literature.

David Searcy's "Science Fictions #3: Bob Goes to Live Under Mary Kay's Pink Cadillac,"
originally appeared in *Shame and Wonder: Essays*, and is reprinted here with permission
from Penguin Random House.

"Ingrained" first appeared in *Southwest Review*, Vol. 89, No. 4 (2004).
"One Turns to One (Walter Cronkite's Head)" first appeared in *Southwest Review*,
    Vol. 106, No. 1 (2021).

Support for this publication has been provided in part by the Summerfield G. Roberts
Foundation and Wordspace.

ISBNs: 978-1-64605-049-9 (paperback) | 978-1-64605-050-5 (ebook)

LIBRARY OF CONGRESS CATALOGING IN PUBLICATION DATA

Names: Trammell, Robert, 1939– author.
Title: Jack Ruby & the origins of the avant-garde in Dallas : and other stories / Robert
Trammell.
Description: First Deep Vellum edition. | Dallas, Texas : Deep Vellum, 2021.
Identifiers: LCCN 2021040325 | ISBN 9781646050499 (trade paperback) | ISBN
    9781646050505 (ebook)
Subjects: LCGFT: Short stories.
Classification: LCC PS3570.R3345 J33 2021 | DDC 813/.54—dc23
LC record available at https://lccn.loc.gov/2021040325

Cover design by Justin Childress | justinchildress.co

Interior Layout and Typesetting by KGT

PRINTED IN THE UNITED STATES OF AMERICA

**This book contains explicit content and
pejorative language, including racial slurs.**

contents

Editor's Note   vii

Foreword by Ben Fountain   1

Jack Ruby & the Origins
   of the Avant-Garde in Dallas   5

The Quiet Man Stories   89

Afterword by David Searcy   349

Editor's Note

Several editions of *Jack Ruby & the Origins of the Avant-Garde in Dallas* were privately printed by Robert Trammell under the Barnburner Press imprimatur. The earliest dates from 1987; the latest, on which this text is based, 2001.

In addition to revising the text and altering the design of *Jack Ruby & the Origins of the Avant-Garde in Dallas* with each printing, Trammell altered the book's dimensions. The 1987 edition measures 11 inches by 4.25 inches—equivalent to a standard sheet of US letter-size paper folded in half along its vertical axis. One might even call these dimensions pamphlet-like.

By comparison, the 2001 edition is more pocket-sized, measuring 4.25 inches by 5.5 inches. It also sports a stiff, laminated cover, much like a guidebook that, frequently consulted, is at serious risk of wearing and tearing. Despite these differences, both editions evoke those Xeroxed treatises, manifestos, and noncanonical histories circulated by assassination enthusiasts in and around Dealey Plaza.

Accordingly, every effort has been made to preserve the layout and pagination of the 2001 edition. Where preservation was not possible, key aspects of the text have been translated for presentation in this format.

The Quiet Man Stories remained unpublished in Robert Trammell's lifetime. However, he clearly conceived of them as a collection. He had extensively revised the majority of these pieces, sequenced them, and drafted a table of contents. "Ingrained" was not included in the manuscript on which the present text is based, but we have incorporated it here as it was composed around the same time and in the same mode as *The Quiet Man Stories.*

—Joe Milazzo

Foreword

"Myth," wrote Maya Deren, "is the facts of the mind made manifest in a fiction of matter." This formula, more powerful than nuclear fission for creating world historical forces, gets a workout when applied to Robert Trammell, born a fifth-generation Texan on 9-9-39, nine days after the start of the Second World War. Myth, facts, mind, matter, the lines blur even before Bob arrived on the scene. One of his ancestors was an East Texas grandee by the name of George Washington Trammell; another, a business associate of the pirate Jean Lafitte, was known as "Hot Horse" for running liberated horses north from the Gulf on Trammell's Trace, a frontier trail memorialized somewhere out there by an official Texas Historical Commission marker. Bob's sister Billye Sue once told me of how she and Bob ended up in an orphanage despite their parents being very much alive and well, and how Bob, already possessed of an inclination to light out for the territory, was planning to run away but ultimately didn't, unable to bear the thought of abandoning his little sister to a crowd that butchered her hair so severely that she covered the bald spots with shoe polish. A few years later, after being separated from his foster family at the Texas State Fair, Bob would navigate his way home on foot by taking his bearings off the red neon Pegasus at the top of the Magnolia Building, at the time the most prominent feature on the Dallas skyline. Later still, while a student at SMU, Bob—bearded and pony-tailed by then—was crossing Hillcrest Avenue and nearly run down by a Cadillac driven by none other than H. L. Hunt, reputedly the richest man in the world and certainly one of the most militant conservatives America has ever produced. Perhaps Bob never actually lived for a while under Mary Kay Ash's pink Cadillac, but he did squat for several months in the public library of Oslo, Norway, and would go on to create a mini-replica of East Texas's Big Thicket in his yard on Mecca Street (yes, he lived on Mecca, one of the shortest streets in Dallas), and got the city code inspectors off his back by giving them a guided tour of his urban jungle, naming each and every plant and its role in the landscape's grand scheme. Did Bob ever go on a Grail-like quest through the Big Thicket in search of Lightnin', legendary maker of transcendent barbecue? What we know for sure is Bob was arrested, tried, and convicted in Dallas in the late 1960s for possessing two thimbles' worth of pot. Sentenced to hard time in a prison no one would mistake for a country club, he survived, discovering the books of Donald Barthelme in the prison library and hitting thirteen jumpshots in a row during an inmate basketball game. The Barnburner Press edition of *Jack Ruby & the*

Origins of the Avant-Garde in Dallas enjoyed robust sales among assassination "buffs" under the impression they were buying a strictly factual account of events, and one wonders how many rabbit holes were plumbed as readers followed the interweaving tales of Jack Ruby, "the situation over at the art museum," the murder of the president, and Charlie Starkweather's bloody tear across the American heartland.

Fictions of matter making manifest the facts of the mind. Sane minds necessarily boggle at the scale and depravity of the act, the murder of a president in broad daylight, in front of thousands, in the center of a major American city. How to make sense of that? How to speak the unspeakable; how to know, or at least grope our way toward knowing, what's essentially unknowable. In desperation we look to the myth that tells us the truth of ourselves, and *Jack Ruby & the Origins of the Avant-Garde in Dallas* is whole truth, nothing but.

Ben Fountain
Dallas
April 2021

*B*efore Jack Ruby's starspangled action Dallas never had any notions about being an International City. The Dallas Museum of Fine Arts had said We don't want to have anything made by International Communists like Picasso and Rivera. The museum board issued a statement: It is not our policy knowingly to acquire or to exhibit the work of a person known by us to be now a Communist or of Communist-Front affiliation.

The Family of Man was in trouble. The trustees got concerned because there were photos by Soviet photographers in the show.

Jack Ruby was not then on the museum board.

Jack Ruby is worried. The Colony Club has Chris Colt, the Girl with the 45s. She is taking business away from his Carousel Club. Royal Earl, the Man with the Talking Guitar, is pulling rock 'n' roll customers from Jack's Vegas Club over to Jimmy's Club. Jack is putting on weight. But what is really getting to him is the situation over at the museum.

It was making Dallas an international laughingstock.
He has to do something. He makes some phone calls.
The museum backs off.

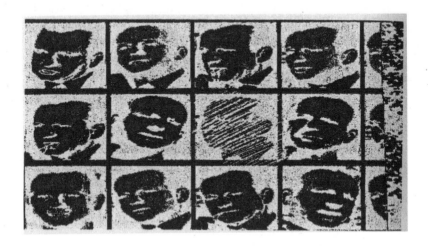

Members of
THE SOUTHWESTERN MEMORIAL ASSOCIATION,
THE DAUGHTERS OF THE AMERICAN
REVOLUTION, THE DAUGHTERS OF 1812, THE
MATHEON CLUB, THE INWOOD LIONS CLUB,
THE BASSETT ART CLUB, THE OAK CLIFF ART
ASSOCIATION, THE FEDERATION OF DALLAS
ARTISTS, THE KLEPPER CLUB, THE REAUGH
ART CLUB, THE VETERANS OF FOREIGN WARS,
THE AMERICAN LEGION (METROPOLITAN POST),
THE PUBLIC AFFAIRS LUNCHEON, THE PRO-
AMERICAN AND THE 1950 STUDY CLUB AND
JOHN MAYO, CHAIRMAN OF THE COMMUNISM-
IN-ARTS COMMITTEE OF THE DALLAS COUNTY
PATRIOTIC COUNCIL
agree to meet with Jack.

Museum Says Reds Can Stay

We are in Bill's '49 Mercury, lowered with Henry J grill, Glass Pac mufflers with a cutout switch, rolled 'n' pleated seats and razor blades welded inside the Fender skirts to cut the fingers off anyone who might try to steal them.

What cha goin to do bout nine o'clock?
Have you heard the news that we goin to rock/
Yes, we going to rock, Clyde McPhatter sings on the radio.

Bill has on a brown suede jacket over his white T-shirt.
I got on my black corduroy Cornel Wilde one.
Mike has his black motorcycle jacket with white sleeves on.

Down at the Carousel the first show is about to begin.

The comedian is nervous tonight.

He sings You don't know what lonesome is until you get to punchin' cows. Have you ever punched a cow? Well, that's lonesome. Have you?

Jack stands in the EXIT sign light takes his billfold out and takes out of that a well-folded picture. He tries to focus on it in the dim, red light. He nearly cries. He cries a lot. He's known for crying but don't dare ask him why he's crying. He feels a twisting inside of himself. From his belly a hot thick liquid boils up into his mouth.

He sees stars.

He bends down and wipes a bit of dirt off his Stacy Adams alligators.

His confidence returns.

TESTIMONY OF CHARLIE STARKWEATHER

Chief Deputy Fahrnbruch later asked Charlie what took place with the King girl after Bob stopped breathing.
Charlie answered Temptation.
What did you do?
Well, I pulled her jeans down, but I didn't screw her.
What did you do to her?
Nothing.
Charlie, you've told the officers different, haven't you?
I didn't screw her . . . I couldn't get to the point . . . it was colder than hell . . . I left her laying there and left . . . I didn't screw her. I'll argue that with you all night long, too.
Later he said I told him I screwed the shit out of that King girl.

You also told him that you went in the rear end?
No.
Well, didn't you screw her?
No. I didn't do nothing to her.
Nobody'd brought up yet the stiletto mutilation job that his girlfriend Caril'd done on the King girl's asshole and cunt?

The lights burned late into the night in the office of the director of the Dallas Museum of Fine Art.

Men slumped and hurried in shadows up stairs and down in jerky quick steps they entered and left the museum.

*E*arlier that day Jack had met a weaselly little guy in Sol's Turf Bar who claimed to be an expert on the International Avant-Garde. He wanted money. Jack said Let's talk. The weaselly guy said Meet me at eight in the morning two days from now in the lobby of the old Texas picture show out in Oak Cliff.

Jack said It won't be open so early.

Look, the guy shot back. Are you interested in a wider view or am I wasting my time?

It was dark in the Texas Theatre's lobby that morning but the door was not locked.

The weaselly guy said This isn't a good place. Meet me tonight at the bowling alley down the street by the donut shop.

At seven.

Shouts of men crash of pins buy beer country & western music playing under the cover of that he said Read this Jack.

> *There can be no real and effective "freedom" in a society based on the power of money, in a society in which the masses of working people live in poverty and the handful of rich live like parasites . . . One cannot live in society and be free from society. The freedom of the bourgeois writer, artist, or actress is simply masked (or hypocritically masked) dependence on the moneybag, on corruption on prostitution.*

Lenin? Right? Jack asked.
It was clear in his mind before it was in anyone else's in Dallas what it meant to be an International City.
He headed out to the Museum.

An Oak Cliff thug said

I was witness to several stabbings and a shooting at the Texas Theatre. One boy attending South Oak Cliff carried a sawed-off shotgun in his car and occasionally used it to blast cars whose drivers wanted to drag race with him. It saved him from having to spend a lot of money to make his car fast. Gangs with names like Lakewood Rats and the Jim Town Gang fought with chains and jagged beer bottles on the grassy knoll or the Trinity River or its muddy banks. Near where Bonnie and Clyde first met.

Down in Trinity Bottoms where the city began.

*D*allas mayor Uncle Bob Thornton got wind of the impending Avant-Garde controversy. He responded with his stock answer If you don't like the traffic then move on to Forney.

But when the mayor met with his staff for a megapower lunch the City Manager showed them pictures of Avant-Garde art.

It made the Gas Man puke.

The Water Man put his hand over his mouth and ran from the table.

They knew Jack Ruby would be there soon and that he would be wanting answers.

Jack Ruby explains to reporters why support for Avant-Garde art is important if Dallas is ever going to be an International City.

President Eisenhower Is Among the Minority Internationalist Republicans

Jack isn't buying it. He bounds down the steps of the Dallas Museum of Fine Art. He was whistling "The Internationale." He nearly starts singing it but decides not to push his luck. So far nobody in Dallas has recognized the song when he's absentmindedly hummed it in business meetings or down at the club.

He uncoils into the cool Dallas night air.

~

A note was found in the Badlands

THIS IS FOR THE COPS OR LAWMEN WHO FINDS US. CARIL
AND I ARE WRITING THIS SO THAT YOU AND EVER BODY

WILL KNOW WHAT HAS HAPPEN. ON TUE. DAY 7 DAYS
BEFOR YOU HAVE SEEN THE BODYS OF MY MOM, DAD AND
BABY SISTER, THERE DEAD BECAUSE OF ME AND CHUCK,
CHUCK CAME DOWN THAT TUE. DAY HAPPY AND FULL
OF JOKE'S BUT WHEN HE CAME IN MOM SAID FOR HIM
TO GET OUR AND NEVER COME BACK, CHUCK LOOK AT
HER, "AND SAY WHY." AT THAT MY DAD GOT MAD AND
BE GIN TO HIT HIM AND WAS PUSHING HIM ALL OVER
THE ROOM THEN CHUCK GOT MAD AND THERE WAS
NO STOPPING HIM, HE HAD HIS GUN WHIT HIM CAUSE
HIM AND MY DAD WAS GOING HUNTING, WELL CHUCK

PULL IT AND THE [DRAWING OF A BULLET] CANE OUT
AND MY DAD DROP TO THE FLOOR, AT THIS MY NON
SAID THAT SHE HAD A [DRAWING OF A KNIFE] AND WAS
GOING TO CUT HIN SHE KNOT THE GUN FROM CHUCKS
HANDS, CHUCK JUST STOOD THERE SAYING HE WAS
SORRY HE DIDN'T WANT TO DO IT. I GOT CHUCKS GUN
AND STOP MY NON FROM KILLING CHUCK. BETTY JEAN
WAS YELLING SO LOUD I HIT HER WITH THE GUN ABOUT
10 TIMES SHE WOULD NOT STOP CHUCK HAD THE [DRAW-
ING OF A KNIFE] SO HE WAS ABOUT 10 STEPS FROM HER,
HE LET IT GO IT STOP SOME WHEN BY HER HEAD. NE
AND CHUCK JUST LOOK AT THEN FOR ABOUT 4 HOURS.

*I*t was a Dick Tracy setup, right down to the snap-brim hat. He'd put an end to these small-town Realists' rough ways. It was time for Dallas to get acquainted with the Twentieth Century. He wanted to do something for the city that would make the Armory Show look like small potatoes.

France would pay attention.

He smiled his best used car salesman smile. That smile that gave him away. When he smiled he was unmasked so he didn't smile much.

Jack was reading *The Elements of a Synthesis*. He'd been preaching Corbusier all over town but nobody would listen. All of a sudden he put the book down and headed over to his Vegas Club. It was the middle of the afternoon and he had some bridges to burn.

Just Another N▮▮▮ Killing

In Lakewood at the 8 Ball Lounge, as Adlai Stevenson starts to speak at the Convention Center, Betty Barry pushes open the heavy red-padded brass-studded door. She is pregnant. She's a preacher's daughter. She takes her time walking over to the table where Chicken Louie Ferrantello is having a drink with some neighborhood pals. She smiles and pulls a .38 Colt Cobra from her purse. Not a big gun. Louie says Let me see it. Where did you get it? Betty says Sorry Louie I ain't goin' to let you see it. I'm going to let you have it and she fires. She's just a couple of feet away and she fires again right into his face. She empties the gun. Puts it on the table. Turns and walks back out the big red door and as Louie slumps dead she gets in her Cadillac, drives to the hospital, and delivers a baby boy. Everbody said Chicken Louie was the Father. Now it looked like she'd be doing time but she gets Tom Howard for her lawyer and he gets her no-billed then marries her.

Other pictures of Jack Ruby were coming into focus.

Jack Ruby is an unsaddled hothead with hero ambitions. That's what Jada said. Shapely Jada who danced for Ruby in the Carousel. An exotic dancer, she had headed the bill there for several months.
He is completely uncontrollable when he is pissed off she said.
She'd left the club after Jack screwed her and hadn't paid for it. She was driving her flashy red Cadillac convertible when she heard on the radio what Jack had done.
She wheeled off the highway at a roadside vegetable stand near Gladewater, perched on an oil drum, and made a phone call.

He's paranoiac. That's not my phrase but I heard some newspaper guy say it.

What about his politics! I remember him as very much for a cause or against it.

I would like to say something good about him. He liked dogs. He used to keep eleven of them in the kitchen. He called them his wife and family. He gave a lot away. He really loved dachshunds. His favorite was Sheba. He told me he gave Candy Barr a dog when she got out of prison.

When Jack drove to the courthouse to shoot Oswald Sheba rode with him.

Ruby? That guy keeps on talking about the International Avant-Garde said a reporter with UPI. I think he was onto something. He's got that big empty room behind the dressing room at the Carousel, all painted International Klein Blue with a blown-up photograph on one of the walls of Klein in Flight. It's like a shrine of some kind.

It is early, a little after two in the morning. Down by the Triple Underpass a man in a long tan spy coat walks up the Grassy Knoll. Near the top he stops. Takes what looks like a map from a pocket inside his coat. He unfolds it to its full size. To the size of a man. He lights a twenty-four-karat gold lighter and in the flickering light he looks down at the image there.

He looks back up Elm Street like he's looking for a spot.
A place for a big piece of sculpture.
He sits down and writes on a piece of parchment paper
the word Tatlin then draws a spiral.

After Betty kills Chicken Louie she needs a good lawyer. Mr. Tom Howard. That's who she got. Master of the
"n████ killing" defense. Using that defense he'd never
lost a client to the chair. He'd get the Grand Jury to
no-bill them and that was that. Who cared if one Black
man killed another. Why take up court time? No different than Betty killing a scumbag small-time hood who'd
done her wrong.
Mr. Tom Howard gets her no-billed then marries her.

She did a triple somersault
and she hit the ground.
She winked at the audience
and then she turned around.

Caril. Did someone turn on the light?
No.
Did you hold the flashlight for him while he was tying
her up?
I don't remember . . . I was looking out the window
and he started stabbing her and she started screaming
and hollering.
Do you know what he stabbed her with?
My mother's knife.

*F*rank and Bill and I decide to have a beer over at the Vegas Club. On our way Bill French inhales smoke then blows perfect smoke rings while he drives drinking a quart of Pabst Blue Ribbon. Mike and I each drink a quart without taking it from our lips. Mike and Bill both have tattoos of skulls in top hats on their biceps. They say I should get one too if I want to be in the Skull Gang. It would mean a trip to Fort Worth. The tattoo parlor is across the street from the Jackson Hotel whorehouse. A tattoo costs about the same as a whore. Nobody ever has enough for both. Up 'til now I've remained tattooless. There's a smell in the hotel that no one would want to smell again and again. The tattoo parlor is full of pain. I finally get my skull but the guy is drunk or tired or blind. When the scabs come off it is a bad tattoo and looking in the mirror at it I can almost smell that smell of the Jackson Hotel.

l have to get it fixed so later when I am hitchhiking through some Louisiana swamps and a guy picks me up who says he is a tattoo artist I listen. He takes me to his house and tells me he'll fix my skull for free. Then he says he and his girlfriend will take me back to the highway. The house is a wreck with empty wine bottles all over. He says Take off your shirt and I'll do it. I ask him if he isn't going to use a stencil. He says I work freehand. I'll make that skull look like it could go to a fancy ball in his new top hat and I'll add crossbones. I ask how he can see through all the blood and ink. He says Don't worry. I'm an artist.

After we finish all the wine I sleep good on the floor.

Noon the next day they take me to the highway. It is so hot they say they'll find me a shade tree. But all the trees have been bulldozed to widen the road. A hundred miles later we find a tree and before long I am home. When the scabs come off I can see that it's still a bad tattoo but it was a damn good ride.

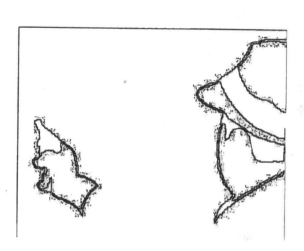

Around that time Richard Speck left Dallas for Chicago where he killed seven nurses. We used to play with him in Tenison Park.

Out in the Badlands Caril was asked Do you know what a penis is?
Yes.
Did he at any time have his penis out of his pants?
Yes.
And what was the reason for that?
Well I don't know what you mean.
All right, did he at any time put his penis up to your sex organs?
Yes.
Did he stick it in very far?
No.
Did he put it in just a little?

He didn't even put it in an inch.
He put it in less than half an inch?
Yes.
And what did he say.
Nothing. He just stopped.
Now then, Caril, you told me previously that he also put
his penis in your rear end. Is that right?
Yes.
And you were undressed at the time?
Well, not all the way . . . I still had my nightgown on.
What sort of nightgown was that.
It was one of them shorties.

In Dallas the assassination of Jack Ruby gets underway.
If they couldn't get him to back off on that whole Avant-
Garde business . . . if they couldn't get him one way
they'd get him another.

The planted stories. The innuendo. What was true?

A story in the *Dallas Times Herald* on November 25
reported . . . aware of Jack's stormy background. There
were vague reports about the mob in Chicago forcing
Jack to leave town. A friend said he often sent large
sums of money back to Chicago. And all those tales of
him knocking customers or performers down the stairs
at the Carousel for trivial reasons. And for the first time
a connection with Billy the Kid was mentioned.

Some of the stuff was made up. Things about his relationship with women, his relationship with men.

They called him a cheap-shot artist. Said he only went after drunks or guys he knew he could beat with his brass knucks or his blackjack or he'd pull his gun or hit them from behind.

To escape all that he goes out to the Dallas Museum of Fine Art for the afternoon. It reminds him of Chicago. It wasn't just Al Capone. Benny Goodman, the Paley Family, Admiral Rickover were neighbors on Maxwell Street.

He has moves left nobody would expect.
and he just got a telegram from Joseph Beuys.

Jack Ruby Knew No Emotional Plateaus

but if somebody mentioned Chicago he'd come unsaddled.
At the museum they knew something else about him.
He tried to keep a low profile in art circles. He was
rarely seen at gallery or museum openings. But he
played a big part behind the scenes in getting the
Museum of Contemporary Art off the ground. There
was a flurry of activity. Claes Oldenburg and Robert
Rauschenberg were seen in town. The Avant-Garde in
Dallas was bolting quickly to its finest moment.

Jack goes into the bathroom and in a stall he reaches
inside his top coat and takes out paper which he
unfolds.

Dallas would become an International City.
Jack would see to that.
He has a plan.
He takes out a large piece of paper and unfolds it until
it is as big as a man.
He's been watching television.
He saw the punk who'd killed the president.
What would Jackie and the children do now?
Jack is mad. He is crying
But he has a plan. He's been working on a manifesto.
He heads to town with his dog.

The Crisis Is Clearly Mirrored

Beuys telegraphed I know what you are going through
Jack. You know the war had a big effect on me but
I knew something had to die. I had to fully reor-
ganize myself constitutionally. I had for too long a
time dragged a body around. At first I was totally
exhausted, but there followed an orderly phase of
renewal. The things inside me had to be totally trans-
planted; a physical change had to take place. Jack I
know you are upset now and you have been through
your own war but let it die. You've got something
important to do. Not just for you. Not just For Dallas.
Not just for art. Jack what you got to do is for the
entire world. I know you feel sick but remember what I
told you:

Illnesses are almost always spiritual crises in life. Old experiences and phases of thought got to be cast off in order to permit positive change.

Lots of people never experience this phase of reorganized action, but when one comes through it, much of what was previously unclear or only vague acquires a totally plausible direction.

Such a crisis is a sign that either there has been a loss of direction or that too many directions have been approached.

Simplify it Jack. Remember what Billy the Kid told you.

Prepare an action.

How Many Times Did She Moan?

Caril how many times did she moan?
More than five.
Was she laying facedown on the bed or faceup.
Facedown.
Now she was laying that way when Charlie tied her
up. Did her hands continue to be tied to the top of the
bed?
No she broke loose when he was stabbing her.
And what had he tied her up with?
A sheet.
What about her feet? Were they still tied to the bottom
of the bed?
Yes.

and then what happened after he had stopped stabbing
her?
He said he didn't think she was going to die.
He said to cut the strips holding her legs.
Did he cover her up? What did he cover her with?
A blanket that laid on the bed. I seen the blood on the
bed but I didn't see the stabs.
You held the flashlight while he was cutting the legs
from the bed?
Yes.
Did you hold the light when he covered her up?
Yes I held it on the floor. He told me to find a clean
shirt for him.
What did you do?

ROBERT TRAMMELL

I went and found him a clean shirt.

Little Jacob Rubenstein tried to disappear, to sink
into the living-room wall. Dingy, dusty, Jewish wall.
His father landed another straight left to his mother's
already swollen head. She screamed and screamed at
him. All Jacob could make out was . . . Joe . . . all those
goddamn children . . . the Czar . . . and another punch
landed and another drink was drunk.
Fannie Turek Rubenstein could dish it out too. She
smashed the bottle against the wall before the next
combination landed and floored her.
Jack Ruby learned to fight at home. Said he could hit
hard as Joe Louis. Call him Kike or Sparkplug and
he'd put out your lights.
To calm himself he'd go to the Art Institute.

covered and   the cut

I seen the blood on

while he was cutting

the   leg

excerpt from Jack's secret testimony

. . . Billy took my hand and put my finger on the wound, on the old scar tissue. He said, "Feel this. It's where Pat Garrett shot me. It covers the bullet hole that was supposed to have killed me. But I didn't die. Billy the Kid died that day but I didn't die Jack. I just got tired of all the killing and decided to fake my death. Pat played his part and fired the woundin bullet. I left the state and headed for Central Texas."
Jack had read the stories about the old man down in Hico who said he had been Billy the Kid but now was Brushy Bill. Jack had been reading stories about The Kid, America's first media star. He had to meet him. Talked his old man into giving him money to buy a bus ticket from Chicago for a few days to visit uncle Billy

who'd moved to Texas a few years earlier. Said he'd
pay it back soon as he got back. He got the money and
bought a ticket to Hico. Brushy Bill was easy to find
and he took to Jack. He let him touch his wound and
while he was doing it he pulled Jack down close and
said Go home to Chicago. Make peace with your old
man and return to Texas. And learn real good how
to use a gun. Jack did all Billy the Kid told him. He
worked hard for Al Capone and other gangsters and
one day he was gone to Texas. Didn't tell anybody. Just
packed, went to the bus station and caught the Dog for
Dallas . . .

I couldn't do the Bop and when Linda asked me to do the Dirty Bop with her, I got away fast as I could. Went to the alley. I learned to like the alley. It was quieter there and I was always surprised when a girl would show up to sit out there with me.

Bill came out and said You're being pathetic. Come on let's go over to the Vegas. We got a couple of hours before it closes. I got some beer to drink driving. Let's go.

Pulling up in front we saw Jack talking to a cop. Over to the side, in darkness he was talking to a cop. Then we saw him slip something into the cop's hands. It looked like a map, a large map. The cop stuck it inside his jacket and walked back to his car. I don't know why that sticks in my mind like it does but I remember something made us hesitate. For a minute we didn't

want to go in. I can remember that moment so clear.
Like sculpture.

We hesitated in the car then got out and went into the
fog of the club.
Into the rock 'n' roll, sax-played, blue-lit darkness.

Jack Ruby was like Dallas's Andy Warhol. Before
Andy Warhol was Andy Warhol Jack was ours.
Bill said he thought Andy Warhol had gotten lots of his
ideas from Jack. But Jack was tougher, I mean phys-
ically. Jack could stand pain. A couple of shots to the
gut and Andy Warhol got scared for the rest of his life.
If any gunsel caused Jack problems he'd slip on his
brass knucks and deal with him right there, then kick
him down the stairs.

Somebody asked Candy Barr about Jack and she answered I don't want to talk about Jack Ruby. She'd been set up and busted for a tiny bit of marijuana and she'd done her time. An Alka Seltzer bottle of it. She could still hear old Lizard Eyes, her prosecutor:

I'll ask you if the defendant pulled any object from her bosom.

And what was it that she pulled from her bosom . . .

All right, sir, did she tell you anything at the time she pulled this from her bosom . . .

Is the person who pulled the marijuana from her bosom . . .

. . . the person who pulled it from her bosom . . .

Her bosom? She remembered when he had told her what great tits she had but the context had changed his language.

Let each stand in his place.
It's a final conflict.
Let each stand in his place.
The International Party unites the human race.

& strike while the iron is hot

& strike while the iron is hot

*T*he Girl with the 45s, Chris Colt, said he was a
man who thought two wrongs make a right, a
swaggering, fat-fingered, sapphire-ringed man. He
was a fanatic about his health who hung out in a little health food store in Oak Lawn. He was part pea-
cock who liked to wear expensive double-breasted suits
to cover his stocky body. He had cold, dark eyes like
grapes about to rot. He wore a hat to cover his head
whose hair had receded into something that looked
like a Mohawk. Once I stopped by his apartment and
caught him with his hair purple. I think he was high
on speed but the next day at work all the purple had
been washed out.

*J*ack had read a lot about the history of Dallas.
He was especially interested in La Réunion, the
Utopian community that had been so important early
on, like 1850. Where those first Communists settled
on the banks of the Trinity. They'd sit out on summer
nights listening to chamber music and poetry. Amongst
Copperheads, Water Moccasins, and Rattlesnakes and
mosquitoes and all sorts of biting things until the State
of Texas got involved and made sure they were shut
down.

Jack wanted revenge for them.

Another score to settle.

He wasn't sure whether his weapon should be art or a
gun. Maybe he could figure a way, an Action where he
could use both. He wrote Beuys for advice.

When Uncle Bob Thornton was mayor everything came down to dollars and cents. Once when he was trying to raise money for the Symphony a writer for the *Dallas Morning News* asked him if he'd ever been he said he hadn't and if he had to he wouldn't help raise another cent. He called that kind of music *The coldest snake I ever touched* but he was convinced that a symphony orchestra was absolutely necessary if Dallas was going to be an International City. That attitude angered Jack. He knew art wasn't just about the bottom line. He looked to the Avant-Garde for answers. And he wasn't so patient. Adding to his anxiety Jack was taking Preludin. It was easy to get and harmless. He was taking it to help him lose weight and it gave him lots of energy.

Jack's Love for John Kennedy Knew No Limits

There had been statements that Jack was homosexual
although there wasn't much evidence. Ruby and Lee
Harvey Oswald had no known sexual relationship.
All the allegations were based on hearsay or derived
from Ruby's lisp or a feeling that some had that Jack
was a "sissy," that he seemed "weird," that he acted
effeminately and sometimes spoke in a high-pitched
voice especially if he got mad. How he dressed when he
was off work shouldn't have been anybody's business.
Then the boy living in a room behind the Carousel, the
one who had eyes that wiggled, was brought up and he
was asked just what was his relation with
his roommate George Senator. Of course his intense
interest in the arts just added fuel to the fire.

"Jack made his customers toe the line. I had a friend
go to the Carousel with his wife. Jack had a gimmick—
he would put a man up on the stage and have the stripper start undressing him. It didn't get very far; when
the fellow's coat and tie were off, the M.C. would take
a Polaroid picture and come on later threatening to
blackmail him. Eventually, he would hand over the picture. Jack chose the men who were put up there carefully—they were ones he knew, or who were with their
wives; not drunks. Even so, when Jack pushed my
friend onstage he whispered to him, in a cold voice,
"Don't touch."

In 1951

After his guitarist, Willis Dickerson, told Ruby to "go
to hell," Ruby knocked Dickerson to the ground, then
pinned him to the wall and kicked him in the groin.
During the scuffle, Dickerson bit Ruby's finger so badly
that the top of his left index finger was amputated.
Around 1955 Ruby beat one of his musicians with
brass knucks; the musician's mouth required numerous stitches.

Jack Got Involved in All Kinds of Shit

How to Build and Sell Log Cabins
         The Silver Spur Beer Joint
books like *How Hollywood Makes Money*
         Little Daddy
      Little Lynn   the art gallery
something had to work for him: punchboards, twist
boards
           the IKB Kleins
The Vegas/Fog Club
English stainless steel razor blades
He put money in a safety box in the Merchants State
Bank
(the Mafia bank)   a couple of Old Masters
prints

He was getting real serious about art, as serious as
he was about strippers. He ran bars: The Silver Spur
where he wore boots and cowboy clothes, The Fog, and
he said I was running the concessions at the Longhorn
Ballroom, selling beer to all those thirsty country
music fans from dry Oak Cliff come pouring over the
river to drink, to listen to Bob Wills, Ernest Tubb,
Hank Williams. Down in Trinity River Bottoms to The
Big D Jamboree in the old tin, rusting Sportatorium,
to some neon honkytonk or the Longhorn. You could
smell the festering, shit-filled river, feel it swelling up
like it might burst out of its banks any minute, up and
over the levee, to rage down Industrial. A big rain on
a Saturday night could drown half the working men in
Dallas.
Down here was the real cultural life of the city and one

way or the other I was going to be a part of it. It kept
me running. From the Longhorn to the Dallas Museum
of Fine Art. Checking out the action. Stopping by
police headquarters, making a living while I corre-
sponded with a bunch of Avant-Garde artists around
the world. On the scene, making the scene. Listening
for hot new Rhythm & Blues musicians to play in The
Fog. Dewey Grooms owned the Longhorn. He told me I
could have the concessions if I wanted it the deal was
mine. I made a little but not enough. Dewey needed
more dough too. I can't remember if it was his or my
idea to fake the robbery, to rob ourselves for the insurance money but I got dressed up like Billy the Kid
that night to stick up Dewey himself. We doubled our
money. I got the holdup money and Dewey got the
insurance. Hank sang it *You got the money Honey* . . .

If Jada Took Off Too Much He'd Turn Off the Lights

Jack was a health nut and a member of Local 20467 of the Scrap Iron and Junk Handlers Union in Chicago.

He'd go down to the *Times Herald,* go into the composing room to try to sell the employees a twist board. It was an exercising device made from two pieces of hardened material joined together by a lazy Susan bearing so one piece could stay still . . .

The Hole
that Sputnik punched in the sky

dreams of invasion. We could feel
the paranoia, we could hear the music. The music won.

> *What cha goin t' say*
> *If I hold your hand?*
> *What cha goin t' say*
> *If I hold your hand?*
> *Will you look me in my eyes*
> *say I'm your loverman.*

Goin t' reel
Goin t' rock
Goin t' dance, drink
have a ball   we cruised to that beat
while Cousin Charlie shot out the stars and moon
some thug in the backroom wondered why Jack
had left so fast

Are my friends mad at me!
That's what Jack wanted to
know.

Hi Jack. All of the girls
told me to tell you they
love you. None of us think
you had anything to do
with . . .

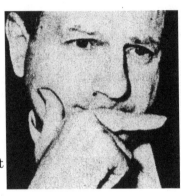

Is that right? Really? I feel
very glad inside, like I want
to cry.

What cha goin t' do about nine o'clock?
What cha goin t' do bout nine o'clock?

Have you heard the news
that we goin t' rock

Yes we goin t' rock
We goin t' rock
Yes we goin to rock

And never stop

*E*lvis Presley didn't have all that much to do with it. He just took it to the bank. All those Rock 'n' Roll visions charged around inside of Jack's brain, his coup at hand. Already known in many International Cities he'd soon be known in the rest. Jack twists his stout neck in a circle cracks his knuckles and fires Avant-Garde glances at the Dallas police in the Carousel. In the wings he takes the man-size map from his jacket, unfolds it, and lays it out on the cold, blood-stained floor.

A death silhouette

Jack walks down the tunnel. The sunlight fades as he walks into the dim nightclub light. Just ahead is a bunch of newsmen, cameramen, his friends the cops.

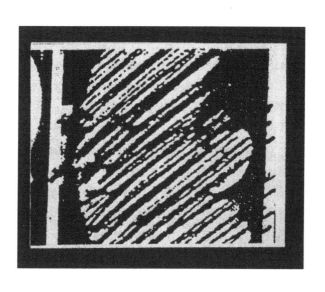

What cha goin t' do when the joints on fire?
What cha goin t' do when the joints on fire?

We're goin turn up the oven
Climb up a little bit higher

Yes a little bit higher
Just a wee bit higher
a little bit higher

We're goin t' keep our promise
'til we begin to fly-y-y-y-y

Jack moved smooth, walked easy through the journal-
ists until he was just a step away, he crouched and
pounced.

*J*ack needs a lawyer. Just somebody to file the papers and do all that lawyer stuff to get him out of jail and have the charges dropped. Somebody who might even be able to get him no-billed. Tom Howard. Tom Howard, that's who he wanted. The guy who got Betty Barry no-billed after she shot Chicken Louie in cold blood. That's right then he married her. Everbody knew Tom Howard, master of the "n██████ killing" defense. Tom agreed. He knew it wouldn't be a routine case but he should be able to get Jack off. He became Jack's First lawyer and stayed his lawyer until fruit boot-wearing Melvin Belli showed up from the West Coast and took over the case, but it wasn't long 'til they ran him back to where he came from and left Jack's defense a shambles.

Left Jack to go mad and die in his cell.

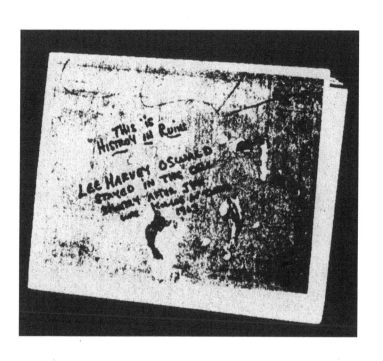

For we, when we feel, evaporate; oh, we
breathe ourselves out and away; from ember
to ember yielding a fainter scent.
>   —*Duino Elegies*, Rainer Marie Rilke

Myth voices in symbolic Figures the psyche
of society. Mythological aspiration is the
high work of the communal imagination,
the "supreme Fiction."
>   —*Unbinding Prometheus*, Donald Cowan

Robert Trammell is author of numerous books of poetry, including *Cicada, Famous Men, Cam I Sole, Epics, No Evidence, Things that Hammer, Things that Cut, Sunflowers,* and *Queen City of the Plains.* His poetry has appeared in *Exquisite Corpse, Southwest Review, Southwest Review*'s Fiftieth Anniversary Issue, the *Dallas Morning News, Another Chicago Magazine, Travois, Temblor, Boxcar, Salt Lick, Giants Play Well in the Drizzle, Veer, texture, Issue, Borderlands, Texas Observer* and a couple of hundred other magazines. Poems have been on public transportation in the Poetry in Motion Series in Dallas and Austin. He won a national competition in 1994 to write and produce ten porcelain/enamel wind panels for the Dallas Area Rapid Transit System's Lovers Lane station. He has been Poet in Residence and has been selected as a Dallas Distinguished Poet. His essays have been in *The America Papers, The Muses,* and *The Angels* from The Dallas Institute of Humanities and Culture, where he is a fellow, and in *Hot Flashes, Picking Up the Tempo,* and *Dallas Arts Revue.* He has given talks on various aspects of culture at Notre Dame, the University of California at Santa Barbara, the University of Texas at Arlington, University of Texas at Dallas, the Dallas Institute of Humanities and Culture, and at Dallas City Hall. He is editor/publisher of Barnburner Press, director of the Dallas-based literary organization WordSpace, and is working on a film documentary on the Civil War with James Hillman.

The Quiet Man

STORIES

contents

D.J.'s Trial   93

Waiting   111

Broadway   122

Spreading the Shine   129

Dallas Bars   141

Benjamin Murchison Hunt Smith   149

Boredom   174

Rudi   190

Benny's Coat   203

Gus   215

Evidence   221

If It Don't Fit Don't Force It   234

One Turns to One
    (Walter Cronkite's Head)   258

The Fastest Man In Texas   266

The Only Song I Know   278

Is Kurt Dead?   287

Ingrained   298

Claudia And Crobar   311

Fill It Up To The Brim   315

Unintended   319

Reunion   326

Juan Acosta's Hearts   334

D.J.'s Trial

"The Revolution has time neither to bury nor mourn its dead."

D.J. knows good and well that if he takes his shoes off there could be trouble. It isn't his sensible black loafers with heavy crepe soles that are the problem. It is D.J. Even after he pulled his shoes and socks off, sighed, and watched his feet nuzzle one another, even then he could have put them under the table and who'd have cared but that isn't his way. Everything is political to him and that includes taking his shoes off. One of his lefty coconspirators once asked if he could think of anything that wasn't political and D.J. answered, "Taking a shit isn't." "But," his cohort answered, "even that is. It matters if you shut the door or not." Why bother to remove his loafers just for a little relief. It has to mean more than that. He plops his bare feet on a chair. He surely couldn't be proud of those fat feet with steaming stink rising from them but still it isn't like anybody really cares about what is on or not on his feet unless he makes an issue of it like he is doing. He knows he could be violating some health code rule but, "Fuck it," he thinks, "this is the sixties. I'm taking my shoes off and I hope somebody tries to stop me." About the only person who is paying any attention is the "philosopher" Bob Brim, who prefers women's feet anyway, but in a pinch men's, even D.J.'s, will do. Not that he is going to stand up for him or even say anything. Bob just leans forward from his seat by the wall trying to get a better look.

D.J. Arnett was one of Dallas's foremost radicals in 1968. Radical as in left-wing. Radical as in Communist, head of Students for a Democratic Society (SDS) at SMU. A protesting, marching, n████loving, dopesmoking, antiwar pinko Commie hippie. Dallas was more hospitable to the John Birch Society, the Klan, any right-wing outfit, even the Nazi party, than it was to anything or anybody from the wrong side of the aisle. Right was right and left was evil.

One of Dallas's favorite politicians was Martin Dies, the East Texas congressman who was the first chair of the House of Representatives' Un-American Activities Committee before Tailgunner Joe used the un-American card in the Senate to blackball anyone who didn't see like he did the Red flood about to drown America. Dies spent a lot of time in Dallas currying favors and raising money to finance his political campaigns and right-wing causes. It wasn't hard to find. He could always put the touch on H. L. Hunt, the richest man in the world, or on the owner of the Dallas Cowboys, Clint Murchison. It wasn't until Joe McCarthy started making a big show of finding half the country in bed with Communists and many others ready to take their clothes off and crawl in too that most Americans became aware of the HUAC developing Star Chamber methods.

He found Communists scattered over the American landscape like amber waves of grain. They were lurking in the military services and in dark corners of government preparing to take over. The movie industry was full of them and it wasn't hard to find Jews like the Rosenbergs who were willing to sell out the USA to the Russians. The Commies were even down at the bowling alley and the scary thing about them was they looked like everbody else. Between strikes, spares, and gutter balls you'd be having an everyday conversation with a teammate when the next thing you knew he was asking you if you didn't feel you were underpaid and didn't you feel exploited by your bosses. And you did and agreed and the next thing you knew you could find yourself in a Communist cell. Every week on television the three lives of Herbert Philbrick were revealed. He was a regular guy, a bowler, as well as a secret Communist and as if that weren't enough he also had a third life as an FBI agent. He was an FBI agent who had a secret room behind a closet in his bedroom where he'd send secret messages to the FBI about what was happening in his Commie cell. Communists were everwhere and they were smarter than just about any American except McCarthy, the FBI, the Hunts, the Murchisons, and their allies. The poor American saps had to be informed before they fell under the evil Red spell. Joe McCarthy knew this and he knew the best way to do it was to get on television. The HUAC got the public's attention. The HUAC would tear America apart.

Dallas wildcatter and owner of America's team, the Dallas Cowboys, Clint Murchison, became one of McCarthy's biggest backers. Loud and crude and high on cocaine with three or four Cowboy cheerleaders in tow, Tailgunner Joe and wildcatter Clint were hard to miss hanging out, drinking in the Playboy Club and other clubs all around Dallas.

If the city of Dallas was hospitable to Tailgunner Joe and his cronies, its major university—Southern Methodist University—was a sanctuary for them. After the Kent State and Jackson State students were gunned down by American soldiers, protests and strikes and sit-ins burst out on college campuses all over the country. But at SMU it was hard to get a dozen students to cut classes to protest those killings. Dallas just wasn't going to have any of that at its schools or in its streets. When big marches were going on all over the South for civil rights or in opposition to the war in Vietnam in Dallas if a couple of dozen people showed up for a demonstration it would be a success for both sides. There were always more cops and FBI agents than protesters.

D.J. is from Chicago. It was never clear why he came to SMU. He would tell different stories. "My father got crossways with the Capone Gang and one of them shot him dead," or there was something to do with the CIA or FBI. But for whatever reason D.J. says he had to leave that city. He is twenty, bright, fat, and trying to invent himself as part Hemingway, part Che Guevara, and he sure can talk. He'll argue with anybody. He gives the impression that he is running or hiding from something. It is an impression that he works on. He might be a spy.

When he isn't agitating at SMU he spends much of his time at The Quiet Man in some debate or other, usually about politics, around the big round table in the middle of the main room. The guy can argue. The table is a big rough round wood cable spindle with a hole in the middle.

There is a patio out front right on the street with six picnic tables and room for fifteen or twenty people but most nights many more pack in. Most bars in Dallas are dark. More cave than garden. A couple of private clubs have swimming pools and member's-only gardens with tables but The Quiet Man is the only public bar with a patio.

All sorts show up at The Quiet Man. Scorpions, Pisanos and once a couple of Hell's Angels which started rumors that they were scouting the town but none come as members of clubs or wear colors. Mostly they come seeking advice from master motorcycle mechanic Bill Jenkins who knows more than all of them put together about what makes motorcycles work and what makes them run fast. He rides a BMW that's so quiet it is hard to hear when he pushes the starter button to turn it on. There is no Harley rumble. Art professors from SMU, artists, writers, street drunks, some pretty women drink here. Preston Jones from the Theater Center is in often. *The Saturday Review of Literature* has just had him on its cover and called him the next Eugene O'Neill. The businessmen who drink during the day generally leave before it gets dark. Oak Cliff Benny is always gone by then.

That summer afternoon D.J. takes off his shoes there is hardly anybody in The Quiet Man yet. He comes in, gets a beer, and sits at a table outside with Seth Riddley. They are soon arguing. As night comes and the place fills their debate heats up but mostly they are just ignored.

Seth always wears a tight black T-shirt to show off his big muscled arms. He is short, in his early twenties. He is a Nazi. We were never sure if he really was a Nazi or if that was just a stance. Maybe he is involved with a Dallas branch of some kind of real Nazi party. He brings other "Nazis" with him occasionally but usually he is alone. He gets along with everyone fine until he starts some racist diatribe. Often D.J. would be the first to take him on and it isn't long until the debate spins out of control but never to the point of violence. What usually happens is nobody cares or even notices them that much or is remotely interested in their tedious discussions.

We usually agree with D.J. in principle but like Seth more even if he is a Nazi. He can hold his own debating D.J. We feel Seth will grow out of it but D.J. is never going to get over being D.J.

It hit 105 earlier that day and it is still 100 even though the sun has gone down. So D.J. takes his shoes off and props his feet up on an empty chair. That in itself is no problem but "no problem" isn't D.J.'s style. He keeps talking and arguing and quoting from *Das Kapital*. It should not be a problem—just another night at The Quiet Man—but there is something in D.J.'s arrogance, in the way he puts his bare feet up. Maybe if he hadn't taken his socks off too.

The owner of The Quiet Man, Mike Carr, is a second-generation Irishman. His father was born near Dublin but he knows really little about the Emerald Isle other than what he's gotten from the movies, especially John Wayne in *The Quiet Man*, and from his dad. He has never been there. There is a green sign on the back wall: *Erin Go Bragh*. One dubious Irish tradition however that he does embrace is on another sign: No Cussing in the Presence of Ladies. He'll put his hands over a lady's ears if cuss words are spoken. Whenever D.J. looks at that sign he just has to cuss, usually to himself but sometimes it spills out of his mouth like spit and he says "motherfucker" or "bullshit" not real loud just loud enough that some lady might hear and think him a great rebel. Outside on the patio there is no restraining him though. Mike usually stays off the patio as if that is some kind of different public place than the inside of his pub. Kinda like the opposite of a cozy in a Dublin bar. Cozies have a table, some chairs, and a door that can be shut and locked. A place where revolution can be fomented in private.

This evening when Mike peeks out the little window on the front wall of the bar where he can see what is going on on the patio he sees D.J. take his shoes off and put his feet up on the chair. When he sees D.J's lips moving he knows he has to be cussing, tainting the air loud enough that a lady at a nearby table might hear. Mike deliberately walks out the door and up to D.J.

"Put your shoes on," Mike orders.

D.J. asks, "Why?"

Mike says, "Because I am asking you to."

D.J. says, "I don't have to."

Mike says, "You are right. You don't have to but if you want to stay in my bar you do."

D.J. answers, "You can't throw me out for that.'

Mike is getting pissed off. "Oh yes I can."

"By what authority?" D.J. demands.

"By the authority of that sign," Mike points.

NO SHOES.
NO SHIRT.
NO SERVICE.

D.J. says, "That don't mean nothing. Like what about boots. What if I had boots on would I be in violation of the sign?"

"Come on man," Mike pleads. "You know what the sign means."

"It isn't a matter of what I know but of what the sign says but even then you can't enforce that. It's just a sign. You can put up any kind of sign you want to. What if you put up one that said,

WE DON'T SERVE COLORED PEOPLE

would that mean anything legally?"

"I'd never do that," Mike responds, "I have nothing against Afro-Americans. Long as they pay as they go."

"Long as they pay as they go. Is that the criteria for colored people? How come just about everbody else in this bar has a tab?"

"I'll tell you why. It is because they are regulars."

"Regulars what? Regular white people?"

"No. Regular customers. I don't care what color they are as long as they are regular customers."

"And it just so happens that all those regular customers are white."

"I can't be responsible for their color."

"Mike tell me. What is a regular?"

"You know, it is someone who comes in regular like at least three times a week."

"And you keep notes or something. Seems like a lot of work."

"I don't keep notes. I just know."

"Kinda like you are your own law. I mean you make up your own law. You can't do that. This is a pub, a public place."

"Yes. And there are laws that I obey and enforce. I'm kinda the sheriff."

"That's where the problem begins. You are not any kind of sheriff. You don't even own this bar. You just lease it. You know what I think I'm going to do is round up some of my Black friends and have them come in here three times in a week and see if you will run tabs on them. Or how many weeks must they come in at least three times before they are eligible for a tab?"

Mike answers, "Until I say they have come in long enough."

"Until you say they have come in long enough. Nothing arbitrary about that. You know what I think I'm going to do. I think I am going to start a sit-in."

"Because you can't take your shoes off?"

"No because of your discriminatory practices in your extension of credit to customers."

"And what will you do during this sit-in? Take your shoes off? Get some of your Negro friends to try to run a tab? Vive la Révolution."

"You know what I think Mike? I think you don't read the newspapers. You do know about the sit-ins in discriminating cafés that only serve white people . . . you know they have worked?"

"Yeah after some people got hit in the head with a baseball bat."

"Or had an ice cream sundae dumped on their head. Mike are you threatening me? You don't want me to make a call to the NAACP do you?"

"No I just want you to leave."

One of the bikers growls, "Come on D.J. Get out of here. You are about to make us all lose our tabs."

D.J. ignores that and says to Mike, "Okay. Okay don't serve me then but you can't throw me out."

Mike says, "Yes I can. You are also in violation of the health code."

"The health code?" D.J. acts innocent.

"That's right D.J. The part of the health code that forbids anyone from being barefoot in a public place."

"What part of the health code are you talking about Mike? Do you have a copy? The law says you got to have a copy of anything that you are going to enforce."

"It does not. I'd have to have a law library to do that. Anyway I don't care. I'm the boss here and you got to go."

"So what if I don't? What are you going to do? You going to call the police?"

"Come on D.J. What if everyone took off their shoes?"

"Yeah, what if?"

"What if? Who knows what kinds of diseases would be spread?"

"Not if you kept your floors clean."

"There are some germs that Pine-Sol will not eliminate."

"I don't follow. So I step in some germs then what? How does that spread the germs?"

"Everywhere you step then there would be germs."

"So? Can't germs spread on the bottom of shoes too?"

Mike answers, "Not as much as on bare feet."

"But if everyone else has their shoes on how could they get diseased?"

"So you are saying as long as you and you alone are exempt from the rule everyone would be safe? But why should you be the only one with that privilege?"

"Okay. What if I leave my shoes off but don't walk around?"

Mike is getting really pissed now. It is his bar. "D.J. leave now," he commands.

"I will not. Call the police."

Mike knows how ridiculous it would be to call the police for something so trivial so he backs off a little. He is quiet for a minute then he says, "Okay I will not call the law but what I will do is arrange a trial for you. Next Sunday after church at one o'clock you will be tried around the big table but for now just get out."

D.J. consents to the trial and reluctantly picks up his shoes and walks to his car. "I'll see you Sunday. How about at three?"

Finally a compromise is reached and Mike agrees, "Okay at two."

"Now how will a jury be selected?"

"You know. The same way we always do. Anybody that is in the bar that wants to be on the jury can. That is anybody sober. We'll turn off the jukebox and your trial can commence."

D.J. says, "It is always off during the day anyway."

Mike responds, "Okay. At two we will convene the jury. You make your argument to them and I'll make mine. Then everyone votes. If you win you may remain barefoot for as long as you want to but if you lose you will be banned for life from The Quiet Man."

D.J. doesn't put his shoes back on but gathers them under his arm and walks into the parking lot where he steps on glass from a broken beer bottle he doesn't see. A trickle of blood drips from his foot as he gets into his old Chevy.

It seems like Sunday will never come as D.J. sits in his apartment smoking dope and reading the health code. When it is time for his trial he is ready.

Only a fool is his own lawyer.

Ken opens up most Sundays but Mike has come in today to open the place himself. He turns on the lights, takes the chairs down, and puts them around the tables. He is putting on the coffee when there comes a banging on the front door. He walks over, pulls back the curtain, and sees D.J.'s smiling face. Mike feels like a huge hand squeezes his stomach. He opens the door and lets the accused in. Mike rarely shows any emotion and he doesn't now as D.J. pushes his big belly past and walks over to the bar. He has a stack of books with him, a briefcase, and is wearing a nice tweed sportscoat over a white shirt and blue jeans. His black shoes are familiar and have just been shined. He walks over to the bar and orders the only thing the bar sells. "Let me have a small draft." As Mike pulls one silently he thinks at least this will be one of the last I'll have to draw for D.J., one of the last anybody is going to pull for him in The Quiet Man.

"Don't give it such a big head," D.J. orders.

He goes over, stacks his books on the table, opens his briefcase, and sits down. Mike hasn't done much research on the health code. Hell he knows it. He wouldn't have been able to stay open if he didn't.

D.J. drinks and reads from a big black legal book. Every fifteen minutes or so he gets another beer. Mike doesn't bring it to him. If D.J. wants a beer he is going to have to haul his ass over to the bar with his mug and get it. When he does Mike takes it and fills it up without washing it. He has some nice frosted glasses in the freezer but he isn't going to get one for D.J. For the next couple of hours it is quiet with no jukebox, no television, no radio, and them not speaking. The Quiet Man grows smaller and more crowded even though it is just the two of them.

Mike doesn't have much to do but he keeps busy waiting for the jury to arrive. Every Sunday, The Quiet Man Regulars go to White Rock Lake to play Red Ball and drink beer. It is not unlike the tennis game in the movie *Blow-up* that is played with no net. About the only rule of the game is it must be played with a Red Ball and that there be two goals. Everything else is up for debate. A little after two the game ends and everyone caravans back to The Quiet Man for D.J.'s trial. The jury takes its place.

There is still a big procedural question. Who is going to be the judge? Someone suggests the bartender Ken who everyone loves and trusts but Ken isn't about to get between D.J. and his boss. How about Bill Jenkins? He has a level head but he says, "No thanks. I'll stick to working with motorcycles." Mike thinks he should be the judge himself after all it is his place. He starts to designate himself but realizes he is already the prosecutor and being both would open things up for an appeal if D.J. lost. As they try to get it resolved Seth Riddley walks in the door. It somehow doesn't seem right to have a Nazi for a judge but no one else will do it and Seth says, "I will," from the back of the room. There doesn't seem much of a choice so Seth moves to sit at the big table. He is in control right off. "Let's start with you D.J. Tell us what happened? Tell us what this is all about. Let's hear your version."

D.J. speaks. "Dallas has no health code per se but in The Dallas City Code under Section 17-7.1. is a Floors, Walls, and Ceilings subsection and under (b) is Special requirements for floors . . ." D.J. continues, "Here, let me read this verbatim: 'A food products establishment shall: (1) construct floors that are water flushed for cleaning, or that receive discharges of liquid from equipment or pressure sprays, and are made of sealed concrete, terrazzo, ceramic tile, or similar material that is graded to a properly installed trapped floor drain.'

"Mike where is your drain?" He is taking no prisoners.

Mike protests. "D.J. what does that have to do with anything?"

Seth is taking his role seriously. "Please do not address one another. Direct your questions and comments to me and the jury." It is going to be interesting to see what kind of procedural rules will be invoked by Judge Riddley.

Mike says, "What D.J. just said is totally irrelevant."

Seth replies, "D.J. what do you mean starting off with something about drains, something seemingly totally irrelevant? This is about you taking your shoes off."

D.J. answers, "I know what this trial is about. It is about how this place is run."

Seth agrees, "Okay. I can see that. D.J.'s question

must be answered." The jury moans. This trial is going to last awhile but at least they can drink while they weigh the evidence.

Mike says, "There is a drain behind the bar."

"But the floor doesn't slant to it," D.J. argues.

Mike says, "No it doesn't. The slant was there when this place was built but over the years the ground swole up and the floor leveled out. Anyway this is a nonissue. The city did an inspection and ruled that because the floor was slanted to begin with it was nobody's fault what the earth did under it to level it out. They said I was in compliance as long as I had a hose with a nozzle strong enough so that I could spray everything toward and down the hole."

D.J. pounces. "I can just see it all washing across your floor: cigarette butts, panties, broken glass, a finger. Did you get that ruling in writing from the inspector Mike?"

Seth is irritated. "I already told you not to address each other. Mike has shown me enough to rule that he is in compliance with the law on drains. Could we now get on to the subject of the trial. D.J., did you or did you not take your shoes off in what Mike calls a violation of the health code or whatever D.J. wants to call it last Friday afternoon?"

D.J. says, "I refuse to answer that question."

Seth is puzzled. "But that is the only question at issue here."

D.J.'s got more. "I don't think so. I would like to introduce now Section 17-23: HYGIENE OF EMPLOYEES: 'If a person who works in a food products establishment prepares food, serves food, or comes in contact with food or a food-contact surface while on duty, the person shall wash hands and forearms with soap and warm water.' Judge, Ken never washes his forearms."

Mike responds, "We are not a food establishment."

D.J. asks, "Yeah. Well then what about those miniature frozen pizzas that you cook up in that little oven behind the bar?"

Seth confusedly says, "Overruled. Shoes D.J. I order you to talk about you taking your shoes off in violation of the health code."

D.J. seems to back off. "Okay. I would like to start with a confession. I did take my shoes off last Friday and refused to put them back on when ordered to by Mike Carr, the owner of The Quiet Man, and I know there might be some obscure law somewhere about it like the law against driving barefoot that is still on the books in some little West Texas town because the brake pedal used to get so hot that when you went to stop before you ran over the kid chasing his ball in front of you you couldn't because you'd burn your foot on the bare metal and so the kid would be run over and maybe killed."

Seth asks, "What are you talking about?"

D.J. answers, "I couldn't find any code that makes taking your shoes off in a bar illegal."

And it goes on like this for going on two hours. Several members of the jury fall asleep and most of the others are drunk when Seth out of nowhere says, "I rule for Mike. D.J. must leave forever." The jury is stunned but they have been so for some time. One of them asks how he could make the ruling he did. It is the jury's job to decide if D.J. is guilty or not.

Seth says, "In most cases it would be but I have

made a special ruling in this one because of the condition of the jury. Now if y'all will just agree to my decision we can wrap this up and get D.J. on his way. The court has ruled and the jury concurs so this trial can end." The decision has as much to do with the fact that they really don't like D.J. as the legalities of the case so they agree. D.J. must go.

D.J. is freaking out. "You can't do this. What kind of trial is this? What kind of judge and jury?"

"The kind that has just found you guilty," Seth responds.

Mike says, "Wait just a minute," and he walks over to the wall where hang the charcoal portrait caricatures that crippled old Bill James has drawn of The Quiet Man Regulars. All the men in the portraits look kind of like men. There are just a couple of women. They don't look as much like men. Mike reaches up and removes D.J.'s portrait from the wall in what looks like the final act but one more follows. Before handing over the drawing Mike removes it from its cheap black plastic frame. He sets the frame aside for the next portrait. He hands D.J. his picture. This time it is for real. D.J. is banned for life. The only other person who has been banned for life is Broadway who definitely deserved it. Now D.J. has become the second. He gathers up his books, closes his briefcase, and asks, "Can I have just one more beer."

It is several weeks after D.J. was found guilty that he dares to come back to the bar. It is a Sunday night, when he knows Mike is never there. He comes for the next several Sundays until Mike shows up unexpectedly. D.J. doesn't know what to expect. Will he call the police? Mike sees D.J. and slowly walks toward him.

When he reaches him he bends down and whispers, "D.J. do you need a job? I need a bartender tonight." D.J. doesn't have anything planned so he says, "Okay." He lasts around six weeks before Mike gets fed up with his constant arguing and reimposes the "banned for life" verdict on him. He doesn't show up again for several weeks.

Waiting

Oak Cliff Benny has been waiting outside since nine for The Quiet Man to open. At ten Ken, the day bartender, invites him in. Behind Benny is a brief shimmering halo that is quickly extinguished when the door shuts the morning sunlight and the world out. It takes a minute for his eyes to adjust from the sun's red glare to the softer, almost blue, light inside. He meekly says, "Hello," then walks straight back to his stool at the end of the little fake leather black-padded bar. He sits on the same stool he has been sitting on Mondays through Fridays from ten in the morning until three in the afternoon for over twelve years. He only gets up to go to the bathroom. On his way he might shyly wave hello to some of the other old men regulars sitting in dark booths but about the only one who he talks to is Ken. Every day at three, to beat the afternoon rush hour, he leaves to catch the bus back to Oak Cliff. He never says goodbye. Is just gone. Today he has on his blue wool Yankees baseball cap so it must be winter.

In summer he wears a plain red baseball cap for reasons that seem to have nothing to do with the seasons;
various long-sleeve naturally wrinkled interchangeable
rough tan, gray, or blue shirts and always khaki pants.
Clothes you don't notice at first. Clothes that tell you
little about the man. His uniform is his disguise. More
like a hide. After the World Series when it gets cold he
changes to a flannel redbrown checked shirt. He wears a
long tan Burberry Goodwill gabardine all-weather top-
coat over it and he changes his plain red cap for his dark
blue Yankees one whose perfectly curved long bill hints
at his past as does his coat. He showed Ken one day how
to get that kind of roll in the cap's bill: Roll the bill into
itself as tight as possible then stretch big rubber bands
around it. Fold the bill into the rest of cap. Wrap more
rubber bands around the whole thing and squeeze it all
into a #303 tin can full of water. Place in freezer for a
month or so. Defrost. Unfold. Dry and wear. Well as Ken
can remember that is what he said. He was kinda busy
getting the bar ready for the day and not able to pay
that much attention to Benny's cap ramble. There is no
cleanup crew so he has to mop up any major spills from
the night before himself. He pours half a bottle of Pine-
Sol disinfectant and some Clorox bleach into his mop
bucket and fills it with water. Tears come to his eyes.
Soon that smell is stronger than the smell of stale beer
in clogged lines. Ken puts a big, not-so-clean mop in the
bucket. Sloshes it around.

Benny must be in his sixties. He doesn't talk much
unless he talks about baseball. Nobody knows more
about baseball than Oak Cliff Benny. He speaks rev-
erently about the Gods of the Diamond: Ruth, Cobb,

Williams, Musial, Mantle, but not The Yankee Clipper. He will not even mention the pompous Joe DiMaggio.

He isn't big or little. One-fifty, five-eight. His eyes are gray. He rarely looks anyone in the eyes but when he does those soft eyes harden, focus. His brownish-yellow hair grows long over his collar. Not as a political statement but a lack of money to get it cut.

He has no past anybody knows about in The Quiet Man but his caps are a hint. Once someone asked him what he had done all his life. He didn't say a word, just got up, turned around and walked straight out the front door. He didn't come back. Not until ten the next morning. It was the only time he'd left before three and the last time anybody asked him about his past. Still he doesn't talk to anyone but Ken unless if someone sits beside him he will be quietly friendly and open to conversation as long as it is about baseball. In his voice is the distant crack of a bat hitting a ball, a fastball stinging the catcher's mitt, the silence of a well-turned double play.

Talking to him you must always remember that baseball is not a metaphor for some greater lesson. He can tell in an instant if you try and the conversation will be over right there. Irony will also end the conversation. The talk is about baseball or there is no talk with him at all. Once when some hippie kid sat beside him and started going on about "how mystical baseball is what with the diamond, nine players (three times three), four square bases, and the horrors of being out at home like being killed in your own front yard," Benny got irritated. ". . . how it, not like most other sports, is not constricted by time . . ." Benny got more and more agitated, twisting his beer glass, a delicate pilsner cone, around and around in his sweating hands on its coaster. By the time the kid got to, "It's like life," Benny was beside himself. He had nearly burned a round hole in the cardboard coaster with the base of his fifteen-cent beer. He finally couldn't take it anymore. He didn't shout although his voice got loud enough that everyone in the bar stopped talking to hear what came next after Benny said, "Baseball is baseball," and silent tears came to his eyes. The dopey kid muttered some kind of defense and something about how "baseball is more than that." Benny said nothing for a minute but turned to Ken and ordered another beer then concluded, "Baseball needs no explanation or the wrong kind of analysis or justification. It is complete in itself except for the statistics and stories. It ain't football." The kid finally shrugged his shoulders at Ken and left the bar.

There are several groups that drink here in the daytime and from ten until three. Benny is a part of them all like the Pine-Sol smell which you don't notice after awhile. The regulars are anomalous stars sparkling in the dark matter of his constellation. When he goes home at three he is forgotten. Gone from the bar's consciousness. Rarely will anyone ask, "Hey. Did you hear what Oak Cliff Benny said today?" With his back to everyone he sees more than is seen, a seer whose reflection in the mirror behind the bar looks out on everything and misses little.

No one knows what he does on weekends. Where he goes. He just catches the bus on Friday and isn't seen in The Quiet Man until Monday. Does he drink alone at home watching the baseball Game of the Week on

Saturdays? Or might there be another bar he goes to to watch and listen to Dizzy Dean and Pee Wee Reese announce the game? No one asks where he lives or speculates but Ken imagines his little cottage across the river in a cedar woods in Oak Cliff. It is clean and neat and cannot be seen from the street.

Today, Monday, after a couple of slow beers Benny asks Ken if he heard what Dizzy Dean said last Saturday.

Ken answers, "I heard he got into some kind of trouble because he said *ain't* instead of *isn't* and gotta lot of high school English teachers all riled up."

Benny says, "Come on Ken that happened a couple of years ago and, I guess, the controversy has cooled down now. Anyway he hasn't stopped saying *ain't* every Saturday over and over, still corrupting the young people of America. Somehow it has become almost okay to say *ain't* now, not proper but acceptable thanks to Dizzy." Benny orders another beer.

Redbeard joins the conversation. He is a disc jockey at a Top 40 radio station. He is not a regular but shows up now and then. He says, "You know it wasn't that long ago anyway that teenagers were invented." Benny loses interest and concentrates on his beer. Ken listens between customers. Redbeard continues, "And they came already corrupted anyway. You know there weren't always teenagers. It was after the war when motorcycle gangs, Marlon Brando, car clubs, teenagers, teenage gangs, juvenile delinquents, rock 'n' roll, and Communism got the country by the short hairs and they all seemed to come from the same evil place. Sometime after Jackie Benson sang 'Rocket 88' in the late forties and before Bill Haley cashed in with 'Rock Around the

Clock,' *Life* magazine did an article on teenagers. It said maybe the first teenage gang, the Lakewood Rats, was right here in Dallas."

Dizzy Dean didn't help the situation. Saying ain't seemed downright un-American. It encouraged Dallas teenage boys who hid portable radios under bedcovers and fell asleep listening to the blues on "Cat's Caravan" to become juvenile delinquents. But Dizzy wasn't worried about being blamed. When he was pitching for the Cardinals he and his teammates formed the Gashouse Gang. They were constantly involved in stunts both on and off the field like once when the team was staying at a hotel they put on carpenter's coveralls and went down to the ballroom, where a businessmen's convention was happening. They came in and started cutting up tables and hammering on stuff totally disrupting the meeting. When the speaker finally asked, "What are y'all doing?" Frankie Frisch answered, "It's okay we're with the hotel," and the meeting had to be ended.

Dizzy made up his own rules. After he became a broadcaster fans would tune in to listen, not just to the ball game, but also to what craziness Dizzy might be up to that week. He often would break into singing "The Orange Blossom Special" but last Saturday he might have gone too far . . .

Ken asks, "What did he say? I missed the game."

Ken lives for baseball climaxes every Sunday on a high school diamond with a bunch of aging and aged guys who always wanted to be major leaguers and still want to but they are far too old now like they ever had a chance anyway. Ken wanted to be a writer or a baseball pitcher but he wound up a social worker who every day after work got a six-pack, went home, kissed his wife, put the beer in the refrigerator, took one out, took off his tie, put his cleats on, and went outside to throw baseballs into a peach basket nailed to his garage door. Fastballs, curves, and changeups that weren't much slower than his curve. He threw until dark and sometimes later. Drinking beer and throwing his best stuff into that basket. He was never happier. He wanted no more from life than that steady routine but his wife did. Everyone loved Ken even his wife. She told him, "I do love you" right after she asked him for a divorce, "but I'm not in love with you." He wasn't sure what the difference was except that one got you a divorce and the other kept your marriage going.

Benny answers Ken: "Dizzy Dean saw a couple kissing and he said right on the radio: He is kissing her on the strikes and she is kissing him on the balls."

Ken says, "Yeah. We had the game on. I guess I just missed it. Hey you know Daffy Dean, Dizzy's brother, has a car lot in Garland. He comes in here every now and then. Sorry Benny I got to go. Got customers."

Near the bar is a big round roughwood old cable spindle table. Rules for the bar are made here on Sundays. Anyone can join in whether they are regulars or not. If Mike Carr, the owner, has his way The Quiet Man will be as quiet as John Wayne in the movie. The jukebox is not allowed on during the day. But Mike leaves every evening and turns the place over to the night manager. The jukebox is turned on before he is out of the parking lot and the place fills quick with a louder crowd. Mike would tell customers, "This is a place for quiet conversation. Men must act like gentlemen and never cuss in the presence of women." He put no restrictions on women. At night though when he leaves his rules leave with him. He must know.

During the day old men sit in dark booths endlessly telling the same stories over and over. Shanghai Jimmy talks about China, chili rice, and ice skating. The story about John Lancaster was that he had been a member of the Clyde Barrow Gang and had spent time in the penitentiary. It isn't something he'll talk about and it is best not to ask him. Pappy Hill sits in the corner. Not as quiet as Benny but not saying much mostly just sitting and dipping snuff and dripping it onto his shirt. Cletis grew up in the country outside of Troup. He has lived in Dallas for most of his life but still has country ways. Jabby lives up to his name yakking away.

At lunchtime a dozen or so men in dark suits cross Knox Street from their office buildings, enter the bar, and take over the big table. They order pitchers of beer, take off their coats, and try to act as if they are not businessmen at all but do not know how. A couple take out and eat sandwiches from brown bags but for most beer is enough. After drinking for awhile they give up trying to be anything more than what they are. They are just louder salesmen than when they came in. Usually they get back to work a little late but sometimes they drink all afternoon keeping an eye out for potential customers passing by on Knox. Ken thinks they sell insurance but he can't afford it so they do not bother him.

Benny usually answers questions about baseball not asks them. But today he deviates from his usual routine. "Ken, how is your curveball coming along?"

There is a small room upstairs that only the owner and a few close friends may enter. Some say he used to live there. There are rumors of a basement.

When Ruth gets off work from her job next door at the cleaners she comes over. She is the only daytime woman regular but she can seem like a crowd at times. Her husband, Jack, is a plumber. He is just about always already drinking before Ruth makes it in.

Shel Hershorn, the best photographer in town, was having an early beer one day when the businessmen came in all agitated. They asked Ken to turn on the television because some maniac was shooting up the University of Texas from the orange tower in the center of the campus. Shel watched for a few minutes, paid his tab, and took off for Austin in his blue Morgan. The sniper had already killed several people and was trying for more when Shel got there. He ducked into a small shop and took a picture of the tower through a bullet hole Charles Whitman had blasted in the plate glass window. A few minutes later a security guard broke in the door behind the sniper and shot him dead. Shel's picture through the bullet hole was on the cover of the next issue of *Life* magazine.

Chief rides a big Harley. He often comes to The Quiet Man to consult with Bill Jenkins who rides a quiet BMW. Jenkins knows more about bikes than all the outlaw bikers in town. In the evenings the Texas Instruments crowd, a couple of Nazis, an industrial glassblower, Bill Knox, the worst artist in town, the actor asshole Broadway, and his cakemaking girlfriend Becky Sloan, wiry Juan Acosta who says the government gave him permission to smoke marijuana, Rudi, that psycho, ex-con, the English car mechanics, Darryl the white shoeshine boy, The Prince of Darkness, drink at The Quiet Man. A couple of Dallas Cowboys, Skip-a-step, the beautiful girl with the bad leg, and Kathy, the girl with three tits, stop by on occasion. The sculptor Bill Verhalst, the tuba player Ev Gilmore, and America's next Eugene O'Neill, Preston Jones, often stop in.

Before it was The Quiet Man it was the Turf Bar with three green neon horses running across the front and vanishing into the dark of the Safeway parking lot and down the street to the Casba.

"They don't know much about me here at The Quiet Man. I ride the bus over every day to drink and talk to no one except about baseball," Benny thinks, "but I know all their stories."

I was a regular there myself for several years. I would stop in after work when I had a job or earlier when I was unemployed which was most of the time. I never had a car. One day as the twilight was fading into night I was riding the bus home from my job downtown and was nearly to The Quiet Man when I . . . I don't know why I turned around and looked back downtown just as the window lights in the tall buildings all blinked out and the city became dark buildings. Then numbers began to flash on those buildings . . . 189 . . . 348 . . . 406. It took awhile for me to realize they were batting averages and getting over the shock of what I was seeing I wondered whose they were . . . 406. Wasn't that what Ted Williams hit when he became the last man to hit over .400? Then there was darkness again. In a moment the window lights were back on. It all happened fast. Was I the only one who had seen those numbers? Before I could say anything to anyone on the bus there was nothing to point out. Now for the first time I am reporting what I think I saw. I was bewildered but when I got to The Quiet Man that night Ken helped clear up what might have caused those mysterious lights. He drew my beer, put it on the bar in front of me, leaned over, and asked, "Did you hear? Oak Cliff Benny died today."

Nobody knew more about baseball than Oak Cliff Benny.

Broadway

You can't kick me out," Broadway keeps it up. "You don't have enough customers as it is and I'm a regular." He's been fucking with El Paso, a day bartender at The Quiet Man, all afternoon. The big Indian standing next to him has finally heard enough though and soon as "regular" spills from his mouth Chief says, "You ain't no regular," as he picks up a full bottle of beer by the neck. "I ain't sure if they can kick you out Broadway but I sure as hell can kick your ass and knock you out," and he swings the bottle so hard that when it hits Broadway's head it explodes—the bottle not his head—shatters into a constellation of thousands of neonsparkling amber shards flying through the moldy atmosphere and landing on tables, in beers, in insurance men's and girls' hair, all over the place. "Yeah I don't think we'll have any trouble kicking you out now." Chief grabs the stiff by the scruff of the neck and seat of the pants and like a cartoon throws it out the front door. Mike, the bar owner, walks over and says to it, "And don't come back. You are banned for life forever."

Broadway's night has been a success. He's gotten banned from another bar but not just another bar. It is not easy to get banned from The Quiet Man, thrown out maybe but getting banned forever is something special and Broadway has just pulled it off. Preston Jones says he'd heard he was going for some kind of record. He is now banned from fourteen bars in Dallas alone.

It's not that rare that someone is banned. There is even a special banning ritual for regulars that involves old crippled Bill James. Near as can be figured out Bill is homeless, sleeping in vacant buildings, on the street, who knows. He makes a little money by drawing portraits of Quiet Man customers. For special customers Mike Carr might decide the drawing can hang on the Wall of Regulars. He buys cheap black frames and hangs your "portrait" on the wall up by the front door. If someone on that wall commits a banning offense his (it is almost always "his") picture will be taken down and the picture removed from the frame (which Mike keeps to use again) and the picture given to the banned one as he leaves. There are degrees of banning ranging from one day to forever. After shorter sentences you may return on a trial basis after your time has been served. But it is about impossible to ever have your portrait returned to the Wall of Regulars once it has been removed. Broadway has never made the wall, has never even been close, so there is no portrait to give him. He is just kicked out.

Preston Jones is a star or was a star. His trilogy of plays—*Lu Ann Hampton Laverty Oberlander*, *The Last*

Meeting of the Knights of the White Magnolia, and *The Oldest Living Graduate*—landed him on the cover of the *The Saturday Review of Literature.* One critic wrote that he might be America's most important playwright since Eugene O'Neill. *Dallas Morning News* columnist Billy Porterfield followed him around town, getting drunk with him before writing a column claiming he was like Boswell to Jones' Samuel Johnson. Then the plays left Texas for Broadway. They didn't exactly bomb but they didn't do very good either. The trilogy closed after only sixty-three performances.

Jones is back home in Dallas now still writing and acting over at the Dallas Theater Center. He is also doing a bit more drinking than he used to. It's at the Theater Center that he gets to know Broadway who has had roles in a couple of plays there and is working on the Jeeter Lester/Tobacco Road role when they meet. It is his first lead role. It is the role that will eat him. Jones is intrigued by Broadway's brashness though and befriends him but never gets to really know him even with as much drinking as they do together. It is hard to get to know much about Broadway because he is such a liar. He'll lie about anything. Ask him where he's from and he'll lie about that. Isn't much he won't lie about. It is his main way of communicating. Probably has something to do with why he is a good actor and the boy can act. Problem is he can't stop.

He's got stuck in the Jeeter Lester role and that Erskine Caldwell character just consumes him. He slowly becomes it. Not just when he's on stage but when he's off. What started as theater becomes his reality. He is stuck in being that ignorant asshole. Or is he acting?

Getting lost in a character like that can cost you permanent IQ points. Broadway's gotten himself to behaving like something between a moron and an idiot but underneath that he keeps hidden a cleverer character. Problem is he gets to liking the stupid character so much he forgets when he's acting and when he's not. It is much easier and more fun to be an asshole anyway. He's the kind of guy who stops drinking and behaves worse than when he was drunk as if his problem is in him and not in the booze.

Jones is in The Quiet Man this afternoon as Broadway is getting thrown out. He does nothing. He figures if he does anything it will be to help Chief throw him out. If there is blood he'll get a bar towel to wipe it up. That's all. Everybody in the bar knows they are both actors in the same company. Broadway has bragged that he is writing a play too but there is never any evidence of it. There is blood. Jones gets a towel, goes outside and hands it to Broadway who is sitting up now leaning against a bench. Mike and Chief have gone back inside. "Here you idiot. You can wipe your own mouth," which he does, smiling . . . no, grinning.

The air is clear on the patio. As it becomes dark Jones gets Broadway up onto a bench. It is a quiet Autumn evening. A Saturday. Pickup trucks and cars slowly pass on Knox Street crushing fall leaves into sadness, turning on headlights as night threatens.

"Give me a ride," Broadway begs Preston.

"I'm not going anywhere Broadway. I came here to drink and here I will get drunk."

"Come on man just over to Oak Lawn to the Nick Farley's Lounge?"

"No. Walk."

"It's too far."

"Okay. You want something nearby. How about walking two blocks down to the Knox Street Pub or that dark old dive across the street whatever it's called. You can see it from here. How about the Casba. Go over to the Casba."

"It's too early. They don't open till later."

"Then sit on the curb and wait for the police."

"Who called the police?"

"That old regular sitting by himself in the back."

"Pappy Hill? What's he doing still here?"

"I think so. I saw him over at the pay phone but it don't matter who . . . okay, I'll walk down to the Pub with you. How have you managed not to be banned from there?"

"Because I respect the place, the history."

"Like what history?"

"I mean like you know who that short dark-haired Russian waitress that just started to work there is don't you?"

"She looks kinda familiar. No, I don't know. Who is she?"

"Man, that's Marina Oswald. Lee Harvey's widow."

"I already said I would go have a drink with you there and let you see if you can get a ride to someplace else or we could drink until the Casba opens. Don't they usually have a band?"

"On weekends. They get some okay bands sometimes."

"What kind of bands?"

"Oh, blues bands. Always blues bands. It's got a dance floor big enough for a dozen couples."

"You got any money Broadway?"

"Of course I have money. It just happens I don't have any on me. I thought maybe you could loan me a couple of dollars . . ."

Days passed into weeks into months and Broadway remained banned. Being exiled from The Quiet Man cut him off from his most important cultural resource. He'd managed to get permanently kicked out of a couple more joints in the meantime. It mattered which places you were banned from. Anybody could get kicked out of some of those killer bars on Columbia. Kicked out or maybe shot. It was a different ethic over there. And anyway who would know? You had to be banned from a bar that everyone would hear about.

Broadway knew Mike just about always went home at five and left The Quiet Man to the night crew so he'd snuck in a few times late at night after checking to make certain Mike was gone. If he was lucky there would be a bartender who'd either not know him or wouldn't fuck with him as long as he didn't get loud which he couldn't. One late night he got out of control arguing with D.J. Arnett and managed to get himself banned again by a bartender who didn't even know him. Even with that he didn't give up but by now all the bartenders knew him and would throw him out soon as he showed his face.

A month passes and Broadway comes up with a plan. He finds old Bill James wandering down Knox Street and convinces him to draw his portrait for which he will pay him in a couple of days. He goes over to the dime store where he steals a cheap black plastic frame and puts his picture in it. He lurks around The Quiet Man for several nights until he sees through the front window an opening. There is a bartender working who doesn't know him. He waits until just before the panic of last call, enters, and goes straight to the bar where he shows the bartender his framed portrait and convinces him that it is okay for it to be hung up and, as it is so busy, he doesn't mind doing it himself. All he needs is to borrow a hammer and nail. The bartender finds the tool-box and gives Broadway what he needs. In the rush to get last drinks nobody pays any attention to him as he hangs his portrait on the Wall of Regulars.

Spreading the Shine

In many traditional societies barbers were holy men, medicine men. The hair is where good and bad spirits enter and leave the body. To cut hair releases spirits. In the eighteenth century, barbers were also surgeons and bloodletters whose sign out front was a pole with two bandages twisted around it—one for wrapping around the arm before blood was sucked out and the other to use after. They also were dentists. In the nineteenth century medicine and dentistry became separate professions and the importance of barbers declined. Soon many were making wigs. By the 1920s barbershops had become places where storytellers and lowlifes hung out to gossip and tell dirty tales to bankers and businessmen. A place where men told stories of the town to keep it alive.

Darryl shines shoes at the barbershop across the street from The Quiet Man and does odd jobs for the barbers. He is a thin pale white shadow moving among the barber chairs. If you look straight at him he just might vaporize. A white janitor is acceptable, maybe preferable, but a white shoeshine boy . . . there cannot be a white shoeshine boy.

No flesh and blood women were allowed in but were replaced with barbershop fantasies of tied and gagged women in torn clothes on the covers of *Men*, *True Men*, and *Real Men*, women who were not there. Barbershops were sanctuaries . . . for men. Places where what could not be said on the courthouse grounds could be uttered in private.

Cavelike with three limegreen leather-over-steel barberchairs in a row. There were mirrors in front and back so sitting in the barberchair you could see yourself(s) disappear reflected into infinity. In the chair the barber cranked you to the right height then shook the barbercloth so it ballooned into the air to float down covering and protecting you. No harm could come while under that shield. Thus the horror when Albert Anastasia, the chief executioner of Murder Inc., was sitting under the cloth with his eyes closed getting a shave and two men suddenly approached and shot him. Even shot he jumped up and tried to grab them with his bare hands but he lunged for their reflections in the infinite mirrors and he died while the real killers ran out the door as his blood spread over the black and white tile floor.

The shop was anchored by a tall shoeshine stand manned by a shoeshine boy . . . a man . . . a boy, a shoeshineboy. Barbershop shoeshine boys were not flashy like those downtown shoeshinestand cats. A barbershop shoeshineboy didn't have to make such a show popping his rag and all . . . *Have your ever passed the corner of*

Fourth and Grand where a little ball of rhythm has a shoeshine stand? . . . He's a great big bundle of joy. He pops a boogie-woogie rag . . . Not that. Your shoes shined as much when you left the barbershop as when you left the stand. But the stand was more. It was usually owned and run by Black men. In downtown Dallas through the 1950s there were several shoeshine stands with three or four shoeshine chairs fit in spaces too small for any other business. If a baseball game was being broadcast it was on the radio; if not, rhythm and blues played. To many of the white customers this was the only time they heard that music but baseball they had in common so they climbed up in those chairs and talked with the Negroes about the game . . . "Boss you need to have these shoes dyed at least once a year. Do you want me to do it now? Then how about a spit shine with sole dressing or I could give you the full treatment with fire. I promise you Boss I won't give you some New York shine." Shining, shining shoes reflecting bright. "Sure Shine give me the full treatment," and his shoes are set on fire.

Old Black Shine swims away to safety from the sinking Titanic.

> *Now when the news got to the port, the great Titanic has sunk.*
> *You won't believe this, but old Shine was on the corner damn near drunk.*

On the wall of one stand across from Neiman's was a sign:

TO BE A SUCCESS IN DALLAS BUSINESS
YOU MUST HAVE SHINED SHOES.

In 1985 Mr. Ego Brown in Washington D.C. gave Ego
Shines at his stand until the government shut him
down citing the 1905 Bootblack Ban which said "No permit shall issue for bootblack stands on public space."
Not 1885 but 1985. At last in 1989 Judge John H. Pratt
declared the ban unconstitutional and enjoined its
enforcement.

It was 1952 and Frank had been shining shoes at the
Lakewood Towers Barbershop for over ten years. He
knew baseball. He loved baseball. He caressed one of
your feet then the other polishing your shoes while
talking about the Cardinals or Dodgers. Everybody in
Lakewood liked Frank and never thought about where
the bus carried him when he left at night. At the bus
stop he seemed changed. He'd say, "Hello," like through
a veil as you walked by but that was about it. He'd just
say, "Sorry I'm waiting for my bus." But you'd go on and
ask, "Do you think the Eagles will win tonight?" and
he'd answer, "Sure do."

And there were young Black kids with homemade
shoeshine kits who danced on pastel chalk sidewalk
drawings in the fading light of downtown streets. And
they danced until the pictures were danced away into
the air in puffs of yellow, pink, and blue as coins were
tossed their way. That was long before you could get topless shoeshines down in massage parlors on Industrial.

Everything had its place but a white shoeshine boy now
that could be disruptive. Not as much as a lady manicurist but who knew. Lady manicurists wore tight skirts

and had red fingernails but nobody had ever seen a white shoeshineboy.

Joe Spruiell, a regular, is talking to Ken, The Quiet Man bartender, one afternoon.

"I got my first haircut when I was three from a barber named Mac. He owned the shop in Lakewood and so worked out of the first chair. He was killed a week after my first haircut when he lost control of his speedboat out at White Rock Lake and hit a dock going full speed. After that the barber in the second chair, Mr. Cole, moved to the first one and gave me my second haircut and for the next twenty-five years he was the most reliable thing in my life. He was the most loved barber in whatever shop he wound up in and there were several that I followed him to even all the way to Oak Cliff. I never could figure why he moved from shop to shop but I didn't think about it much either. Over the years as the price of a haircut went up he always charged me fifty cents, the same as for my first haircut, slipping coins under the barbersheet into my hand along with a piece of candy. I went to him until he died about the same time that many white men stopped getting their hair cut and started getting it styled by white women.

"Mr. Cole died when I was twenty-five and I didn't get a haircut for a year. I just couldn't go in a barbershop if Mr. Cole wasn't there. My mother finally said she'd pay for me to go to a hairstylist. I wasn't sure of what a hairstylist was and what was wrong with barbers anyway but she was paying so she made an appointment for me and I got dressed up and my sister and my mother and me went to the parlor in NorthPark Mall. Man it sure was different. There was a woman sitting at a desk in a small waiting room and no sign of whoever it was that was going to cut my hair. I signed in and waited until a door opened and the stylist said 'Come in.' It was just her and me in there and no barber chair just a regular metal chair. I sat and she spread the cloth over me. It was dark blue. I felt no protection under it. When she brushed her tits against my arm it was unnerving."

A boy's father took him for his first haircut. Maybe his mother would come along. The only other women in the shop were those passing through to the beauty shop in back. They did not linger but headed back to get permanent waves put in their hair. Few knew that the machine used to put the waves in was invented by a Black woman. Marjorie Stewart Joyner was the grandchild of slaves. She started as a hairdresser and worked her way up to owning a chain of Madam Walker beauty stores and schools. As a beautician one of her biggest problems was figuring a way to give women hairdos that would last more than a day. She came up with a permanent wave machine. The prototype used sixteen pot roast rods hooked to an old-fashion hair dryer and joined together through an electric cord that would heat the rods.

Ken sympathized with Joe: "I know. My barbershop was not that different. It wasn't that women were not allowed in it, it was just that there was nothing there for them unless they wanted to be bound, gagged, and savaged by the men."

Joe says: "Everything was as it should be in my

barbershop until one day when I was about fourteen I went in for a trim and there was a woman in the shop, not passing through, but sitting in the back at a little desk. Frank's stand was in the front window. Who was she? As I waited my turn for Mr. Cole I couldn't keep my eyes off her. She might as well have been a panther. When our eyes met she smiled and I looked away. Finally covered and the chair cranked to the right height I asked Mr. Cole who she was and he told me, 'She's our new manicurist. She cleans and cuts men's fingernails,' and he smiled, 'puts a little polish on them.' 'Polish?' 'Yes but don't worry it's clear.' 'What kind of men would have that done?' I asked, 'sissies?' But what would a sissy be doing in the barbershop? Mr. Cole said, 'No. Not sissies. Regular men. Tough men. You have to be tough to get a manicure. Tough like a gangster.' He asked, 'You know your father has his nails done?' I said, 'No he doesn't,' but I knew Mr. Cole would not lie. 'My dad gets his nails done?'

"Manicurists usually did not stay around long. Seemed soon as you got to know their name and grudgingly accept them they would be gone. Her name was Loretta, the one in Mr. Cole's shop. She was real pretty and real disruptive. How could you have an intimate talk with your barber if there was a woman only a few feet away? Other than gangsters and my father everyone was glad when she left and our normal lives could resume.

"I stopped by that shop nearly daily. Not to get haircuts every time but to talk to my friend Frank. He was the shoeshine boy and was like an uncle in a way, a Black uncle to Mr. Cole's white father. My biological father abandoned me, my mother, my sister, our family for another woman when I was five. I would never again have one father but parts of fathers. Specialized fathers. Mother's boyfriends who gave her money for food. Providers. Mother's boyfriends like Oscar who drove a blue Cadillac convertible and knew Hank Williams. Mother's boyfriends like the golf pro, the inventor, the rich man, the judge. Like Frank. I looked without knowing I was looking for these partial fathers everywhere and a few times found them but Frank was more than an uncle or part-father. He was my friend. We made small bets on baseball games. The color of his skin was the least important thing about him. At least to me, at least until we went to an Eagles game together. On the streetcar there I never thought about us not being able to sit together. We were the only passengers but he had to sit behind the little metal sign on the seat that said 'Coloreds' on one side and 'Whites' on the other. He had to sit behind that. I sat in front of it. It was really idiotic. He sat right behind me but we couldn't sit in the same seat or even across from each other. Those little 'Coloreds/Whites' signs were movable so if there got to be more Blacks than whites they could be moved forward to make more seats available or vice versa. We put up with that to get to Burnett Field. I asked at the ticket booth for two together but just before I got the tickets they said, 'Oh no. He has to sit in the Colored Section way down the left field line.' I could buy a ticket to sit anywhere but there. I should have known, been forewarned, by the 'Whites/Coloreds' sign on the streetcar but wasn't. How could I have not known. I said goodbye to him at the ticket booth and suggested we meet up after the game to ride back together but he never showed up. Of course not he lived in a different part of town.

"My granddaddies on both sides were racists and my father was too although he ran a grocery store on the Black side of town and had more Black friends than white. My mother's father was a carpenter, a respected man, a good man. The president of his Sunday school class who slept through church. He was quiet and humble: a builder. Worked hard as his men but just a little smarter. He had no obvious flaws so when Jackie Robinson broke the color line and became the first Black baseball player in the major leagues my grandfather Big Daddy's behavior was way out of line for him. He was beside himself: How could they let a n█████ play in the big leagues. They have their own league don't they? Why do they have to play in our leagues? I'd heard the word 'n█████' before but never out of Big Daddy's mouth. My father's father was a much more hard-core racist. He told stories of n█████ lynchings and he said he saw more than one n█████'s body float down the river near his home in East Texas. He was in the Ku Klux Klan. A Grand Klugal or somesuchshit. He asked me if I knew what trains said as they passed through town. I answered, 'Chug, chug . . . choo, choo, choo . . . No granddaddy what do trains say?' He said, 'They say: Catch a n█████, black and dirty. Catch a n█████ black and dirty. Catch a n█████ black and dirty' as he used those trains to drill his racism into me and it worked until I got old enough to learn better."

Ken brings him up short, changing the conversation back to where it should be. "Who do you think is the best pitcher in baseball?" But Joe has to finish what he was saying: "You know the funny thing is that the Dallas Eagles became the first Texas League team to have a Black player when they put Dave Hoskins on the mound.

"Oh absolutely. You know it was nearly him that did what Jackie Robinson got famous for."

"How's that?"

"In 1945 three Black ballplayers—Sam Jethro, Dave Hoskins, and Jackie Robinson—were chosen to go to a tryout to see who would be the first African American in the big leagues. Hoskins got hurt and couldn't make the trip. Jackie Robinson caught everyone's eye and he was chosen. When Dave became the first Black ballplayer in the Texas League it wasn't always nice what with 'n███ this' and 'n███ that' but he was such a good guy that his team rallied around him. He was 22 and 10 that first year."

"How'd he get hurt?"

"I can't remember. It wasn't anything too serious. He was able to play again soon. Everybody forgets but he was about as good a hitter as he was a pitcher."

"He sure was. Man what a team the '52 Eagles were. Ty Cobb, Dizzy Dean, Tris Speaker, Mickey Cochrane: all Eagles."

"Yeah I saw that team. I went to the game in the Cotton Bowl with 53,747 other people. It was the biggest crowd ever for a minor league game. Dave Hoskins pitched but nobody came to see him or worry about what color he was. They came to see those old all-stars. Cobb and them took the field against the Tulsa Drillers shuffling into positions as the crowd settled in to watch them play, to see if they had anything left. Dizzy Dean took the mound. He wound up and threw a strike and that was it. The old-timers just left the field after only one pitch. The crowd was stunned. Not one out even just one pitch. But a better team took their place. The regular Eagles came out and Dave Hoskins took the mound. He pitched a great game but my disappointment over getting short-changed by the all-stars lingered so I made up the game in my head and played it and still play it over and over again before going to sleep. 'Crack,' Ty Cobb lines a single to right field but he doesn't stop at first base he rounds it and heads to second sliding in with sharpened spikes high . . . and I fall asleep . . ."

There is some kind of commotion at the front door of The Quiet Man. People are getting out of their seats for a better look. Somebody says, "It's Darryl. He's fallen." The air is charged almost as good as a fight breaking out. The normal routine is broken but isn't that what you go to bars for anyway. Some kind of break, some entertainment and Darryl is providing it. He's fallen. He can't breathe. He moans, "Call the fire department. Have a fire truck sent." He needs oxygen. It happens every couple of weeks. Maybe he does. Maybe he really needs oxygen. When the fire truck arrives they find Darryl slumped on the curb gasping. They know the routine but who knows maybe this time it is for real so they give him oxygen and soon he is better. It could have something to do with bleach.

Joe says, "I was talking to him one day about cheap ways to get drunk. Darryl told me, 'I've tried them all. You know: canned heat, shoe polish strained through white bread, vanilla extract . . .'

"'Isn't that stuff bad for you? All that cheap alcohol? Have you ever tried nutmeg or sunflower seeds? I heard if you put banana peels in the oven, bake them a little, and eat them they give you a nice little buzz.'

"Darryl dismisses all that with, 'I don't want to get a nice little buzz I want to get fucked up and the best way I've found to do that is with lots of beer and a little bleach. Now don't go out and get a big bottle of bleach and gulp it down. That could hurt you. What you got to do is buy a case of the cheapest beer you can find and a little bottle, a pint, of Clorox. I like Clorox better than Purex. It doesn't burn as much. Have a sip with each beer and if you do it right you will finish the beer and the bleach at the same time and pass out. One problem is if you do it alone you might die so I drink some bleach before I go out to a bar where somebody can call for the fire truck.'"

Joe says, "Most everybody thought it was just a way for him to get attention. Maybe it was. He got tired of being at the barbershop and treated like something less than a n███. A big red fire truck helped him be seen but there was more to it than that. Man, I think Darryl was drinking bleach to get whiter."

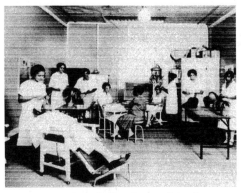

A Madam Walker Beauty School

Dallas Bars

The bartender puts his hand on the bar and in one smooth move hurdles it. Before the drunk can get any real trouble started he is yanked off his barstool and thrown out the front door. A frontiersman sitting at the bar dressed in dirty brown fringed buckskin slowly turns his head to follow the action for a moment then turns back and takes a drink from his beer. No one else bothers to do that much. The bartender who looks like the Republic Pictures' B cowboy moviestar Rod Cameron walks surely, silently back behind the bar. Everything is silent except for the swishing sound of a car passing by outside in the light rain. He stands under the stuffed head of a wild hog waiting for one of the drunks to order another drink. He probably will not have to toss anyone else out tonight. He rarely throws more than one drunk a night out of the Dallas Buckhorn.

Albert Friedrich opened the original Buckhorn Tavern down in San Antonio in 1881 with a standing offer that anyone bringing in a rack of deer antlers or a rattlesnake rattle could get a free shot of whiskey. Teddy Roosevelt and his Roughriders came to drink as did Will Rogers and O. Henry. The world-record, seventy-eight-point buck was bought, mounted, and put on display. Now there are schools of fish in the Hall of Fins and congregations of birds in the Hall of Feathers. The Guard, a huge black gorilla, stands at the front door. He has never denied anyone admission. There are foxes, javelinas, wolf heads and most nearly any other kind of Texas varmint you can think of stuffed and staring through glass eyes. Birds of prey circle. And there are guns, pistols, rifles, shotguns displayed on fake red velvet in glass cases and hung on the walls. There are no signs warning against bringing a gun in. There are plenty already there. The place sprawls across old wooden floors scuffed and blackened by the leather of thousands of boots walking, dancing, fighting on them. Windows that are as much wall are swung up. A big cantina. The farther north in Texas you travel the more enclosed the bars are until by the time you get to Dallas there are few windows at all.

In Dallas the Buckhorn North is a seedier place. Not a saloon or anything as exotic as a cantina. It is a sleazy bar on a dark downtown Dallas side street. Animal fur droops like Spanish moss from stuffed heads on the walls and drips onto the floor, the tables, and sometimes into drinks. Some of the guns are rusted but many still work. In a few places where some have been removed their outline, their image remains lighter than the smoked wall—like ghosts of guns. Stories are told, made up, about why that Winchester is gone, who took it down,

who got shot. And there are stories few remember about
what a ghost gun is needed for.

Above the bar is a huge barn owl with wings spread
wide, a rat in its mouth. At night around the Hour of
the Wolf, long after the bar has closed, it swoops from
its perch and dives to catch rodents or anything else living and creeping about. But there is always more than
it can get. It would take a parliament of owls to clean
this place. Most of the customers are drunks working on
becoming winos. The beer is cheap. The jukebox has a
great selection of Hank Williams, Lefty Frizzell, Webb
Pierce, Patsy Cline. But it broke tonight and plays only
"Lemon Tree" over and over.

> *Lemon tree very pretty and the lemon*
> *flower is sweet*
> *but the fruit of the poor lemon is impossi-*
> *ble to eat.*

> *Lemon tree very pretty and the lemon*
> *flower is sweet*
> *but the fruit . . .*

Until the bartender goes over and jerks the plug from
the wall turning out its flashing lights and leaving the
place quiet as death. He could have used the volume
control/on/off switch behind the bar but it wouldn't be
nearly as dramatic.

A small, not-so-clean customer already about obliter-
ated on Mad Dog 20/20 comes in and puts enough coins
on the bar for a beer. He doesn't like beer but knows
that he can sit in the warm, dry Buckhorn as long as he

buys one or two. He nurses the first one for an hour or so until he thinks he sees the owl's wings slightly move which he takes as a signal that it's about closing time or that he has had too much to drink. His now empty glass has been removed by the bartender who has put one hand on the bar and is glaring at him. A light rain has started outside and he wants to stay dry a little longer so he digs in his pockets and finds a crumpled dollar bill. He orders one more beer and looks at, longs for, the Colt revolver displayed behind the bar. Yellow city night light is darkened to brown oozing through the front plate glass window which hasn't been washed in years. In that dull air the owl's wings slowly open wide and the bartender shouts, "Last call."

Across the street from Neiman Marcus is a small blue neon sign in a window of a black building that reads Zoo Bar. It is darker inside than in other bars and all the customers always men watch you as you come in but you can't see them. Sol's Turf Bar is a cop hangout. Abe Weinstein's Colony Club is the kind of burlesque club which Jack Ruby aspires to. It is classier than his Carousel. And tucked away down other side streets are a couple of Porters and Waiters. They have great soul food, no white customers, and jukeboxes from which Percy Sledge sings: "At the dark end of the street. That's where we always meet. Hiding in shadows." There are private clubs high up in buildings that are not so private. If you can find them and are white and clean you can drink in most of them after purchasing a cheap membership that may cost nothing more than your signature. They do not have neon signs out front. Someone must tell you about them. You can get already mixed cocktails in them. It's not until 1970 that an amendment to the Texas Constitution makes liquor by the drink legal in Texas for the first time since before Prohibition. Otherwise it's just beer or bring your own in a brown bag and order setups. There are clubs though for the Dallas elite that only the rich can be members of.

The Quiet Man was a twenty-minute bus ride from downtown or a ten-minute drive down Central Expressway or a five-minute drive from SMU. All the downtown bars were minor distractions which did not often tempt me on my regular visits to The Quiet Man. It was a new sort of bar. A Irish bar. An early concept bar. It had been a regular bar before called the Turf Bar with three neon green horses galloping across the outside front wall and into the night parking lot. When Irish Mike Carr bought it he did not intend for it to become what it became. He knew little about Ireland but figured an *Erin Go Bragh* banner on the back wall would make it seem that he did. He wanted an Irish bar where talk was more important than music. A bar where men were gentlemen and women were grateful.

Bars were bars in Dallas unless they were nightclubs where you had to dress up. You went to a bar to drink. You went to a nightclub to show off your clothes, your date, your money. But something happened at The Quiet Man that set it apart. Maybe it was the sixties. Maybe it was the drugs. Carr owned it and thought he ran it but he didn't. The real action happened when he left for the day at six. Maybe it was when the first person showed up on acid and ordered a Dr Pepper instead of a beer. Maybe it was because nobody knew for sure what bars were becoming. Anyone and everyone felt comfortable in The Quiet Man. And they told their friends and their friends came. During the day old men and insurance men and plumbers who should have been working and criminals and just plain drunks pretending to be something more than they were or just relaxing and being exactly what they were drank there.

There was rarely trouble at least physical trouble. Fights hardly ever happened but when they did usually Chief was involved. Chief was hooked up with a gang of bikers who drank at the Little White Cloud but on occasion he would ride down to The Quiet Man. Everybody said bikers were cool when they were alone. It was when they were with their gang that they had to show off though you should never call them gangs. I meant to say clubs. Chief often came alone. He was a big Indian who rode a big Harley. Nobody messed with him most of the time but one night (the story went) Chief tangled with the wrong guy who slammed him into the jukebox and wiped the place up with him. It was hard to find eyewitnesses or determine just when this happened or who the guy was that kicked Chief's ass. It just became part of the bar's mythology. It was not a good idea to bring that fight up with Chief.

I was gone for over five years, gone to prison. Then I escaped the USA to Norway where I met a guy in a bar who invited me home but instead of sleeping with him I wound up with his wife Siren and while he cried on the living room couch we fucked in their bed. But it wasn't just some overnight deal. She left him for me. She was real smart and even more beautiful. When I met her the Beatles' "Norwegian Wood" played: I once had a girl, or should I say, she once had me. She was a librarian who told me if I ever got lost from her I should go to a library, tell the librarian there I was a writer, and she would take care of me which made me realize how far I was from Texas. She spoke four languages, hung out with artists, and slept with anyone she wished to, man or woman. When I came back from Norway she said she would follow as soon as she could. I didn't believe her. After I landed in New York with no money I called some friends in Brooklyn who said I could sleep on their couch for a few weeks until I could make some money and get my own place. I got a job as a messenger for a bunch of lawyers which gave me access to their offices and had no idea what I was going to do next. After a couple of weeks I got a call from Siren. She was in New York. The first night she was there I took her up to the lawyers' offices on the fiftieth floor and we made love on the long board table with the lights of Manhattan shining all around us. She wanted to see Texas so we got a car to drive to Dallas. We stayed with my mother. I had no idea what The Quiet Man might be and it hadn't changed. We didn't know what we would do next but weren't worried about it. She had the money and I had the time.

At The Quiet Man I introduced her to Chief. He was the first Indian she had ever met. She was a little intrigued. He was more mystified. I wasn't worried as he started hitting on her thinking she could handle whatever bullshit he came up with and she did, she handled it so good that he got frustrated and did something stupid. He picked up a salt shaker and for some odd reason shook salt on her head. She just smiled and picked up one of her own, unscrewed the lid, stood up, and dumped the whole thing on Chief's head. It wasn't a good idea to one-up him like that so everybody in the bar turned to watch to see how he would go after her or me for being with her and nothing moved and nothing made a sound and everyone waited. Ken the bartender put his hand on the bar to push himself as far as possible from any trouble and it was real quiet.

Benjamin Murchison
Hunt Smith

houses & fathers

He was sitting alone in The Quiet Man wearing faded old clothes that were khaki or gray. He could have been in his fifties. The only thing that stood out about him was his deep blue wool New York Yankee cap with the bill elegantly curved. On the stool next to him was a lightweight red, gray, and yellow checked gabardine jacket that must have been cheap like some Goodwill bargain. It wasn't until later in better light that I saw it was a fine but old Burberry coat. I sat one barstool away from him. We were the only ones in the place. I ordered a beer and said, "Hello." He nodded, "Hello," back. There was a baseball game on the radio. I asked him the score and he said the Cardinals were just coming to bat in the bottom of the first. It was nothing to nothing. We talked about baseball for awhile, then, I can't recall how, the subject changed and he launched into a tale that turned a searing light into some dark corners of my city's history. I grew up here in Dallas too and wove a couple of stories around his that seemed to amuse him but really I was just trying to keep him going. Once he got going there was a sense of urgency in what he had to tell me. He said he was a regular in this bar but wasn't sure if he'd be back after today. He talked fast and mumbled and every now and then he'd let go with a razor-pitched laugh that stopped time. After awhile he calmed down and settled into a rhythm. I'm not sure which was more interesting: the stories or the teller.

After a couple more beers which I paid for we got to talking about where we were from.

He said, "Mount Vernon."

"Mount Vernon, Texas?" I asked.

"No," he answered.

"Well the only other Mount Vernon I know of in Texas is Sam Houston's home outside Huntsville which has come to be called our own Mount Vernon. It was no more than a cabin in the woods but it was the Father of Texas's home. You from there?" I asked.

"No."

"You are from Texas though aren't you?"

"Yes. I'm from right in Dallas and the Mount Vernon I'm talking about is here too."

"You mean Mount Vernon like George Washington's home?"

The question irritated him, "Well yes but I'm not talking about the Father of the Country's home or the Father of Texas's either. I'm talking about my daddy's. Funny thing is lots of people think he copied Washington's Mount Vernon but just had his place built just twice as big like some comicstrip Texas brag: *Everything is bigger in Texas.* I'll tell you something though. Daddy didn't build that house. It was already there, built in 1930 by Mr. Thomas Y. Pickett. Daddy bought it in 1937. It came with ten acres of land, two peacocks, chickens, a cow, and one calf. He paid $69,000 for it. I never heard him say anything about who Mr. Pickett was. But then again I never heard him say much of anything.

> *When it suddenly awakes the peacock cries out*
> *because it thinks its beauty has been lost.*

"Well Daddy was soon rid of the livestock. The chickens were eaten, fried. The cow and calf sold. Only the peacocks were kept, for awhile anyway, because they made such a terrifying scream scaring away anyone who came on to the grounds. After awhile though he got tired of their racket, cut their heads off, and had them cooked and served for Sunday dinner. In the place of chicken it was a spectacular dish. When the servants served them on silver platters the family was amazed what with those opalescent green and gold jeweled tails spread open and sparkling like small constellations but the meat was dry and hard and not near as good as chicken. A week after that meal thieves snuck onto the grounds and in the silence there broke into the house and made off with all the silver trays.

"Daddy's Mount Vernon was everything he dreamed it should be. Classic American architecture and up on a hill overlooking White Rock Lake like Washington's Mount Vernon overlooked the Potomac. He got up early and raised the American flag every morning himself. I bet George Washington didn't do that."

"So do you know if there are any more Mount Vernons?" I asked.

"Yes, there are plenty more scattered around the country."

"Who was Vernon anyway?"

"He was an admiral in the British Navy. I bet you didn't know that George Washington didn't build his Mount Vernon either. His great granddaddy did. In 1674. It was passed down to George's half brother Lawrence who named it after his commanding officer Admiral Edward Vernon in the British Navy. George got it after Lawrence's widow died."

"How do you know all this stuff?"

"I've had lots of time to study. You're from here aren't you? Do you know my daddy's house?"

"Sure I've seen it, driven, walked by it many times. It has that long green lawn that rolls forever down to the road that runs around White Rock Lake."

"Neither Washington's nor daddy's Mount Vernons have many trees," he tells me, "but both have those huge lawns. I always thought they should have more trees. Sam Houston's Mount Vernon had lots of trees, wasn't on a hill, and overlooked nothing but a little fishing pond nearby."

"Yes I know the Mount Vernon you are talking about. I know the place, at least from a distance. I mean who in Dallas doesn't? It is the home of the richest man in the world."

"The richest man in the world? Some say he was. *Forbes* magazine once called him the richest man in America but let me tell you something about him. Every morning 'the richest man in the world' got up, went out to the tall flagpole in front of Mount Vernon, and raised the flag of the USA himself. He'd eat a little breakfast then get into his ordinary Oldsmobile sedan with Gastromagic advertising stuck on the side . . . He'd gotten into the food business with a line of cheap canned food called HLH Parade and then he got into the flatulence business when he came out with Gastromagic to neutralize the gas that his food gave you. I knew more about my daddy than he ever could have imagined."

"Did you spy on him or something?"

"No I didn't spy on him but I would go by his mansion every now and then. I could see it from the road and longed to go inside but knew that probably was never going to happen. I might as well have been the garbage man. No not even that. Most of the time it seemed he didn't even acknowledge my existence. I stayed upset with him. The few times I saw him he promised he'd take me up in a blimp that a friend of his owned or we'd go to a baseball game and sit in the best seats in the house right behind the dugout. But he would never show up when he said he was going to. I guess I did spy on him. I'd watch him in the morning raising that fucking flag and putting his brown paper bag lunch on the seat beside him and driving off to work. He about always went straight to work but he did not always stay there. Sometimes he'd just disappear. Be gone a day, a week, a month. On business."

"I always wanted to see the inside of that mansion," I told him, "but the closest I ever got to it was once after an office Christmas party where I was working. I should not drink Scotch. I knew that. I know that. But for that matter I've had problems with rum and I've had problems with gin. The first thing I got drunk on was gin. It still about makes me throw up just smelling it. Bourbon, Everclear, even beer. I've drunk too much of just about any alcohol you can think of. Saké, Jack Daniels but for some reason I never had a problem with vodka. Anyway I had gotten real drunk on Scotch at the party and wasn't sure exactly what I had done or said but knew I'd done something for which I best leave the party before I lost my job. There are some things that go beyond the limits of even a Christmas party. When I drink Scotch I just can't remember what they are.

"My coworker Homer Haroldson said he'd give me a ride home. He asked where I lived and I told him right out by White Rock Lake. I don't know what got into me but I directed him to Mount Vernon. As we pulled up the long driveway he saw the place and said, 'You don't live here.' I said, 'Yes I do,' and that was kind of funny but I should have stopped right there and said, 'I'm kidding. Let's get out of here,' and gotten him to take me to where I really lived in a little garage apartment but I just said, 'Thank you for the ride' and got out of the car. As he drove back down the drive it started to snow as I stood there at Mount Vernon waiting to go in like some drunk beggar at America's front door. Soon as Homer's taillights disappeared I took off walking fast down the driveway before someone saw me and called the cops.

"It was a long way home and I was lost in a snowy, Scotch haze for I don't know how long, thirty or forty minutes, when I saw a 7-Eleven. Warm and familiar. I loosened my tie, went in and bought a six-pack. Coming out the door though I saw some cops and thought they were watching me from their cruiser like maybe they had been called by someone at Mount Vernon so I took off running. I held on to the six-pack for awhile until I ran into a barbwire fence. The beer floated from my hands. I started to pick it up but couldn't see it in the dark. I stumbled, fell through the fence, out of my mind. The barbs tore my suit coat and my white shirt all the way through to rip my flesh but I didn't stop to watch the blood. I got to my feet and ran fast as I could through the field on the other side of the fence until I came to a stream and before I could see a thing the ground was gone from beneath my feet. I fell in. It was just a small stream, mostly mud. I crawled out and got to running again like in a bad dream. By this point I had forgotten even why I was running. I was just going fast as I could but moving slower. I was walking. I thought I saw a bull but it was too dark to tell for sure. It started snowing harder and it was the night before Christmas. I tried to run but collapsed. I was ready to lie down and freeze to death or be killed by the bull but as I sat there just before giving up I saw a row of lights not far away. It looked like small houses. I managed to get up and stumble through the snow toward them. As I got closer I saw yellow lights burning in curtained windows of modest frame houses and red and green Christmas lights around the porches. Several had Christmas trees in the front windows but only one had a tree with bubble lights. That was the one I made my way to brushing at the debris on my suit coat, wiping what blood off I could, running my fingers through my hair. I walked up to the door. An old man so frail he seemed transparent responded to my knocking. He looked at me, smiled, and said, 'Come inside,' like he was expecting me. I opened the screen door and entered, He said, 'Sit down,' and I sat in a big soft chair. Soon an old woman with long gray hair brought me a towel and asked if I would like something warm to drink. I said, 'Yes,' and as green and red lights blinked and bubbled she brought me a cup of hot chocolate. I dried off as much as I could with the towel then as I sat in front of a space heater out of the blue the old man politely said to me, 'It seems you have had a rough night.' I answered, 'I have had a rough life.' He said, 'Would you like to change all that?' and I said, 'Sure.' He said, 'If you would like to maybe you are ready tonight to accept the Lord Jesus Christ as your personal savior?' I didn't hesitate, 'Sure. I will but if I do would you call me a cab.' He said he would. It wouldn't be the first time I had let the Lord into my life. I had done it several times as well as having been baptized twice just to make sure it took. I had it done in a Baptist and Methodist church. I later accepted Buddha, Krishna, and Hank Williams and I don't know how many other gods. I saw no reason to limit the number.

"I repeated, 'Yes. Yes,' to the old man. 'I do take the Lord Jesus Christ as my personal savior,' it being Christmas Eve and all and as I was wiping more blood from my pants I passed out. I guess I got home in a cab but I don't remember for sure anyway the next morning I was in my own bed. I lay there trying to reconstruct the night before and remembered the old couple and accepting the Lord. I wondered what it means that I was drunk when I did it. Did it still count? I argued with myself and won. I concluded that it only counts as long as I stay drunk which I sort of still was. Piecing the night before together I remembered leaving the office party and somehow being at the home of the richest man in the world. I'm pretty sure I didn't get in. There was a hole in what I remembered from the time I left Mount Vernon to the time I got to the 7-Eleven and I'm not even sure how much of that was true.

"That big old mansion just haunted me for some reason when I was a kid. It wasn't until a few years ago at my father's funeral that Uncle George, my father's brother showed me a picture that helped me understand why. It was a creased, ragged, and aged brown photograph of the family home in Marshall. I knew they had lots of money which they lost in the Depression but had no idea they had such a mansion. And in the photograph lying, propped on a casual elbow on its long green lawn was my handsome father. He must have been around twenty. This mansion wasn't as big as Hunt's but had that plantation look too like another Mount Vernon. After he showed me the photograph my uncle folded it back up and put it in his wallet. He said, 'You've got to come visit me sometimes and I will tell you stories of your grandparents' house,' but I never went. Recently I heard he had died but I didn't know when he did so hadn't made it to his funeral. He was the last member of that generation of my father's side of my family to pass away. I don't know what happened with the photo but like so much history it is just gone and we are left alone in a world of ancestors' shadows."

So he asked me, "When you were out at the lake in front of Mount Vernon did you ever see anyone around the house?"

I answered, "I never saw a living person there during the day and at night it was mostly dark inside except for a lamp burning in what must have been the parlor."

"So in the daytime? You never saw my father on the lawn or around the house?"

"No. Never but I heard tales of what went on inside. I heard his wife had lots of church parties in the sixties. Later I found out there were darker things happening there around that time."

"Like what?"

"You must know how crazy things were at that time right before John Kennedy was shot."

"I know some things but what are you talking about? Do you mean things that involved my daddy?"

"I do. Like the meeting that happened the night before the assassination when Richard Nixon, J. Edgar Hoover and his boyfriend Clyde Tolson, Mayor Bob Thornton, your daddy, and a bunch of other people even the gossip columnist for the *Dallas Times Herald* Val Imm met at Clint Murchison's house for something more than a social get-together."

"How do you know about that?"

"From Madeleine Brown."

"You mean Lyndon Johnson's mistress?"

"Yes. She was there when Vice President Johnson himself arrived late that night and immediately went into a room with the other big shots and shut the door. After he came out he was . . . 'squeezing my hand so hard, it felt crushed from the pressure, he whispered into my ear words I'll always remember: "After tomorrow those goddamn Kennedys will never embarrass me again. That's no threat. That's a promise."'"

"I think that is more than I want to know."

"So tell me what was it like inside."

"I don't know. I used to walk past too but I never got inside."

"How's that? You never were in your own daddy's house?"

"Never."

"I never got to go in because I was not part of the family that lived there. You know my daddy had more than one family and that he had kids with all them. He tried to keep them from knowing about each other but he didn't always try too hard. He even moved the second family into a house just a couple of blocks from Mount Vernon. I got to admit my daddy seemed like some kind of sex maniac but I heard a story that it wasn't sex that interested him so much as that he wanted to have lots of children to carry on his name. The amazing thing about him was that he was able to keep all those balls in the air at the same time. I reckon though if you had as much money as he had you can do most anything you want to. If you were in either of those families you were taken care of but I was born into a fourth."

"A fourth family?"

"Yeah there was a fourth family if you could call it a family. Maybe there were more. I don't know? Nobody but Daddy and Mother and me knew about it. I mean it wasn't a family really. My mother didn't raise me. I was passed from uncle to aunt to a family in Oak Cliff. My daddy would anonymously send cash to whoever I was living with to pay for room and board. You'd think that was easy enough to do if you were the richest man in the world but he was real tight. He drove that old Oldsmobile with advertisement glued all over it. It was embarrassing to everyone but him. Carrying his lunch to work in a paper bag acting like he couldn't afford to eat out or even to have a proper lunchpail."

"Maybe he was trying to make up for his wild youth."

"You know it wasn't just that he was wild but he was mean and conniving too. He was a liar and a cheat. He'd traveled all over the West cheating at cards, driving mules, just all sorts of halfway legal stuff. He started off in the oil business by swindling Dad Joiner out of the Daisy Bradford #3 down in Gregg County. You know that oil well kicked off the biggest oil field in the world and my daddy cashed in. He could more than hold his own amongst the other con artists there. He was a gambler. But all that was a long time ago, long before he got religion and joined the First Baptist Church in Dallas. He wanted to look legitimate not like some kind of kook but that was hard to do. He'd started all those right-wing talk shows like *Facts Forum* and *Life Line* and with his sons Lamar and Nelson Bunker he'd set up an outfit called the International Committee for the Defense of Christian Culture. And then he connived a way that he could pay for them with tax write-offs. He wound up paying hardly any taxes while getting his political views aired for free. John Kennedy didn't like that and got legislation passed to stop that kind of activity. That and Kennedy's efforts to have the oil depletion allowance eliminated made my daddy hate John Kennedy. He was taking money out of his pocket. And then the president was coming to town. There are many stories about him which I could tell you but I'm not sure which are true and which were made up. Once when I got older I asked about some of the stories I had heard about him and all he'd say was, 'They are just stories. I was a wildcatter after all.'"

"An oil wildcatter?"

"Yeah. A gambler. Then he took his riches, moved to Dallas, and bought Mount Vernon."

"So you are . . ."

"A Hunt.

"Yes. Yes. Yes. I am the son of the richest man in the world but I never saw any of that money. He paid for my mother's maternity bills, gave her a few hundred dollars, then disappeared. Like I said he did make sure whoever was taking care of me got money and when I got older he had a small trust fund set up for me so I never really had to work. I had lots of time. I bought a little house in Oak Cliff and have lived a simple life. About the only thing I have any passion for anymore is baseball. All I wanted to do was listen to games on the radio, watch the Game of the Week on Saturday, and ever now and then go see the old Dallas Eagles play at Burnett Field which wasn't far from my house. The only time I'd read the newspaper was during baseball season. If you ask me America started going downhill when football became bigger than baseball."

"I agree. There is no poetry in football. Football is all prose."

"You might even say the decline started when baseball games started being televised but I got to admit I love watching Dizzy Dean and the Game of the Week."

"Sure. I think maybe because Dizzy treated television like it was radio."

"What do you mean?"

"He was like a storyteller in your living room more than a television announcer. So, anyway, baseball is your passion?"

"Yeah. I've been riding the bus over to this bar for several years because it is a safe place and because of Ken. He loves baseball as much as I do and he doesn't pry into my life."

"So your name is Hunt? What's your first name?"

"Benjamin but everybody calls me Oak Cliff Benny."

"Benjamin Hunt?"

"No. Just Oak Cliff Benny. Hunt wasn't even the name I was given at birth. I was born a Murchison in a shack outside Athens."

"Greece?"

"Come on. You know I mean Athens, Texas."

"Okay. If your daddy was H. L. Hunt who was your mother then?"

"She was a Murchison and that's all I'm going to tell you about her."

I didn't try to get more out of him about that except I did ask, "Then you were part of the two richest families in Dallas?"

"Biologically. That's all. I really had no family. They just named me Benjamin Smith."

"That's what it says on your birth certificate."

"I asked my mother once about it and she said there wasn't one and had never been one. I was born way out in the woods and the only people who even knew about me was my mother, Daddy, and an old Black woman midwife. There was this rumor that I had Negro blood but in East Texas that rumor was spread about lots of white children. You know who I think started that about me?"

"Who?"

"I think it was my daddy."

"Why?"

"Because if I was Black I couldn't be Mr. Hunt's son."

"How's that? It just takes one parent to make you black."

"Don't try to make sense out of it. It's just racist bull-shit. When I was a kid I went along with a lot of it. Back then there was the old Miscegenation Law which had it that only 1/16 of your blood had to be Black for you to be. It was like Black blood was so strong that it took just 1/16 to make you Black. Anyway the story was that if I were Black I couldn't be H. L. Hunt's son because he would never have sex with a Black woman cause if he did and there were children there could be like a Black Hunt empire and a white one. It's pretty farfetched but that's how they used to think.

"You know though I got to say my daddy did come up with some pretty good ideas like all the way back in the thirties he was in favor of a shorter work week but it was like he couldn't leave a good idea alone and by the sixties he'd written this book *Alpaca* about a perfect society where the most votes would go to the oldest and the wealthiest. Citizens younger than twenty-two would get one vote. Older voters would get two. The top twenty-five percent of taxpayers would get an extra two votes. I read it once."

"Talking about your daddy's children were you his first born?"

"No. His first born was H. L. Hunt III. He called him Hassie and he was his favorite child. It's a sad story. He looks just like Daddy. Dresses like him and had in Daddy's opinion an almost mystical ability to find oil. By the time he was twenty-one he was already a millionaire with his own company that Daddy helped organize but then Hassie cracked up, just lost it, couldn't stand the pressure or whatever. Maybe he'd wound up with Daddy's crazy genes and none of the good ones. Hassie. He was real shy. Never talked much but you could see it in his eyes—pain, confusion. I don't know maybe he just went crazy. Back then in Dallas psychiatrists were considered not much better than Communists but something had to be done. Daddy had him sent to the best head doctors in the country and he got diagnosed as being schizophrenic. He tried everything to cure him. Got to thinking maybe it had something to do with Hassie's sexuality or lack of it. He hired whores for him like kind of to prime the pump but it didn't. Daddy wanted grandchildren. He wanted a Hunt dynasty. You know Daddy had fourteen children but the one that counted most with him was Hassie. It is hard to estimate how hurt Daddy was by the way he turned out. After he tried everything he could think of he finally pretty much gave up on Hassie being the next head of the dynasty. He finally gave in and did something drastic. He had him lobotomized. He figured, you know, Hassie would either be better after having his brain scrambled or he'd be a vegetable and that's how he wound up. Calm. He had to have around-the-clock care after that and about the only time he left the grounds of Mount Vernon was to walk along the lake."

"So whatever happened to him?"

"I used to see him walking out along the road in front of the house. It was creepy. He was dressed just like my dad in his black suit, white shirt, and bow tie. He looked just like him. It was as if though he was not a separate being but was some part of Daddy that had broken off, disconnected. Just walking, just walking. You know I think that what happened with Hassie really hurt Daddy more than he ever let on and made him a bitter old man out to take his revenge on the world. About the only other thing I ever heard of that affected him as much happened in 1937, the same year he bought Mount Vernon. He wasn't one to let on . . . to let his feelings show but what happened back then had to get to him . . . even make him feel guilty. I mean he felt guilty about a lot of stuff like his secret families and his shady business dealings but what happened then ate at him the rest of his life."

"1937? What happened then?"

"Man that was the year all those kids got blown up down in East Texas in New London when nearly four hundred children were killed."

"Oh yeah. When the school blew up but what did that have to do with your father?

"I'll tell you the story. It was a real pretty spring

day in, I think, March, right at the end of the school day at the New London High School. The students were getting ready to go home when everything blew up. Huge slabs of concrete, desks, doors, tile, blackboards, brooms, glass, children, iron girders were blown sky-high. I read that there was a sound right before of something in the earth rumbling and then a flash and a huge BOOM then a few seconds later arms, legs, bloody torsos were falling from the sky. This guy who was there said it was just one great big puff. In no time hundreds of men showed up to dig with their hands or whatever tool they could find in the rubble for survivors. Fire trucks, doctors and nurses, ambulances rushed in from hundreds of miles around.

"This one student said he had been in the basement wood workshop and saw his teacher unplug an electric sanding machine which was by a partially opened door right before he saw a burst of light and fire and then the explosion like thunder that blew the floors and ceiling of the entire building into the sky."

"Oh I've read about it. It was horrible but what did that have to do with your daddy?"

"What caused the explosion was residue from one of his oil pipelines. It is hard to know just what happened but one thing for sure is that it was gas. Propane gas in the basement that had built up down there and waited for a spark. The gas leaked from the pipeline of Excelsior Refining Company. You know back then you couldn't smell natural gas so you wouldn't even know it was there. It wasn't long after that the government passed a law requiring mercaptan to be put in the gas to give it a smell. The company that ran Excelsior was

Daddy's Placid Oil. After that horrible day he changed the name of his company to Parade Refining Company.

"Far as I know Daddy never talked about what happened that day. I don't think he could."

"So that and what happened with Hassie, those really changed him."

"Not that he showed it but yes. It had to."

"You never got to know Hassie did you?"

"Not really. I'd see him out walking. You know he walked real slow. I'd say hello but he had no idea who I was. Not that it mattered. He never answered, I don't even know if he could still talk. I did have a picture in my mind though of him and Daddy sitting in Mount Vernon's living room at dusk. Just sitting there. Neither of them saying a word until the nurse came to put Hassie to bed. Funny thing is though Daddy set up a company for Hassie which he couldn't really run. Good oil-men were hired to run it and it made more money than any of Daddy's other companies. Hassie was rich."

"Is he still alive?"

"Oh yes. He is although it is like his soul or spirit or something left his body years ago maybe during the lobotomy. He still walks along the lake usually with a nurse but there have been some reports of him wandering by himself very late at night like he was looking for something. Maybe the Lady of the Lake? "

"The Lady of the Lake?"

"You know about the Lady of the Lake don't you? It is an old story, told in many places but with different details. Sometimes it is a hitchhiker who disappears out of the front seat after he has been given a ride at night. Sometimes it is Jesus but in Dallas it is the Lady of the Lake but, you know, it is just a story, a myth, a legend . . . I know you've heard the story."

"I have."

"And what story did you hear?"

"I heard one about this Doctor Echols who was driving home after a couple of drinks at the Lakewood Country Club on a Saturday night when he saw a woman in a beautiful dress standing along the road motioning for him to stop. He did and she asked him for a ride over to a house on Gaston Avenue. The front seat of his car was full so she got in the back. When they got to the address he turned around to say to the woman that they were there but she was gone and where she had been was just a puddle of water. He sat there for awhile then went up to the house. The doctor asked him if he knew anything about the young woman who had given him this address. The man at the door stopped him: 'I know it has happened several times and always on Saturday. Someone comes to my door with a story like yours. I am tired and don't want to talk about it but two years ago my daughter died in a boating accident at White Rock.'"

"Well I don't know if I believe that," Benjamin said. "Maybe the doctor just made it up. Maybe but there are other versions about the Lady."

"I know. There is the couple who worked at Neiman Marcus who gave her a ride in 1935. That is supposed to be the true story but who knows. So yes I know the stories but what is your point?"

"What I mean is it is like those two spirits haunt the lake. Hassie and the Lady exist somewhere between the living and the dead. And there is this other story an old fisherman told me. He said Hassie was not aimlessly

wandering by the lake. He had a purpose. He was looking for the Lady. And the fisherman told me some believe
he found her . . . found her not in this world but in some
other half-world . . . I mean more than found her. They
liked each other right off and over the years became
quiet close. Old man Hunt never knew that when he
was hiring whores for him Hassie already had a better
teacher. But she was a ghost and Hassie was a living
human. Hassie has a human body but when he'd had
those lobotomies his spirit, or something broke free and
out of his physical body. It was like he was doubled. A
spirit body and a still-living physical body, but I think
I've talked enough today and heard enough. I'm going to
have to be going."

"Okay, but before you go let me ask you about one
more story. I've heard there was a child."

Benjamin stood up. "That's enough."

"Don't you want to know who that child was?"

"No. I don't want to hear anymore," and he turned
and left.

I wish he had stayed around so I could have told
him about the mysterious flag raisings that happened
at Mount Vernon after his daddy died. I can't remember
the first time I heard it but the second was from Red,
the guy who runs the bait shop on Garland Road where
I was buying some nightcrawlers. He said he knew Mr.
H. L. Hunt and thought him a fine fellow.

It was like Ken, the bartender, had read my mind.
He said, "I'd like to hear about that flag raising."

I hesitated for a minute before telling him but so what
it was just a story. "What I got from him," I told Ken,
"was this. He said, 'I was usually at the lake even before

the fishermen because they would need bait. Before the sun was up I'd drive along the lake road right in front of Mount Vernon on my way to work. When he was still alive I often saw the old man raise the American flag. After he died the job was passed around among the servants. One morning Mrs. Hunt asked if the flag was up. The servant said, "No. It isn't," but he would go do it. When he got out there though the flag was already at the top of the pole.'

"How do you know that?, I asked him.

"'I know,' Red said, 'because that servant used to get worms from me. We got to know each other pretty good. He's the one who told me. He said it happened more than once too that flag seeming to raise itself.'

"'Did anybody have any idea about what happened?' I asked.

"He said, 'Of course somebody always has a story. One that was told to me was by a jeweler named James Echols. He rarely bought anything but always had a tale to tell. One afternoon I asked him if he'd ever heard anything about those flag raisings.'

""'You are asking the right man," he answered. "You know I live near the lake on Coronado. Close enough to it that on many mornings I go for a walk there. One foggy morning as I passed the mansion I saw the flag going up the pole. Nothing unusual about that but when I looked for who was raising it I could see no one through the heavy fog but then the sun broke through for a moment and I could make out a person. They were a dressed in a small black suit, white shirt, and black bow tie. Was it a child or a small man? I couldn't make it out but when the sun illuminated the figure better it was clear that it was a boy. As I continued to watch that child turned to look right into my eyes. I was transfixed for a moment before the fog closed back in. I tried to see but it was not possible until I stepped through the fence railing and walked up the long lawn to get a closer look. When I got near the house where I could see the bottom of the flagpole I saw nothing . . . no one.'"

"Red said, 'I asked him who or what he thought he had seen that morning.'

"Mr. Echols answered that he had nothing to add, at least that morning, to what he had just told but that child sure looked like Hassie.

"'But Hassie was a grown man by then, wasn't he?' Red said he asked Mr Echols.

"'Yes he was.'"

Ken says, "Wow I've heard a story from a customer something like that."

"And what was that?"

He asked me, "Do you know who Rosemary Thornton was? Probably not. She was the eccentric daughter of Mayor Robert Thornton. She still lived at her parents' home, a small medieval castle, down in a hollow near the lake. It was hard to see from the road for the trees and iron fence around it. There was nothing in Dallas like it. Not like Mount Vernon for all to see up on that hill—the mayor's castle was for none to see but family and a few friends. Enough of a turret stuck up above the trees for a passerby to see. Rosemary was a weaver who spent most of her time alone in her room in one of the castle's towers with her loom and spinning wheel. She did not go down to the lake often but one morning in the same spring of 1962 when a full moon shone through her window and woke her before the sun came up she felt pulled there. She got dressed and set out in the bright moonlight. It was a long walk before she got to Mount Vernon. In faint early morning shadows she saw the flag going up and she saw who was raising it. A child. A girl dressed in an expensive blue dress, like one from Neiman's. When the flag reached the top the child turned and started walking toward Rosemary. The child called her name. 'Rosemary. Rosemary,' and approached but just as she got right up to her the first morning sun-rays hit the child and she blurred and shimmered for a moment and then was gone."

I wanted to know more at first but when Ken said, "I got to work it's getting busy," I realized I had heard enough for one day.

On the radio the Old Scotsman, Gordon McClendon, was still broadcasting the Cubs and Cardinals game. It was the bottom of the seventh and the score was tied. I wondered if Benjamin would make it home to hear its conclusion.

Boredom

Jimmy Day should have gone home by now. He started drinking before three. It is after six and all the daytime regulars have left but him. The insurance salesmen who came in for lunch at noon had just got started drinking good when they realized it was after one so decided to stay until two. A little after two they pulled their ties tight around their necks, put on their suit coats and nearly got run over crossing Knox Street walking back to work. The old men regulars who've been arguing since noon, drinking, sleeping, and telling lies have become a gray molten mass with heads and arms dissolving into dark back booths. At four before they disappear completely they lift and push and try to pull themselves apart from one another and at last standing they stumble, separating, and get up. Grumbling they lurch toward the door, leaving in time to get home and listen to Walter Cronkite telling them what happened in the world while they were away drinking. It is best that Mike Carr, the bar owner, doesn't usually allow the television on during the day because if they could watch the news there the old men might never go home. He also doesn't let the jukebox be plugged in until after dark. Baseball games can be played on the little silver radio behind the bar long as it isn't turned up too high. No other programs, certainly no rock 'n' roll, psychedelic music, or any other sports but baseball can be on the radio. The television is for just in case of some kind of emergency is telecast and for Saturday afternoon when the Dizzy Dean/ Pee Wee Reese Game of the Week can be tuned in. On Sundays Mike says that some church service as long as it is Catholic can be watched. D.J. says that would be illegal unless some kind of Protestant service gets equal time and Mike knows the problems D.J. could cause so he just says, "No television on Sunday," like someone might have been interested anyway in coming to a bar and hearing a sermon especially if they have just left one at home. He says, "Okay. There can be a Catholic service on one Sunday and a Protestant on the next." Jughead Walensky asks, "How can you leave the Church of Christ out?" Ken asks, "You're kidding right?' but then he realizes it is Jughead asking the question so he explains to him, "Church of Christers are Protestants too." Jughead asks, "They are? I didn't know." Mike says, "So that is how it will be: Catholic then Protestant," but nobody really wants either so Mike concludes, "Okay the jukebox can be turned on on Sunday afternoons but not loud." Before he can finish the sentence "Hey Jude," left over unfinished on the jukebox from Saturday night, plays.

Mike turned on the television as Ken turned on the radio when a customer came in and told them the president had been shot in downtown Dallas. And they both stayed on all that day and even after the bar closed they were left on all night broadcasting and telecasting, electronic waves bouncing off the walls of The Quiet Man and out the front door, up into the Akashic record, when Ken opened up the next day. After some discussion Mike said, "Yes," they would stay open, "but no beers would be sold until Happy Hour at four." Both the radio and television were left on until Oswald was shot by Jack Ruby, LBJ was president, and Kennedy's body was flown back to Washington.

On August the first, 1966, just before noon in the second inning of an early baseball game on the radio we heard, ". . . and we interrupt this game to bring you a breaking story from Austin, Texas. Someone has climbed to the top of the University of Texas tower, to the observation deck, and is shooting at people on the ground from the twenty-eighth floor. Oh God . . ." Charles Whitman had taken his guns to the top of the Texas tower that morning. The night before he'd choked his mother, Margaret, with a piece of rubber hose then stabbed her in the chest until she was dead. He then went home and stabbed his wife to death as she lay in bed. It was around 3:00 AM. He spent the rest of the night and morning packing a footlocker he'd gotten when he was a Marine. In it he'd put:

- Channel Master 14 Transistor AM/FM Radio
- Robinson Reminder Notebook (blank)
- white 3 1/2-gallon water jug (full)
- red 3 1/2-gallon plastic gas jug (full)
- sales slip from Davis Hardware dated 1 August 1966

- four "C" cell flashlight batteries
- several lengths of cotton and nylon rope
- plastic Wonda-Scope compass
- Paper Mate black ballpoint pen
- one Gun-Tector green rifle scabbard
- hatchet
- Nesco machete with green scabbard
- Hercules hammer
- green ammunition box with gun cleaning equipment
- Gene brand alarm clock
- cigarette lighter
- canteen with water
- binoculars
- green Sears rifle scabbard
- Camillus hunting knife with brown scabbard and whetstone
- large Randall knife with bone handle with the name "Charles J. Whitman" on the blade with brown scabbard and whetstone
- large pocketknife with lock blade
- ten-inch pipe wrench
- eyeglasses with brown case
- box of kitchen matches
- twelve assorted cans of food and a jar of honey
- two cans of Sego
- can of charcoal starter
- white and green six-volt flashlight
- set of ear plugs
- two rolls of white adhesive tape
- solid steel bar (one foot long)
- Army green rubber duffel bag

- green extension cord
- lengths of clothesline wire and yellow electric wire
- gray gloves
- deer bag
- bread, sweet rolls, Spam, Planters Peanuts, sandwiches, a box of raisins
- plastic bottle of Mennen spray deodorant
- toilet paper

He also brought a .30-caliber M1 carbine, a .357 Magnum Smith & Wesson revolver, a 9mm Luger, a Galesi-Brescia pistol, a .35-caliber Remington rifle, a sawed-off Sears twelve-gauge shotgun, a 6mm Remington bolt-action rifle with a four-power Leupold scope, and over 700 rounds of ammunition.

Charlie put the footlocker into the trunk of his car and drove to the tower. He arrived at 11:30 AM. At a checkpoint on the edge of the campus he showed guard Jack Rodman his Carrier Identification Card that he'd been issued for his job as a research assistant at UT and said he would be unloading some equipment. Rodman gave him a forty-minute loading permit. He parked his car and unloaded the footlocker at 11:35. He took the elevator to the twenty-seventh floor where he hit the receptionist Edna Townsley in the head twice and drug her body behind a couch. She died a couple of hours later. At 11:50 Cheryl Botts and Don Walden found Charlie leaning over the couch holding two guns. They hurriedly got on the elevator and left. A few minutes later M.J. and Mary Gabour with their two sons Mark and Mike along with William and Marguerite Lamport walked up the stairs to the twenty-seventh floor. They found the door to the receptionist area blocked. The boys pushed the door open, looked in, and saw Charlie, who immediately fired at them with his sawed-off shotgun. He killed Mark. He then fired down the stairwell three times at Marguerite, who had run, and killed her. Mary Gabour and Mike were bleeding but still alive. William Lamport and M.J. Gabour ran for help.

Whitman ran up the stairs with his footlocker to the observation deck. He wasted no time getting his M1 out, screwing a scope on, taking aim, and firing. His first target was a pregnant eighteen-year-old. Claire Wilson's unborn child's skull was fractured by the bullet. Nobody was safe. He shot people running and he hit people hiding and he gunned down a couple who were holding hands. Mike Carr turned the television set on and the radio off. Black Star photographer Shel Hershorn had just ordered his first beer of the day at 11:30 AM and watched as plumes from guns billowed out from all sides of the tower. It wasn't clear whether there was more than one person firing. Maybe it was a gang or some revolutionary cell starting the revolution or maybe it was just some crazy guy with an arsenal. Shel finished his beer in one swallow, got in his Alfa-Romeo, and sped all the way to Austin listening to reports on the radio as fear oozed from that tower and rolled across the University campus. What was up in there? Fear crystallized into hysteria. It was as if the whole state was in Whitman's crosshairs and anyone could get hit. Ken said he heard it was the brother of Charlie Starkweather. Starkweather whose rampage of killings and rape across the Badlands constellated the dark side of fifties America. What James Dean played at Charlie did for real priming the country for the revolutions of the sixties. Charlie had no brothers. The shots were coming faster.

The best view in Austin is from the observation deck. The tower is higher than the state capital building. It lights up orange when the Longhorns win. No building in Austin is more loved. Three more shots from the tower. Walking across the campus late to her next class another girl was shot down. Shel got to Austin a little after two and found a place where he could see the tower. He got out of his car and scrambled behind a green Ford pickup looking for a picture, looking for a shot. He didn't know that the sniper was already dead. People were still ducking and hiding. Shel aimed his camera and fired. He ducked into a shop whose front plate-glass window had been shattered. The photograph he shot of the tower visible in the distance between two clean bullet holes became the cover of the August 12 issue of *Life*.

After the shooting stopped the television station cut to a soap opera. Mike turned it off and turned up the volume on an all-news radio station. Customers pleaded with him to turn the TV back on and try another station. After nearly an hour he gave in. "Turn the son-of-a-bitch on." A newsman is giving the final score. Sixteen dead and thirty injured.

After ninety minutes, as Charlie was reloading his M1, the door to the observation deck was broken down and Officer Houston McCoy busted in with a twelve-gauge shotgun loaded with double-aught buckshot. He fired and hit Whitman in the head. His body was blasted back and nearly off the tower. He fell and shook twice and he was dead. Officer Ramiro Martinez then rushed in and grabbed the shotgun from McCoy. He fired the other shell into the dead man nearly blowing off his right arm. It was 1:24 PM.

Ruth, Jimmy's wife, came in to The Quiet Man at five as usual after she got off her job at the cleaners. She just wanted to have a beer or two with her husband but he wanted to tell her about the shootings. She didn't want to know and that set off a quiet but intense argument. They normally left a little after six but by six thirty Ruthie had gone home leaving Jimmy at the bar alone.

After work every weekday Jimmy and Ruth drank at the bar not at a table or in a booth. Jimmy didn't like to feel pinned in. He was a plumber and nobody around here ever thought of him as anything else and even though there was something unplumberish about him nobody paid much attention to it. He was too hand-some. Ruthie was no beauty but much loved. Jimmy had dark moods and his khakis were never dirty. He said he was a plumber and that was enough. What reason could anyone possibly have to claim to be a plumber if they weren't one? Still he wasn't born a plumber and some-times between being born and becoming a plumber it was pretty clear he was up to something that he never talked about. He was glad he was with Ruthie now. She comforted him. She bored him. He figured he had had enough excitement in his life. He didn't have to worry about Ruth giving him any more.

Jimmy told me he'd been coming to The Quiet Man for over twelve years. Claimed he came to the place back before it even was The Quiet Man, when it was called the Turf Bar. He told me there used to be three green neon horses that galloped across the outside front of the building and into the dark parking lot next door. I recalled having seen the Turf Bar from the bus I rode on my way to work. It always seemed out of place like it belonged in New Jersey or in some New York City neighborhood where gambling on horse races was legal. Where there was pari-mutuel betting. Not that horse racing didn't go on in tracks off red dirt back roads in East Texas and at quarter horse tracks in West Texas . . . really all over the state. It was legal to race but it was illegal to bet on the races so, of course, there was lots of money bet on horse races. But still . . . maybe it was the name. While the Turf Bar didn't sound like something that belonged in Dallas that was not hard because Dallas never knew what belonged in it itself either except money and fashion. It had Neiman Marcus and sports and after that money. It wasn't even a cow-town. Fort Worth, just thirty miles west, always knew better what it was. It wasn't ashamed of liking Hank Williams. It didn't have to try to be cultured because it had culture. It didn't have to make it up. Dallas Mayor Uncle Bob Thornton once said, "I'll give money to the symphony but don't expect me to go. I went once and let me tell you, it was the coldest snake I ever touched." Dallas always wanted to be known as an international city. After Kennedy was killed here it got its reputation but not what it wanted. It became internationally known as the City of Hate. Oswald and Ruby and a bunch of other conspirators made it happen. Dallas got its place in history. Conspiracies multiplied. But still the city did not give in. It built an ugly monument to Kennedy but otherwise it could never figure a way to celebrate or mourn that death. Maybe a JFK assassination theme bar that served Bloody Rubys while the TV above the bar showed over and over Ruby killing Oswald. Call it Conspiracies and they would come.

Jimmy had met Ruth in The Quiet Man nine years ago or as she liked to say in the last century. She remembered the time better than Jimmy did. She'd just got a job at the cleaners. She came to Dallas from Troup in East Texas and had arrived in Dallas, in the big city, like so many girls from little towns down there . . . to find a husband. Some did but many just found dead-end jobs. Some got office jobs and many moved into apartments on Gaston Avenue built especially for them. But many couldn't do shorthand or file that good so wound up in the service industry which included everything from strippers to waitresses to girls working in cleaners. They told Ruth when she first went to work that she wouldn't be washing and ironing for long but that if she worked hard and showed up on time she'd be a cashier in no time. They lied to her. Nine years ago she was optimistic and very much in search of a husband to rescue her from the cleaners. Very much in search of a husband to fulfill the promise that Dallas had held out to her. Not that it was obvious because she was shy and didn't know the first thing about what to do in her husband search except try to find a young, single man somewhere. She tried church. Joined a singles class that bored her. She'd been to a couple of bars already but she wasn't a big drinker and would get sick before she got drunk and lost her inhibitions. She'd tried the wrong bars, places like the It'll Do Lounge and the Why

Not?, real dives that she didn't go back to a second time.
When she found The Quiet Man she was relieved. It was
a pretty funky-looking little neighborhood bar but it was
right next door to the cleaners and it was comfortable
and people were friendly. It felt more like a big living
room than a bar. Jimmy comforted Ruth. Sometimes he
scared her. She liked his looks right off but felt she had
little chance with him. He was too good-looking with his
black hair that shined so nice in bar lights. His dark
brown eyes were deep enough that she could drown in
them. And there was something just scary enough about
him. She'd surprised herself when she broke the ice and
said, "Hello," and stumbled into a conversation with
him asking what he did. He said, "I used to be a forest
ranger but I'm getting into the construction business."
She didn't care what he did. And he didn't ask her what
she did. He comforted her. They were soon married.

He never talked about his work to her or she to him.
Even if she had wanted to what could she say about
washing and ironing hundreds of blouses pants-shirts-
skirts except that it was hot work. She came here to The
Quiet Man to forget about that and she found a husband.

I am the first of the nighttime regulars to come in
today. I sit at the far end of the bar from Jimmy and order
a beer. I ask Ken how many are dead and he says he has
lost count but last he heard they'd killed the guy doing
the shooting. Jimmy is not watching the television but
staring vacant-eyed at a stack of cases of empty beer bottles. I ask Ken what is going on with him. He says, "Ruth
and him got into it about the shooting soon as she came
in today. She hadn't had a good day and didn't want to
hear any bad news. I don't know just what happened but

before I knew it she was jumping on him and he wasn't taking it. They hissed low, dreadful words like only people who have been married for a long time can do. After one beer Ruth got up and I heard her tell Jimmy she didn't even care if he came home tonight and she left and he asked, 'How about if I never come home.'"

Jimmy is still a handsome man somewhere on the far side of forty. Slim in tan khakis that set off his sunbrowned skin. His thick black hair hides some gray. Ruthie must have been born with gray hair. No one can remember when it wasn't. She's put on weight over the years.

At six thirty Jimmy orders whiskey. Ken reminds him they don't have whiskey, that this is a beer bar, and that if he wants whiskey he has to bring his own bottle. Jimmy knows all that of course. He knows all there is to know about when and where and how whiskey can be served in Texas. He orders a pitcher of beer. Pours a glass. Drinks it. Pours another. Drinks it. And one more. Ken asks him if everything is okay but he doesn't answer.

By seven Jimmy Day is as close to being drunk as he can get on beer. Jim Kent comes in. Everbody likes Jim but nobody loves him and nobody knows much about him either. It isn't like he is mysterious there just doesn't seem much worth knowing. He always has money. Not a lot but enough to buy drinks for the house every now and then. We have no idea what he does, if he has a job or what but nobody is all that curious about it either. He's one of those people you like for being no more than what they appear to be. His clothes are clean. Usually bluejeans and a shirt, maybe checkered, but a couple of times he'd showed up in a military outfit that looked kind of like an Air Force one. He wasn't asked why he was wearing it. Maybe he was in some kind of reserves.

Jim likes books. All books. Not just good ones. He is never seen reading though and he never talks about literature. He must read some. Maybe the books matter to him more than the words. Like if he just owns, just carries them around he will gain something. The owner, Mike Carr, let him put a couple of shelves up near the front of the bar that he can put books on as a little lending library. It is rarely used. The books gather dust. Every now and then Jim changes them out. Nobody would notice if he left and never came back. Days, weeks would pass, months and nobody would say a thing. Memories of him would fade before anyone noticed him missing. The books he had put up on the shelf would become no more than decoration. Jim comes in and takes a seat by Jimmy but Jimmy makes it clear with one look that he doesn't want company.

At seven thirty there are several more customers. Jimmy is still at the bar and he still hasn't said anything to anyone other than to order more beer.

The place is about half full by eight. First and second beers have been drunk and pitchers ordered. The jukebox has been plugged in but Ken has turned the volume way down with the switch behind the bar. Everyone is talking about the sniper when the front door suddenly explodes open so hard it is knocked off its top hinge and hangs on, then is kicked off the bottom hinge and slams into a table knocking beers off tables and breaking on the floor. A couple of girls in chairs are knocked over. It is Raphael. After busting in he stands there in the opening haloed by the night lights from outside. It is not surprising that it is him. He doesn't come in that often but when he does he often causes trouble. He can seem like the most sensible guy you could meet one minute then be absolutely psychotic the next. His wife is a beautiful Mexican woman named Carmen. They live in the apartment above Ken the bartender. Her hair is black as a starless, moonless night and flows down to her waist. She usually wears it up. She likes the crowd at The Quiet Man but he doesn't like her being here or in any other bar without him. She has tried to tell him that The Quiet Man is not like other bars and that the people are nice. What he hears her say is that she likes the men in the place. So as to avoid any problems Raphael has told her to stay away from it but if she just has to after she fixes his supper he might give her permission. Today though her friend Patricia had come by around four and talked her into going out for a beer and they came to The Quiet Man. She got to talking and enjoying herself. She lost track of the time. She let her hair down.

When he gets home that evening Raphael is pissed off the minute he opens the door and can't smell food cooking and when he can't find her in the apartment he loses control. There is more to it than that of course. It also has to do with him getting older and the kind of family he was raised in and that he doesn't make enough money and those gray hairs that are spreading through his hair. Carmen's hair is still black as it ever was and full. Every night she brushes it with a soft brush 150 times.

He goes out looking for her. He drives straight to The Quiet Man, gets out of his car, walks over, looks in the window and sees her sitting with two guys.

When I was over at Ken's one evening I heard them

fighting upstairs. They were yelling and cussing. She kept her end of the fight up pretty good until we could hear things broken and what sounded like a heavy bag being punched over and over. We could hear her screams which were soon muffled and then there was silence. Ken said, "It happens a lot but what can I do? It is his wife after all."

Raphael stands in the doorway looking at her and the two guys she is sitting with. He knows they are talking about sex. He doesn't know that their girlfriends have gone to the bathroom. Those guys should have done something. Everybody in the bar should have done something to stop him but nobody moves when Raphael growls, "Come on any of you chickenshit, cocksucking pussies why don't you try to stop me?" and everyone acts like he couldn't be talking to them. They know what he might do to Carmen but they want no part of him. They could get hurt. It is not their fight.

Raphael doesn't speak to Carmen. He just slaps the shit out of her, knocking her to the floor. He says to her, "Here I'll help you out of this place," and he grabs a handful of her long black hair, wraps it around his fist and drags her out. We watch and are quiet.

There isn't a sound for a few minutes. The jukebox got unplugged in the melee. The radio is off. Cars pass on the wet street. Nobody speaks. Finally Jim Kent jumps up from his barstool and runs outside. He slips down rounding the corner of the building and falls onto the wet black asphalt. Soon as he gets up he sees a big, old Buick Dynaflow pull out and bounce fast into the street. He can hear Raphael screaming at Carmen. Jim yells into the night, "Come back you bastard. Leave her alone," but they are long gone so he trudges back in to the bar and announces, "I tried to catch them but they got away." Then he orders a round of drinks for the house.

When they get home Carmen cooks spaghetti for Raphael and spits in it while he watches the news on television. He comes into the kitchen during a commercial and from behind he puts his arms around her waist then lets his hands drift up to her breasts. She knows there is a reason she used to love him but she can't remember what it is. While he fucks her the spaghetti sauce burns.

Jimmy Day hadn't moved during the fracas. He didn't even turn around but watched what was happening in the bar mirror. He saw Raphael hit Carmen and knock her to the floor. He could see him grab her by the hair but some tables and chairs were in the way so he couldn't see him drag her out the door. He was probably the only person in the bar that could have stopped Raphael but after his fight with Ruth he didn't want any more trouble. He was already upset and after what happened to Carmen he got mad. He'd never hit Ruth but now he had a target for his anger. He has always liked Carmen. She is about the most exotic woman he knows anymore. She's always friendly to him. He has a .38 Special in his pickup's toolbox. He knows where she lives. He gets in his truck, takes the pistol, and puts it in the seat beside him. They are still talking about Whitman on the radio. He's heard enough. He turns it off and drives toward home and Ruth which is in the same general direction as Carmen's. At Belmont and Henderson if he goes straight he will be headed toward his house. If he takes a left he will be going toward Raphael and Carmen's. He touches his gun. He's finally got some options.

Rudi

The big red horse stands stone-still for a moment then falls spilling the highrider, struggling to draw his rifle from its scabbard, crashing to the ground. The heavy horse lies on the rider's leg. Neither moves. Bosses in nearby fields ride fast to help. They are not sure what happened. They just saw the horse go down like it was shot. A horse doesn't just fall over like that on its own. Is a bustout starting? When the riders get to the downed pair they see a convict in his white prison jumpsuit standing over them. What is he doing there? Is he just looking? It's unlikely but is he there to help? Or is he in some way responsible for the fallen man and his horse? Warden Carl Luther MacAdams-Beartracks knows what happened though. He knows everything.

Rudi James had always vexed everyone who tried to help him when he was a kid. He was smart, plenty smart. When he went to school he did good. He just didn't go to school that much. He didn't get in lots of trouble but he got in enough. Mostly for fighting. By the time he

was seventeen he had a reputation for being the baddest
cat in Oak Cliff, maybe in all of Dallas. His fights were
legendary. He feared no one. Once he hit a Lakewood
Rat in the back of the head so hard he knocked one of
his eyeballs out. Another time when a couple of thugs
got in his face he listened while he finished a cigarette
which he dropped to the ground. He lowered his eyes to
watch it fall and so did they. That was all the opening he
needed. It was hard to count the blows he landed. They
were on the ground before they knew what was happening. He gave them a couple of kicks and then, standing over them, said, "Okay motherfuckers next time you
better come with more than two."

He was five eleven and nearly two hundred pounds
of muscle but he seemed bigger. His hair was red and
Medusa-wiry which he'd manage to sweep back into
snarling ducktails. There was nothing round about his
face. It was as full of angles as a geometry book. It was
his eyes though that'd get you. They were green and
had red flakes that grew bigger the longer you looked at
them. If it seemed like there was going to be trouble all
he had to do was look at the trouble and it would usually go away. He wore bluejeans, white T-shirts whose
sleeves nearly tore when he flexed his biceps, and motorcycle boots. It would have to get real cold before he'd
put on his black suede jacket. Even the weather feared
him. He never used weapons other than his fists until
he killed a man one night with a hatchet and cut up
and mauled a couple of other assailants who had come
at him out of the dark in the woods down in the Trinity
River Bottoms where he was camping. At his trial the
question was whether he'd brought the hatchet to fight

with him or had he been doing something else with it like using it for a tool to chop up kindling for a campfire. Rudi loved to go camping by himself. That and fighting were his two favorite pastimes and he was very good at both. He got fifteen years in the state penitentiary for manslaughter.

Rudi wasn't running. He wasn't trying to escape. He'd just had enough of Beartracks's flunky highriders staying on his ass all the time. He worked as hard as any man in the field. Warden MacAdams knew that and he knew Rudi was smart and knew he was bad. Just the kind of challenge the warden liked. He'd broken worse and he'd break Rudi too but he'd toy with him like a cat playing with a mouse for hours before biting its head off. One morning out of the blue he told Rudi not to go to the fields. He was going to make him a rowtender. Basically what a rowtender was was an enforcer of the warden's will. It was one of the best jobs a convict could get. You got made a first-class trustee and didn't have to do much work other than making sure all the cells on your row were clean and then you could lie around in your cell or watch television or play basketball in the gym a lot. Ever now and then a boss'd have you break some troublesome convict on the row to keep order. Rudi did what the job demanded but kept that defiant look in his eye. Then BOOM after a couple of months Beartracks took that good job away for a bullshit reason like that was his plan from the get-go. He busted him from first class and put him on a flat-hoeing squad where all day a heavy aggie was used to chop grass flat. Rudi didn't let Beartracks see him flinch. He just hit the door first the next morning and jumped on the wagon to the field. He was first off and first to pick up his aggie and first to be ready to work. He got tired by the end of the day because lying about in his cell he'd got a little out of shape. He lifted weights in the gym but that wasn't the same as working in the fields. It was the difference between practice and the game. Rudi always had been able to outwork anybody but he couldn't outwork a whole squad. Until he got accepted by the squad he couldn't be a leader of it. Everybody was Black but him. To get to be part of the team he had to learn to sing the work songs. He had to learn those helping rhythms. He never could sing before but he learned to good enough anyway to be part of the workforce. He even got to lead a song ever now and again. His favorite song went:

> I wanna to tell you a story 'bout a Grizzly Bear
> I wanna to tell you a story 'bout a Grizzly Bear
> He was a great big grizzly, Grizzly Bear
> He was a great big grizzly, Grizzly Bear
> You know people got a-scared a the Grizzly Bear
> You know people got a-scared a the Grizzly Bear
> He stood ten feet tall like a Grizzly Bear
> He had a big bone paw Grizzly Bear

with the hoe coming down at the end of each line. The last couple of verses ended though with:

> You know I ain't a-scared a no bear, Grizzly Bear
> Because the workin' squad they killed him there, Grizzly Bear
> Well-a grizzly, grizzly, Grizzly Bear
> Well Lord have mercy, Grizzly Bear

Even Beartracks liked that song except the last verses which the squad wouldn't sing when he was near.

Rudi's hard work got him the respect of the squad. He couldn't be denied. Beartracks had to make him squad leader. He was at it again with Rudi. He did make him squad leader. And he let him stay in that revered position long enough for him to get comfortable with it. Then he busted him again. This time he didn't even give him a reason. He just said, "You got a new job," and sent him down to do some serious work chopping sugarcane with a machete in the heat and steam of the primordial Brazos River Bottoms where mosquitoes were as big as your imagination and there were cottonmouths and copperheads and rattlers and all sorts of thorns and briars that ripped your skin. Then you got to hacking the sugarcane and the sharp leaves sliced spiderwebs of blood on your arms that would become nearly invisible scars. The mosquitoes got giddy zeroing in for the feast. In summer it was so bad that nothing moved but mosquitoes and convicts. In the cane fields you worked alone at your own pace. There was no team. No songs. It didn't make any sense to sing by yourself. It was just you against the cane and the highriders from sunup until sundown.

Rudi did it though. He even took pride in the swarm of fresh cuts that sliced up the skin on his arm. He'd been chopping the cane for a few months when one day he was abruptly taken out of the field by a gang of screws and beaten nearly to death with baseball bats and then thrown in the hole for six months where there was no light or much food or even a toilet except for a hole in the floor. They said it was for insubordination and that was that. There wasn't a trial or even an explanation.

There just was a verdict and a sentence. He knew there was no reason to argue and he knew he could do the solitary time. He kept that defiant look in his eyes as Beartracks sat on his horse in the woods and watched Rudi get beat. Most times he liked to do the beating himself but this time he let the screws do it. Nobody talked back to Warden MacAdams with either their tongue or eyes or body or anything else. He was the meanest warden in the system. Rudi hadn't said a word to him. He'd just been looking old Beartracks right in the eye for too long. Finally there was no option. He had Rudi beat in front of the other convicts.

The Ellis Farm where Rudi served most of his sentence was the toughest in the system. Beartracks made sure it stayed that way. He handled most of the bad discipline problems himself with a bat he called Justice. He had an office in the prison but didn't spend much time there. He was out in the fields on his black horse Diablo most days. He was there in the field the day the red horse fell over. He saw everything. It was Rudi. He'd just spent a month in solitary and was going back. Beartracks knew when he got out of the hole he would get the hardest job he could and he'd build his body back strong again. He got put on an ax squad. Steady chopping wood all day and singing. He could do that and he was when the highrider called him over as Beartracks watched through binoculars. The rider told Rudi the warden had a new job for him. Rudi'd had enough. His green eyes became red. He wasn't going to let Beartracks take him down again though without a fight. "Fuck you," he told the rider which got him hit across the face with the horse's metal-studded reins.

Beartracks rode up slow to the downed horse and rider and watched as the horse kicked struggling to its feet. The rider tried to get up too but he couldn't stand. His leg was broken. Beartracks didn't waste any time. He ordered the other riders to put Rudi in chains, throw him on the wagon, and take him to the hole. The investigation got started. He'd seen Rudi walk over to the rider but couldn't see clearly what happened after that. He got one of his snitches aside and asked him what he'd seen. Beartracks had told the riders that morning to stay on Rudi, to see if the time in the hole had softened him and if he could be broke now or at least sent back to the hole for more training. It wasn't the heat or the work or the hole or even the rider. None of that. It was Beartracks. Rudi knew that if he didn't make a play now Beartracks would do whatever he wanted to him. Maybe even kill him. He wouldn't be the first convict beaten to death with a baseball bat and the standard explanation to the family would be that a tree had fallen on him. But he didn't explode. He calmly, slowly walked over to the rider who looked down and started in on him. Rudi stood there for awhile taking the abuse answering, "Yes boss," and "No boss." He didn't snap though. He waited then struck fast. So fast that it was hard to see and harder to believe. "Warden," one of Beartracks's snitches told him, "Rudi knocked that horse over with his fist. A boss rode over toward him, stopped, leaned over, and jumped his case for something. I couldn't hear what he said. Rudi just kept swinging his ax and that boss just stayed on his ass saying 'Get over here old thing. Come over here you asshole,' and such shit. He told Rudi to put his ax down and walk over to him.

Finally Rudi did what he was told to. He stood right beside that horse and the rider hit him with those metal-studded reins tight across his face. Rudi didn't flinch. I think that pissed off the rider 'cause then he kicked him in the head with his boot." "Now," Beartracks said, "he didn't kick him," and the snitch gave in. "Okay then Rudi just turned his head for some reason. Then he turned back and looked that rider straight in the eye. The rider put his hand on his rifle. It was then that Rudi hit the horse. I can't say I exactly saw the horse get hit 'cause I was on the other side but I saw it fall and then I saw Rudi standing right there and he didn't have a club or anything in his hands and his ax was on the ground. You know boss what a punch he has. You've seen him in the gym hitting that heavy bag. You put him on the boxing team. He hit that horse one time and knocked him down to the ground." There was too much admiration in the snitch's voice. Beartracks just said, "Okay. Get back to work."

But he didn't need to use a snitch. Rudi's work squad saw clearly what happened and they weren't shy about telling Beartracks that they saw the blow. They knew something was brewing that day. Sometimes it was like the screws knew everything. More of the time the convicts did. Everybody stopped working to watch. They had trouble at first believing what they saw. They saw Rudi hit the horse. With his fist. It all happened so fast.

After he got out of the hole he was The Man to the other prisoners. But Rudi was smart and he didn't want to spend the rest of his life behind walls. He was starting to like it too much. He'd met too many longtime convicts who told him they'd rather be in prison than in the world. They were better taken care of and it was safer. Real lifers. Rudi could understand that but he didn't want to get there. He wanted out and he knew he wasn't going to ever get out unless he somehow figured a way to get along with Beartracks so he tried to show him some respect. Beartracks thought it was just another round in their fight but Rudi stayed out of trouble after he got out of the hole and was put back in population and sent back to the fields. That defiant look in his eye softened when he talked to the warden. Was he broken? Or smart? Beartracks played along waiting for him to blow up. He waited as months went by but Rudi stayed straight. He joined the prison Alcoholics Anonymous chapter and started going to church. Beartracks was taken in. At first it was pride. He had broken Rudi. Then it turned into something else. Shit he got to liking him. Not that he could show it. He'd always respected his toughness and all but now it even surprised him when he started to like him. He started giving him breaks that were more than just setups. Nobody could remember Beartracks backing off like that on a convict but he gave Rudi a chance and Rudi took it. After knocking the horse out and spending as much time in the hole as he had he didn't have nothing to prove to anybody or himself anymore. He worked in the fields for a year. He kept his mouth shut even when the screws fucked with him. He finally got a job in the kitchen. He now had time to improve himself even more. He got books from the library. It was a little library but it had an amazing collection of books. Things he would never have read before. He found out later that the reason there was such an interesting bunch of books was because they had come from a little bookstore in a nearby town that had gone out of business and sold the prison all its books. There were novels. He read everything from Tolstoy to Barthelme and he got into Eastern religion books. He got made trustee again and after ten flat years he was paroled to Dallas.

He still had those gunfighter eyes and street-tough walk when he got out of the joint but there was something more to him than that. He learned to cover up that tough appearance. He didn't go to ex-con bars where he'd have to act bad, where he could get into trouble. He wanted to put all that behind him. He wanted to try out that Eastern religion he'd learned in prison in the world. He found The Quiet Man but it took him awhile. A couple of years. He had to make a living so he hired himself out as a bodyguard to rock stars visiting Dallas. He didn't tell us that when we first met him. He let us find out. There were other things though that he let no one find out but when we saw the prison tattoo on his forearm of a ball and chain with THE HOLE above it and '59 and '60 below we started to figure out that he'd done some serious time.

He was out riding his Indian Chief red motorcycle when he first saw The Quiet Man. He rode on but a few days later he was drawn back. There was no big sign out front, nothing announcing what it was but it looked right. It was just a small brick building in the front of a Safeway parking lot with lots of parking all around it and all the things that that allows. The parking lot was like an extra room. The Quiet Man was the kind of place you'd like to discover on a cold winter night. Like everything else in the sixties bars were changing but what made a bar a good bar remained the same. As always the reason you went to one was to talk. If you wanted to just drink you might as well stay at home where it was cheaper.

The Quiet Man was named for the John Ford/John Wayne fifties movie. It was a great name for a bar but not a great movie. Soaked in Irish nostalgia all it lacked was four-leaf clovers and some Bing Crosby songs. Other than the *Erin Go Bragh* banner on the back wall though the bar had little to do with either the movie or Ireland. Mike, the owner, was second-generation and had never been to Ireland so knew little about it other than what he got from movies and his father but the bar was everything a bar should be but not like some old honky-tonk. This was a place where talk was as important as music. Mike didn't allow cussing especially around women. Once when a guy started talking dirty around the big, round table Mike covered Linda's ears. After it was open for a couple of years a front patio was added. It held four picnic tables. A hole was cut in the front window for the bartender to pass drinks through.

It is a Thursday afternoon when Rudi parks his bike and walks in. Nobody lets on that they notice him. Not the insurance men or the old men. He tells Ken that he doesn't usually drink but could he have a beer anyway. Ken is a great bartender. Even-tempered. Friendly. In an article in a 1959 issue of *Fortune* magazine on what young Americans wanted there he was a full-page photo of him in his navy uniform in Hong Kong. He was good-looking. I can't remember what he said he wanted. After the navy though he got it into his mind to be a writer or a baseball player, a pitcher, but that didn't happen. He had some

talent as a writer but never worked at it until all his talent had faded away. He could pitch good enough to be on
a high school team and wound up playing in a game every
Sunday with a bunch of guys who were never going to
make the pros. He drank beer every night but he did it in
such a controlled way that he rarely seemed drunk. Like
they say, the more you drink, the more you know how to
behave as a drunk. Like I see two doorknobs instead of
one and from past experience I know the real one is the
one on the left. Rudi took to Ken like everybody did. He
didn't talk to anyone else that day and didn't stay long
but he knew he would be back. One night a week later
when Rudi came back he saw a different place than the
one he had first visited. For one thing there were some
good-looking women there now. It wasn't long before he
was working his way through them. Mostly one-night
stands. But then he met Petri. She was German. Smart
and gorgeous. Everyone was surprised when he moved in
with her. She was something more than Rudi was used
to, more than a one-night stand. One thing he'd known
about relationships with women was that they'd end.
Even if he got married it would be like a long, one-life-
time stand. Petri had been around The Quiet Man for
awhile and had slept with several of the customers but
it wasn't ever serious. That is the fucking was serious
but there was no commitment and she didn't intend to
make any to Rudi but he didn't give her a choice. He was
a strong man and she liked it. At least for awhile.

I don't know what possessed us that night other than
the LSD. I was attracted to Petri like every other man in
the bar and some of the women but she was Rudi's girlfriend. I'd been sentenced to ten years in prison for drugs

and was just waiting to go down. I was living on the second
floor of an old house in Oak Lawn. Downstairs or in the
little servant's quarters out back someone was always on
acid. Rudi was out of town the day Petri stopped by. We
talked for a while before she asked me if I had any LSD.
I told her I had some I could give her but it was pretty
strong. I thought she wanted to take it but she asked me
if I'd like to do it with her. I didn't have any plans for the
day so I said, "Sure," and we took half a tab each. We
spent much of the afternoon walking around the neighborhood and seeing things we'd never seen before. Some
were there. Some not. We weren't fucked up. Just the
opposite. We were seeing as clearly as we ever had in our
lives and we felt it wasn't just the drug. We felt real close.
It was getting dark when we made it back to the house.
Several people were downstairs writing on the walls so
we went upstairs and watched the sun go down an hour
after it had. I put on a record. I asked her if she knew
where The Doors got their name. She said, "No." I said,
"It comes from a William Blake line: 'If the doors of per-
ception were cleansed, every thing would appear as it is,
infinite.'" I heated water on my little stove and made tea.
It seemed hours before we saw the sun go down again. It
was around midnight.

I was sitting at my desk and she was sitting on it. I
can't remember who took their clothes off first. I should
have been thinking about Rudi and what could happen
to me if he found out. Then he was there. I whispered
to her, "What should we do now?" She answered, "Why
don't we just make him disappear?" And we did. Then
for the rest of the night everything was infinite.

Benny's Coat

Something is wrong with Oak Cliff Benny. Weekday mornings he's always the first customer. When Ken opens the front door of The Quiet Man at ten he enters and goes straight to his seat at the end of the bar. He sits and waits as Ken turns on the lights, prepares the cash register then draws him a small beer. He sips on it for a half hour before ordering another. He has ten more slow pilsners before he leaves at three to catch the bus back to Oak Cliff. Today though it is nearly eleven before he shows up. He surprises Ken when he orders a mug and drinks it fast. It is a warm fall day but he has his overcoat under his arm. He always has it with him. When it is hot he carries it. When it is cold he wears it and it is his raincoat when it storms. He never hangs it on the coat rack but puts it on the barstool beside him where he can reach over and touch it and it can keep anyone from sitting beside him. When he goes to the bathroom it goes with him. His coat is one of the few distinguishing things about him. It is plaid black, camel, and gray with occasional thin red stripes, is old but not frayed. It is difficult to imagine him without it. It is his and he is it.

Benny is just a guy drinking alone at the bar. Like his coat he's worn but not worn-out. While there is nothing unusual about him he is somehow hard to forget. He is not big, maybe 150 pounds, but the way he stands and carries himself makes him seem smaller. He bends over and hunches his shoulders like some children do when they run from danger trying to disappear into themselves. His round face reveals few secrets for a man in his early fifties. He could be older. He won't look you straight in the eyes but that is overrated anyway. There is a fine line between being shifty-eyed and being shy. His skin is a mottled brown veil over a deeper gray except for a touch of red in his cheeks and on his nose. He usually has a stubble of gray whiskers. He shaves once a week if he remembers to. His mouth has shrunk from lack of talking or maybe to cover bad teeth which are yellowish but not that bad otherwise except for his long-gone dog teeth. His ears are big with long lobes. His yellowing hair matches his skin which matches his coat. Some people grow to resemble their dogs. Benny grows to resemble his coat. More hair grows from his ears now than from his head. His eyebrows threaten his nose. He is a quiet man who says little except to Ken and even then he mostly will only talk about baseball. Rarely anything personal. He talks soft except for occasional bursts of a screeching laugh. He is hard to understand but Ken does. It is one of the things that makes him such a good bartender. He listens. Benny listens too. Some days they spend just listening to each other.

When Benny shows up today after he demands a mug, drinks it, and orders another Ken asks, "Are you okay?" He doesn't answer just points to his empty glass.

He gets drunk but stays quiet. The only way to tell he is drunk is that he doesn't take his coat to the bathroom with him after which he walks straight out of the bar. It is only one. Something seems to have caused his internal clock to go haywire. A good game between the Cardinals and Dodgers is on the little silver radio behind the bar. It is tied in the bottom of the fifth when Bennie gets up abruptly and is gone without even telling Ken goodbye. Ken looks at another daytime regular, shrugs his shoulders and walks from behind the bar to clean a table. As he is coming back he notices Benny's coat still there on the barstool. He picks it up and runs out to see if he can catch him at the bus stop only to see the bus headed down Knox to Oak Cliff. He brings the coat back in and starts to hang it on the coat rack but stops knowing Benny'd never do that so he carries it behind the bar, carefully folds it, and puts it in a paper sack on a stack of boxes of empty beer bottles. Ken has been seeing that coat for so long that he no longer sees it. It is just Benny's coat. It doesn't coordinate with his other indifferent tan and gray clothes and certainly not with the blue Yankee baseball cap he always wears which doesn't go with the rest of the clothes either. Likely he got the coat at Goodwill or some secondhand shop. No one can remember when he didn't have it. It is not fashionable but classy. As Ken folds it he notices the label on which is a charging white knight with a banner unfurling against a black field. Above the knight stenciled letters spell BURBERRY. That knight arouses Ken's interest. It is a fine noble knight which seems it could charge off the label and right into the bar.

Toward evening after work Grigory Yefimitch, who everyone calls George, comes to the bar. He is a Russian-American who came to America with his parents in the forties to escape Stalin's purges. They landed in New York and moved to Dallas a couple of years later when his father had gotten a job with an airline. When he was a kid in Russia George had taken dance lessons at the Bolshoi school. In America he had tried to continue his dancing but couldn't find teachers as good as his Russian ones. He got bored and gave up what might have been a career. When he was nineteen he enrolled in the Parsons School of Design where he studied clothes design and marketing, He got his degree in the history of fabrics then moved to Dallas to join his parents. George Yefimitch is the best-dressed regular at The Quiet Man. He sells clothes at Volk's, a very good men's clothing store, about one rung below the transcendent Neiman Marcus. At work he must wear his store's clothes but soon as he is off he changes into his hand-tailored or Neiman Marcus ones. He has many regular customers who will only buy their clothes from him. He spends lots of time carefully measuring the men and boys for perfect fits. He is especially good with trousers. If the customer is handsome it takes him a little longer to measure the inseam. He lingers at the crotch before stretching his tape down to the cuff. He loves fabrics and reads any book or magazine article he can get his hands on about them and their histories.

George prefers to drink in private men's clubs. He doesn't come to The Quiet Man that much just barely enough to be a regular. It is near his apartment in Highland Park. He really isn't a beer drinker but as that is all there is that is what he drinks. This afternoon there are only a few customers when he comes in. He and Ken talk briefly before it occurs to Ken to ask him about that Burberry label.

"Sure I know it," George Yefimitch tells him. "It is gabardine."

Ken says, "I've heard of gabardine but I don't know what it is."

George gushes, "It is a wondrous durable cloth. Rain rolls right off."

"How?"

"The fabric is waterproofed tightly woven Egyptian cotton. Over a hundred years ago a fellow in England named George Burberry invented it. It wasn't some fine cloth for expensive clothes. It was for making all-weather coats for men who worked outdoors."

Ken wonders. Maybe Benny did get it at some resale shop but didn't realize what he'd gotten. But he must have. It looked like none of his clothes. It was checks. All his other clothes are plain, simple, one color, unadorned. But this coat . . . there was something more to it than what was on the surface, like Benny himself.

ENGLAND FINALLY HAS A WORLD-CLASS
BRAND TO CALL ITS OWN: THE NEW BURBERRY.

The squarest possible clothes in the world were women's plaid pants. My ex-wife's father used to send her plaid pants. She'd wear them to do housework in. Even if Audrey Hepburn wore Burberry in *Breakfast at Tiffany's*? Still. Checks?

But that was years ago. In 2004 Burberry is arisen. The knight is charging across the fashion landscape again. Below him on the label is the word *Prorsum*, Latin for "forward." At the turn of the twenty-first century England had no big-time fashion designers. Not like Italy or France. The last big thing in England was Twiggy, the first supermodel, but that was over forty years ago.

In 1998 an American, Rose Marie Bravo, left her job as president of Saks, Inc., to run Burberry. The company had managed to survive for over a hundred years but it had become more a brand than a thriving business. That brand was known all over the world, but the image was staid and boring. The first thing Ms. Bravo did after she took over the company was to hire designer Roberto Menichetti, a motorcycle-riding, pony-tailed man who'd worked for Claude Montana, to remake the image, to redesign the clothes. He wasn't long on the job before he came across another of Mr. Burberry's creations: the trench coat. It had proved itself as an all-weather, durable garment when it was worn by thousands of soldiers in the trenches of World War I. Bravo and Menchetti shook Burberry with new designs. The company took off. While continuing to produce traditional Burberry coats, pants, and scarves they expanded into other things like dog clothes, iPod holders, and perfume. Sir Ernest Shackleton and Robert Scott wore gabardine overalls to Antarctica.

WE'RE SELLING OVER 200 PLAID BANDANAS A DAY.

Amundsen left a gabardine tent to let Scott know he had been there first.

When young Prince William gave his first press conference in 2002 he wore Burberry.

Now some Burberry clothes are not even plaid.

There is a four-story Burberry store in the middle of Tokyo.

When Ken asks, "Where did plaids come from anyway?" George tells him how Scottish highlanders were the first to wear plaid in the mid-1500s. They were fierce warriors who wore plaid pants and kilts that went down to their ankles. The British tried to suppress them but couldn't. Their plaids became symbols of defiance. When the lowlanders started copying that fashion the British acted passing the Clothes Laws which outlawed kilts altogether. The highlanders and the lowlanders ignored those laws.

Burberry plaid, all the rage now in 2003, is considered the design of thugs by Scottish bar owners and bouncers, so much so that they will refuse to let anyone in wearing the plaid. Burberry has become the badge of thuggery.

The daytime crowd left a couple of hours ago. The nighttime crowd is starting to drift in. Ken is getting busy and can listen to George no more but what he has heard has changed the way he sees Benny. He knows it will do no good to ask him about his coat. Not directly anyway.

When Benny comes in the next day around noon though he isn't in any mood to talk. He doesn't order a beer he just asks for his coat. He puts it under his arm and leaves.

•

Benny doesn't know what hits him in his chest. As he opens the front gate to his cottage in Oak Cliff he hears a rustling in the nearby woods. He turns to look when it strikes him, something like a big rock or a hard horse apple. He doesn't have time to think about it though. He falls back crashing through his picket fence. His body floats down snapping crisp dry Texas Star branches, crashing down and down through the golden sunset landing on, crushing a bed of lamb's ears and lies there, still. It is his heart. He can feel his blood pumping out onto his Burberry coat. He is worried about his coat as he lies dying. He is worried about the bloodstains and he dies with petals of blue Texas Star flowers drifting down onto his body.

It was a bullet, a big bullet from a Winchester .30-.30 but Benny never knew. It tore a hole in his coat and burst his heart. As his body lies there in the darkening day though it becomes suspended somewhere between liquid and solid. Then the bullet hole grows together as if woven so well by some invisible weaver that it disappears. His coat shivers and wraps itself closely around his metamorphosing body. Faint vertical red stripes begin to appear on his skin. Then horizontal black, camel, and gray ones. Checks. His body merges with his coat or it with him and collapses flat on the lamb's ears.

The police get a call to investigate a gunshot. They arrive at the woods. It takes awhile to find a path to

Benny's cottage. When they finally find his place they first see the broken-down fence and the lamb's ears crushed by a plaid coat lying on them. They look around for a body but find none. They check the cottage but it is locked up and nothing seems disturbed. If there was a crime they can't figure what it might have been and they have other crimes to solve so write a brief report and leave. The crime scene guys show up a couple of hours later and find no evidence at all. There is no body and now the coat that was mentioned in the patrolmen's report is missing. And the fence not broken. They use a passkey and enter the house. It is smaller inside than outside. There is a living-slash-bedroom, a bathroom and a tiny kitchen. There are no pictures on the wall but on a small desk there is an old yellowing picture of a boy and an older man. The man's face is mostly hidden by his upraised hand. The boy is looking up at him. The man looks familiar but they can't recall who it is. They have no idea who the boy is either. Could he be the missing victim? If there is one. Later when they check for who held the title for the house they are surprised to see it is owned by H. L. Hunt, the richest man in the world. Hunt is a philanderer who rumor has it has three families. He has children by each wife. There are stories of others. Could this child in the photograph be one? They want to investigate more but receive orders from someone way high up in the command not just to drop the investigation but to leave no evidence that one has even been opened. There is no body so it is not hard for them to do as they are commanded. A couple of weeks later out of curiosity they drive back by the little cottage and find it boarded up. They wonder who did it and would like to investigate but this time they are told if they want to keep their jobs they must drop it and keep their mouths shut. They do as they are told to do.

•

The Houston Street Viaduct is an old concrete and stone bridge that crosses the dark and polluted Trinity River whose waters flow slow with trash and tires and old cars between two levees. Benny crossed it twice a day on the bus on his way to The Quiet Man. Down there in the Trinity River Bottoms was the best place in Dallas to dump bodies. Not long after Benny was killed Jack Holmes, a vice-president at Republic Bank, told his wife that when he was driving home he saw a nice looking checked coat hanging on the concrete railing of the bridge. He stopped his car and went back to get it but it was gone. The sun had just about left the sky and the bottoms were cast in long shadows but Jack Holmes said he could have sworn when he looked down there he saw that coat on a man walking along the river. In the months and years after that other travelers across the bridge at twilight saw the coat moving down in the bottoms, behaving as if it had its own body but no one was able to get close before the coat disappeared into the dark. The story was told and spread in Oak Cliff of a ghost coat that haunted the Trinity River. Drunk teenage boys drove over the levee and along dirt roads in the setting sun to search for it. Several claimed they did but soon as it got dark they would get into their cars and fishtail out on the dirt road. They found what they didn't know they were looking for. They found stories.

A few homeless people live up under the arches of the bridge. Randall Johanson has been on the streets ever since he quit riding the rails. He hasn't been sober in over twenty years. Drunkenness is his normal existence and he handles it well. At dusk one cold, windy night he was walking home from begging downtown. He'd made enough for a loaf of bread, some American cheese slices, and a bottle of Mad Dog 20-20. He was trying to get to his cardboard home before he froze when he saw something come floating down through the orange air from the bridge. He watched it descend. It landed right at his feet. It was a coat. He didn't pay any attention to what kind or color of coat it was. He didn't care. It was warm. It was plaid.

Every morning when Ken opens up The Quiet Man he looks for Benny but he doesn't show up for a week, a month. He is worried about him but doesn't know what to do. He doesn't even know his last name. He calls hospitals and the police but they tell him they have no record of an Oak Cliff Benny.

A few months after Benny disappears a disheveled fellow comes into The Quiet Man shortly after Ken has opened up. Even by The Quiet Man's low standards he stands out. He smells bad and is already drunk. Under his arm is a big brown paper sack. Ken starts to tell him he can't stay when the guy begs, "I just want a beer, just one beer."

Ken says, "A little one is twenty cents."

The guy says, "I don't have any money."

"I'm sorry," Ken tells him, "but we do not give out free beer."

The fellow asks, "Could I run a tab?"

Ken is a very trusting man but he doesn't trust this guy. He says, "No tabs," which isn't exactly true. What he means is, "I will not start a tab for you."

The guy says, "I really want a beer. I'll tell you what: I've got this coat which I will not be using any longer as the cold weather is over this year. Would you like to see it?"

Ken asks "What sort of coat is it?"

The guy says, "It says Barberry or something like that on the label but I don't know anything else about it. It's a good coat though. It kept me warm all winter but it did more than that. It became like a companion, almost a friend. I could swear at times it seemed alive."

Ken says, "Sure. If you say. Then why are you willing to sell your friend now?"

"Like I said because it is spring and I need a drink more than a coat or even a friend."

"Let's see it."

The guy opens the paper sack and starts to take its contents out. It is a coat all right but it isn't a Burberry. It is a dull tan car coat. He looks surprised and says, "This is not what I put in this morning."

Ken tells him, "I'll give you a couple of beers for the thing."

The guy can't figure what happened to the coat but much of the time he can't figure out what happened to him yesterday and he is more thirsty than curious so he agrees, drinks his beers, and leaves.

As soon as he is gone Ken puts the coat in the trash.

Gus

Gus Bondolo keeps Knox Street swept. Most mornings he is out there with his brooms neatly arranged in a wheeled tool holder. It is a round tin barrel painted urban gray with reflecting yellow horizontal stripes at the top and bottom which looks like it might be or have been official City of Dallas equipment. In it is a push broom, a regular straight straw one, a narrow one for corners, two or three whose bristles are worn down to uselessness, and some handles. There are a couple of whisk brooms and other small brooms in a metal pocket that Jenkins has welded onto the side of the barrel. There are two large wheels and a kickstand in back to lean the contraption against when he has to leave it to go into The Quiet Man for a beer.

Bill Jenkins builds motorcycles. Although there are several very good mechanics who hang out here they all defer to Bill when it comes to motorcycles. Tommy Spangler has a small garage near the bar. He is good and inexpensive and who most of The Quiet Man regulars go to for repairs on their cars. If not him then Charley Whiteside who used to be a schoolteacher but gave it up to work mostly on Volkswagen Bugs in a small garage behind his house. He will fix minor problems like changing spark plugs, belts or replacing a radiator on any car. There are several English mechanics who specialize in foreign cars. Ken, the bartender, bought an old Volvo when he was in high school. It is the only car he has ever owned. The English chaps keep it running for him. Pisanos, Scorpions, and other bikers consult with Jenkins on how to improve their bikes' performance. He will not mess around with ape hangers, extended front forks, and aesthetic stuff like that. It is all mechanics with him and they know that. They do not come as a group to talk with him but one at a time like samurai visiting the master sword maker in hopes he will make a great sword for them.

Jenkins wears an old black-and-white helmet that looks like some worn-out cop one. On the back of it hangs a tail. Probably Ace's. Ace was the raccoon who lived with him in a big, metal warehouse four or five blocks from The Quiet Man. He was a menace, staying high up in the rafters and only coming down to eat or steal Bill's dope. Bill had been complaining about him for months, questioning why he ever got him in the first place and what a useless pet he was then one day Ace was gone. Bill would never talk about what might have happened to him but now from the back of his helmet there hung a raccoon tail. Jenkins himself rides a very quiet, very efficient BMW.

Bill was working on building a bike that would set some obscure land speed record out on the Bonneville

Salt Flats in Utah. When he wasn't at The Quiet Man he was usually in his building working. If he took some time off from motorcycles it was most often to build something else with an engine. Like motorized barstools. He and the mechanics came up with the idea and within weeks they had built several which they'd race around the Safeway parking lot next door. The only restriction was that it had to be able to drive up to the bar.

Gus Bondolo sweeps in front of The Quiet Man more than any other part of the street. He is rarely over a block away. He is a relic like the knife sharpener who whistles a knife sharpener tune as he wheels through neighborhoods. If he gets a job sharpening someone's knives or scissors he flips the wheel over so it becomes a grinding wheel. He charges a dollar a blade and when he is done he flips his wheel back over and whistles his tune vanishing down the street and back fifty years into the past when there were horse-drawn milk wagons in Dallas.

Gus lives in one room of Billy Joe Branson's big old two-story wood rooming house around the corner from The Quiet Man. Billy Joe is a born-again Christian who drinks as much as anybody. Several Quiet Man regulars rent rooms from him. It is almost certain Gus doesn't work for the city. Maybe he had at one time been a street sweeper but the city now uses street sweeping trucks to keep the streets clean although how clean is debatable. There are two big wheels with steel bristles that scrub the surface. Then a water truck follows washing down what the sweeper stirred up. Maybe Gus lost his job to those trucks but has refused to stop sweeping. There is suspicion that Jenkins made his wheeled broom holder but he will never admit to it.

Gus is out there sweeping in front of The Quiet Man every morning. When the bar opens he parks his equipment in front and comes in for a beer. His clothes are never clean but are cleaner than him. In mornings they are not that bad but often by afternoon he has pissed his pants and will not be allowed inside so he sits out front having a beer before he goes back to work. It is not long before he's tired again, he is a pretty old guy, and needs another beer which he has to get through the window.

The guy can talk. When some group lets him sit at their table with them he does all he can to hold up his end of the conversation and more. While he can talk he can't be understood. It isn't just the alcohol. He mumbles fast interrupting himself with a whole range of contrapuntal sounds interrupted by a laugh that starts as a giggle and rises to a roar. He seems not to need to pause to breathe riffing up and down the scale from a sparrow chirp to a cannon roar. Occasionally an understandable word springs from his mouth like a rabbit breaking out of a trap. He is nearly as hard to understand first thing in the morning as he is later in the afternoon. If he still has money for beer in the evening or can bum some he'll ask Barnett or one of the other day bartenders if he can park his brooms in the back room. If Barnett is in a good mood he might let him as long as he parks himself out front at one of the picnic tables. When he can Gus will invite himself to sit with people he often doesn't even know and join right in with whatever conversation is going on. He gets so caught up in his own stories that he forgets to go pee. Most of the regulars don't listen to him anymore but newcomers will sit and try to figure out what he is saying for awhile until they give up and ignore him which doesn't stop him talking though. And when he finally realizes no one is listening to him he goes inside, collects his brooms, and pushes them down Knox Street to his room in Billy Joe's, smiling, thinking what a glorious evening of conversation he's had at The Quiet Man.

Evidence

Nobody wanted to go home. Nobody ever wanted to go home.
At least not to their own home. At least not alone.

A light too bright to be looked into came on shortly after midnight. There was chaos. Everyone should have known what was coming. When Barnett the bartender announced, "Fifteen minutes until closing time, drink up" his words got stuck in the tangle of words growing louder, the music from the jukebox turned up high as it would go, and the rattle of glasses that had jelled into a jellyfish-like density of noise about an hour ago. Shortly after he made his first announcement he made his second. Sounding more like a fire-and-brimstone preacher this time he shouted a "Last call," that warned all this fun was ending and that it was time to get your affairs in order because if you wait until the light comes on you will get no more beer. Everyone heard that. Anxiety and urgency blurred into desperation. The ten-minute-fast clock on the wall behind the bar throbbed larger. Time was running out. The doom of midnight closing in. Customers rushed about to get to the bar, to get Barnett's attention, to get one more drink which, when they did, they then took back to their tables and drank slowly. Then it was over. The music turned off and that light suddenly switched on. Some covered their eyes, others froze as if poleaxed. "Finish up." They staggered to the bar and pleaded for another beer but it was too late. The bar was shut down and Barnett concluded with, "All glasses off tables." Some begged but he just about never gave in to them. They must try though and, to keep it interesting, on rare occasions he might . . . They could only hope for compassion for him.

Answered Prayers

If you are a super-regular who comes in nearly every day or a friend of the bartender there is an outside chance that if you hang quietly alone at the dark end of the bar and wait humbly until everyone else has left, the front door locked, and the bartender wanting to wind down after the horrible light has been turned out he might not say anything but go to the tap and draw a free beer for both of you. It is story time and, if your stories are good enough, who knows how late you might stay and drink.

But that is a long shot. The next best thing is to get a six-pack to go and hope someone says bravely or drunkenly, "Let's go to my house." What then follows is considerable standing around outside the bar trying to finish stories that never end and waiting for someone to step up as the cops cruise by. Dave and Elizabeth Stout are often the ones willing to sacrifice their home. They both do something with computers for which they are well-paid out at Texas Instruments. They must be at work by seven in the morning so it is hard to figure how they manage to stay up until all hours drinking several nights a week and still make it in on time.

Tonight though Dave and Elizabeth have begged off. She's been getting sick and he, for once, admits to needing sleep. It is Tuesday, too early in the week for someone else to say something like, "We can go to my house but we must not get too loud because my wife is asleep." John Simon asks, "Can we think of anyone who might open their door to us? We got beer." Bill Standard says, "Probably anybody we know who is interested in staying up all night is amongst us here." So they give up and one by one and in pairs drift off to their cars and go home.

Don Sloan and Joe Savage came in around nine. They have not drunk enough to lose their reason so at closing time are ready to go home. Don is a fading prodigy who can do anything: paint, draw, write poetry, and play the piano and sing something like an old blues singer if he is in the right mood and what can get him in the right mood is cheap vodka chased with Mountain Dew. They met for the first time at Peter and Susie Heck's rambling house in exclusive Highland Park. Peter was a big-time advertising guy. Susie was a red-haired former debutante from Oklahoma City who carried a pistol in her boot. Every Monday they opened their house to whoever showed up for drinking, talking, and listening to Frank Zappa, Bob Dylan, Donovan. Joe was older by a couple of years, had graduated from college and been to jail several times. When Don announced, "I have something in the car I'd like to show y'all. It is like nothing you have ever seen," Joe feigned disinterest and stood at the back of the group as Don brought it in and set on the floor a machine that he said could move an object back in time one minute. It was a wire pyramid with a heavier wire hanging straight down from the apex at the end of which was a leather sling. He set it up, adjusted it, and lay a wooden marble into the sling and said, "Keep your eye on the marble. Watch closely. You must concentrate. NOW THERE! Did you see that? Did you see it move?" Peter said, "No. It is still where it was," and Don answered, "Of course you didn't see it move because it is still where it was in space but now it is moved back in time one minute."

Joe is not sure. If it moved back say a million years it might be detectable in its decomposing or with carbon-14 dating but one minute is too short a time to measure. "Why don't you move it back a hundred years then," he asks Don who explains, "So far one minute is all that I've been able to achieve. I don't know if that may not be all I should try to do." He is justifiably concerned because while fooling around with other experiments he has often achieved more than he intended.

Once he and Jimmy Lynch were dueling with proto-neon Geissler tubes when they struck them together causing a frightening burst of electrically charged light. And there was the electromagnetic nail-firing device that worked too well driving a 10d nail through his mother's kitchen wall. One night using some archaic text he'd conjured cloud-like spirits that floated high in his bedroom before vaporizing. He told Peter, "I should not fool around with time much more than what I have. And I'm not sure how those near the device are affected. I have not been able to determine the radius of its influence. If I somehow move you back one minute there should be little problem, but a week, a year who knows?"

Joe was a little older than Don when they met but if he stayed around that machine much who knows? They could wind up the same age. Joe was impressed but couldn't let on. Maybe it was just some bullshit anyway. Maybe it was the story that mattered more anyway like what went on in Major Amos B. Hoople's attic in the *Our Boarding House* comic strip when he transformed junk into wonderful artifacts with his stories about them. A piece of decaying wood with a big old rusted nail sticking through it became, as Major Hoople told the story, something more. He might began with, "And this piece of wood is all that remains after the fire that burned down the house and do you know whose house that was?"

Since meeting at the Heck's Don and Joe had become friends. Tonight after the bright light comes on Don asks Joe if he needs a ride home and Joe says, "Yeah. I do." Don has an old Volkswagen painted Army green. On each door is a yellow circle with a yellow line bisecting it at a fifteen-degree angle which makes it look like it might be some kind of odd government vehicle which is the point. Like it is from some secret branch of the military but then if it is secret why is it marked at all. It is an ambiguous secret vehicle that announces it is a secret thing but keeps its secret to itself. The kind of markings that, if the police stop Don, they might look at the circle, scratch their heads, and let him go.

Soon as they are in the car Don pulls out a pint of cheap vodka from under the seat and they have a sip. Don washes it down with Mountain Dew. Joe just takes it straight. They sit in the parking lot for a little bit sipping from the pint, waiting for the car to warm up, and making up stories before Don puts his Bug in reverse and backs out. He needs gas so goes to a Texaco a block away. The station is lit bright as day by high-intensity lights on tall poles. After getting gas he pulls out. He needs no headlights to see in the station but, just as he gets into the street, and as he reaches to turn them on, the cops who have been watching them since they left The Quiet Man, just waiting for them to break some law, have seen all they need to and pull them over.

One cop stands at the back of the car with his hand on his gun while another walks up to Don's window and says, "I'm stopping you because you did not have your headlights on."

Joe looks at Don and asks, "Did they say something about us having head lice?"

The cop says, "Shut up! Don't talk to each other. Get out of the car."

Don says, "I was just getting ready to turn them on."

"Get out of the car, both of you. Bend over the hood."

You have to bend a long way down to reach the hood of a Volkswagen Bug but they try slipping down the incline of it. It makes them laugh which is something no cop likes to see. He says, "Stop that. Not that hood. Get over here. Bend over my hood."

"Are you going to check us for head lice?" Joe can't help himself. He's had this problem all his life like when he found out his grandmother had a middle name which she hated so much that it must never be uttered he could not control himself. He was five. It was a cold East Texas morning but in Little Momma's kitchen it was warm. She was fixing his breakfast and he was sitting at the porcelain-topped table close to the fire when he said it, not once but twice, "Della Zulla, Della Zulla." She didn't slap him away from the table. She didn't need to. He left on his own. It was a week before she fixed breakfast for him again. He loved Little Momma a lot and it made him sad that he had upset her. He hadn't intended to but it was like he had no control sometimes over what came out of his mouth.

Joe's granddaddy, Big Daddy, was a thin ropehard German carpenter. With one hand he could roll Bull Durham tobacco into a cigarette shaken from a cloth pouch with a red string thread which he pulled with his teeth to close. He rarely smoked. He didn't talk, didn't say much, beyond the blessing when he could make it home for lunch. His blessing was the same one every time—heartfelt but not easy to understand especially the part at the end. "We umbless for Christ's sake. Amen." What the heck did that mean? Joe figured maybe something in German. And even when he was, which he often was, the foreman on a job he was friendly to his men and didn't have to talk much to them because he always hired good men. He put his overalls on, picked up his wood toolbox, and went to work. He needed no blueprint. He was president of his Sunday school class and slept through church. On Sundays he read Joe and his sister the funnies. After Sunday school and lunch on many Sundays he would back his car from the tin-roofed garage in Jacksonville and they would go on rides to visit relatives in Troup or Black Jack. One trip to Tyler to visit Aunt Lucille, Big Daddy turned around near Bullard and told Joe, "You talk too much. You run everything into the ground," and Joe had a clear image of a big round wooden stake with bands of colors around it being driven into the ground by him and he couldn't figure what that had to do with anything. At the same time he knew exactly what Big Daddy meant. These two things often fought in Joe's head with each other What was meant to be heard and what he chose to hear.

"Put your hands behind your backs," the cop says and he cuffs them. "How much have you had to drink?"

"A couple of beers," Don answers not revealing the vodka drunk because he figures vodka can't be smelled so why admit to it.

"Sit down. Sit there on the curb. What kind of car is this anyway?"

"A Volkswagen."

"I know it's a Volkswagen. You know damnfucking good and well what I'm asking. What's that circle on the door for?"

"Nothing. It's just a circle."

Now a sergeant drives up. The three cops talk to each other out of hearing of Joe and Don. First they divide them up. Don gets the sergeant. Joe gets the mean young red-haired one who had originally stopped them. Joe is put in one and Don in the other cop car where they are questioned about what they are up to. Joe asks, "Up to? You mean driving out of a gas station with our lights not yet on? Is that some kind of serious crime?" The sergeant says, "Serious enough to get you thrown in jail if you've been drinking and you obviously have." Really though they have nothing on them other than that until they search Don's car and find burglary tools. The cops pull Joe and Don out of the squad cars to show them what they've found.

Don says, "I can explain."

The red-haired cop says, "Explain it to the judge."

Joe asks, "Where is he? Should we go to his house or . . ."

Don shoots a *shut up* look and then explains to the cops, "Those are not burglary tools those are dental tools." He is a connoisseur of fine tools and weapons. He's had his friend and master craftsman Tim Coursey make a beautiful wood-lined-with-velvet case for these instruments to fit into but to the cops the picks and pliers and all are no more than lock-picking devices. They cannot begin to understand why he would have them otherwise. The dental tool excuse just doesn't wash with them.

"Oh. So you are a dentist?"

"No sir. I am a student."

"Yeah. I bet. You are probably a student of breaking and entering."

Just then the young cop has found something else in the car. A gun. As if he needed anything more. He gets on his radio and calls for a wrecker to come haul the Army green Volkswagen in to the station where it can be thoroughly checked out.

"Okay, Mr. Student. Explain this and don't try to tell me it is not a gun but a hammer or something."

"No sir. It is certainly a gun but not much of one. Just a little .22."

Don starts to explain but neither cop is interested. The older one says to the younger one, "I'll take them down," and he then opens the door and helps them into the back seat of his squad car. Before the cop gets in to drive them to jail Don tells Joe, "That gun belongs to Lynch. He was going to try to blow his brains out with it so I took it from him . . ."

Before they take off the other cop hurries over. He is holding a red bandanna. He asks Don, "Is this yours?"

"Yes sir."

Good Lord, Joe thinks, *we are going to be taken downtown for head lice, dentist tools, and a red bandanna. Oh and a gun.* Don asks the mean young cop, "What's the problem with having a bandanna?" The cop puts his hand up to cover his mouth and nose. It takes a minute for them to figure out that what he is doing is showing them how the bandanna could have been used like an old-time cowboy bank robber would. "Well Joe," says Don, "I reckon they got you now."

"Shut up. You are both going to jail." Don recognizes the "evidence" they have but they have not told him exactly what crime he is accused of. He asks, "For what exactly?"

"For life, if I had my way," the red-haired cop barks. Joe Savage wonders if he is implicated along with Don. He tries to keep his mouth shut.

"They'll tell you downtown what the charges are." Joe has wondered why cops do this. What difference is it going to make if they are told what they are suspected of. Maybe it is just to keep you guessing or a way to show who is in charge.

"Please tell us now."

The cop answers, "The more you ask the worse it is going to be." But Joe can't help himself. "For head lice?"

The cop has heard enough from him and pulls the squad car over. "Oh shit," Joe says as the cop gets out. In his hand is a length of rubber hose. When it strikes the body it leaves no marks, no bruises. All the injuries will be invisible, internal. He jerks Joe out, slams him against the hood, and hits him five or six times in the kidneys. Don thinks he will be next but Joe is just pushed back in the car. The cop gets in and takes them downtown.

The ramp down under the police station to the booking desk is familiar. They walk in through the same sliding glass door that Oswald came out of to be gunned down by Jack Ruby. Joe and Don are separated. They are both in trouble but different kinds. Joe because he has a big mouth and Don for a whole list of things from driving at night with no headlights on to illegal possession of a gun and burglary. "Call them what you will and put them in the finest case," the sergeant tells Don, "burglary tools are burglary tools."

Don is fingerprinted, his mug is shot, and he is led into a small white room whose walls haven't been washed in decades where two detectives sit waiting to talk to him. They are polite and seem just to be trying to sort things out and see what Don is guilty of. They struggle with what the red bandanna was used for. Holdup men haven't used them in over a hundred years. Maybe Don is a second-story man, a cat burglar, and Joe is his accomplice, his getaway driver? Don thinks cat burglars don't use bandanna masks but has the good sense to keep his opinion to himself. As Don's interrogation continues Joe has been sent on to the bullpen with the other drunks and petty criminals.

One of the detectives asks Don, "Who was the dentist?"

The other detective follows up with, "And who did you say was going to kill himself with that pistol?"

"What makes you think you know so much anyway?"

"You college boys got it all figured out don't you?"

"You think 'cause you go to a fancy school that you got a free pass to do whatever the hell you want to in the world including robbing and creeping in through people's windows at night, but let me tell you whatever you were doing we are going to find out. We know a crime has been committed by you and all we got to do now is find out what it was and where it happened. You can keep up your innocent routine but we are going to break it down. I'll tell you one fucking thing, believe me, you'll give us some answers or else."

Don asks, "Is that a question?"

"No."

Don asks, "What about the red bandanna?"

"I think the officers explained that to you."

The questioning continues for another hour. Nothing getting resolved. There just gets to be a time when it needs to end so the detectives can go on to their next case. They call off their interrogation but one of them tells Don, "By morning we should have something to charge you with and we'll have you indicted in a day or two. You'll be getting your own private cell in a little bit as soon as it is made up and ready for you but for now maybe you'd like to visit your friend in the bullpen." They take him from the interrogation room and drop him off in the holding tank—the bullpen where Joe is locked up along with about fifty other guys. There are not enough benches for all the prisoners to sit on so there are bodies squatting and sitting all over the place. A few who are still drunk from the night before, some who are too tired and some who are used to it, have found room on the floor to lie down and some are even asleep. There is one nasty toilet in the back corner that someone is always sitting on taking a shit or using to throw up in when they can make it there otherwise they just vomit on the floor. Groups form for protection from other groups or to intimidate other prisoners. Alliances shift. All kinds of threats are thrown around. Every morning the floors are hosed down but it does nothing to remove the stench of sweat, shit, unwashed bodies, filthy clothes, and vomit.

After the steel door shuts behind him Don looks for Joe and finds him standing against a wall where three Black guys seem to be harassing him. Maybe they are just getting to know each other. Whatever, when Don walks over they move away but not too far. Joe asks Don what they have charged him with and Joe tells him just for being drunk and disorderly and that his mother is already on the way down to bail him out. "What about you?" Joe asks Don. "Are they going to charge you with anything?" Don doesn't answer.

After he has been in the bullpen for an hour or so the red-haired cop who arrested them shows up and motions Don over to the bars where he asks him, "You want to know what sunk your ship boy? It was your car. We've been watching you for some time. You think you're so smart with that yellow circle. Like you think if you confuse us enough we'll just give up. Well we got a man down here who knows every symbol in the world and if he doesn't know one he knows someone who does." He says, "We are close. We'll have you by sundown. We know what that thing means. It either means nothing or it's some sort of subversive sign."

"Goddamn," Don pleads, "Try the first. That's some

crazy evidence y'all got. I mean it's not a lot. A bandanna, some dentist's tools . . ."

The detective says, "You're right it is not that much . . . Oh don't forget the gun. Not much. Just enough. And we got some other things from your car that are not going to help your case."

Don asks, "Like what?" But they won't tell him.

They wind up charging Don with half a dozen things but can't make any of them stick. They know he is guilty but can't find the crime he is supposed to have committed so after keeping him in jail for over a week they finally have to let him go. They do not apologize. When he goes to pick up his Bug out at the pound that afternoon the first thing he notices is that the symbol on the side of the door has been altered. Where there had just been one yellow line that bisected the circle there now was another which crossed the first to form an X. It just didn't work. It was too obviously someone trying to be cute. Whoever had done it had been able to match the paint color exactly and that was impressive but an X. The next day Don took it in to Maaco, a cheap car-painting outfit, had it painted gray and traded it in on a five-year-old black Ford F-150 pickup.

If It Don't Fit
Don't Force It

Jolene Goforth needs more than a beer but that will have to do for now. She pulls her old limping piece of shit Chevrolet pickup into a space in the Safeway parking lot. She doesn't have to turn it off. It dies on its own. She should have bought a Ford. She knew better. Her daddy told her stick with Fords but a Mexican she worked with was only asking five hundred for the Chevy. He said, "Maybe it don't look so good but it runs okay." Under its dull green peeling paint were patches of a 1954 red layer peeling away revealing a '51 black layer. Some restraining rope was stretched across the space where a tailgate had been. Dents and scratches competed for the little virgin sheet metal left. It was muddy but that was no big thing. She could wash it with her garden hose when she got home. It smoked a little but she needed some wheels. The Mexican told her she could pay it out a hundred dollars a month and if it stopped running before she paid it off he'd buy it back for a couple of hundred. She wasn't sure but when she said, "I'll give you four hundred," and he agreed, she had herself a truck.

She untwists the bailing wire holding the door shut, gets out, and has to slam the fucking thing four times before it latches. She walks down an alley to The Quiet Man, goes in and orders a Lone Star, drinks it fast and orders another. This bar is not the kind she usually drinks in. Too many college kids and hippies but she likes Ken the bartender and some biker friends who usually drink at the Little White Cloud show up now and then. She orders another Lone Star.

Ken comforts her. Talking to him smooths out her wrinkles. After a couple more beers she is smooth as burlap. She has thought about fucking him but doesn't want to mess up their relationship. She leans over the bar to get a little closer. Her problems had floated away after her fourth beer. Her smile that had grown into a soft laugh from deep in her throat is choked back when she feels a sudden tap on her shoulder. She doesn't turn around but looks in the bar mirror to see who is tapping and disturbing her. It is some blonde woman in a suit. She doesn't know women who wear suits. Women in suits are usually after something she doesn't want to give them like money. Informed she half turns her head to see what the fuck the woman wants and stops right before she bumps into a pair of big tits under a silk blouse that have been thrust into her turning radius. Before she can pull back she recognizes them. It is Candy Metcalf. Good Lord. Jolene looks up and sees her still-pretty round face, not beautiful but pretty as it ever was. She hasn't seen her since high school except at their ten-year reunion. Hasn't even thought about her at least not that much. She'd been a stuck-up pain in the ass when Jolene first got to knowing her in high school, going on about her new car or where her daddy was going to take her skiing next Christmas. She always wore expensive, tailored clothes and had her hair and nails done once a week. She even got pedicures. She put herself on a pedestal but Jolene and her friends Joyce Demetros and badass Red Rock Taylor's little sister Linda had plans to kick it out from under her and knock her down to their level. It wasn't hard. Just one serious talking to in the parking lot after school as she was getting into her new Oldsmobile Rocket 88 convinced Candy that they were not impressed with how much money her daddy had. It didn't make her any better than them. Other than money Jolene and Joyce and Linda had lots going on. They were teenage queens of the underworld. All were real good-looking in a give-a-fuck kinda way. Joyce would spend just enough time in front of a mirror to get her ducktails right and to check out how her ass looked in her too-tight long skirt and her white boy's shirt with collar turned up in back. Linda didn't look tough with her long blonde hair. She was skinny but every day her tits grew not so much bigger but prettier. Jolene had country girl looks and was proud of them. She had recently bleached her hair blonde and was the strongest of them all. She could beat most boys at arm wrestling. None of them spent hours in front of mirrors. They didn't have to. And they were bad. They modeled themselves on the sweater-wearing girls on the covers of juvenile delinquent novels and carried switchblade knives in their purses. Nobody fucked with those three and Candy wasn't going to set any precedents.

Candy stopped talking about what all her daddy bought her at Neiman's and ski trips to Aspen around them anymore, but it wasn't easy as she didn't know any other way to act but rich. Jolene and them came from poor families. They thought being poor was normal and anybody who wasn't poor wasn't normal. They were as mean as their lives. Joyce and Linda liked fucking with Candy better than Jolene did who didn't know where her compassion came from. It felt all wrong and she sure couldn't let on that something was going on with her and the way she felt about Candy, something physical that bugged her and that she couldn't understand. Candy picked up that vibe from Jolene but wasn't quite sure what the feeling was either. As for the other two she just did what she had to to keep them off her back. She gave them rides and big bottles of private-label liquor from her daddy's liquor closet. She tried to change the way she dressed to look more like them but tight skirts didn't work for her. It wasn't that her ass was too big. It was maybe too broad but not fat. Not real fat but too fat for the kind of mid-thigh tight skirt that required a perfectly curved girdle-free ass. And leather motorcycle jackets just didn't work with silk. She really wanted to be hip like them but it didn't come natural to her. Hipness wasn't just something you could just take up like a new dress. You had it or you didn't.

They played Candy. Treated her nice when they wanted another bottle of booze. She knew if they asked for something it was in her best interest to get it for them. She wanted to keep them happy. Not only out of fear. She wanted to be friends but she was their monkey and they all knew it. Candy had a good reputation as much as she had any before she got tangled up with them. She was a virgin. Boys made panting jokes about her tits but few got any closer than to "accidentally" bump into them in the hall. She was mixed-up about them herself in a way that girls with little tits could never understand. Boys had trouble looking her in the eyes. It was like her tits set up some kind of barrier around the real her but they were her. As much as she wasn't hip she was a girl with very big tits. The kind that would sag as she grew older but sure weren't sagging yet. She knew she should be grateful but standing naked in front of her full-length closet mirror she wondered if she wouldn't trade them in to be thin. She wasn't all that fat. The one boy who she'd let take the silk away and touch the naked flesh of them had asked her out on a date, had acted like he really liked her, but it soon became clear . . . She was tired of saying no but did not push his hands away as he unbuttoned her blouse and fumbled with the in-front clasp . . . He couldn't get it undone and she had to do it herself while acting like she was still resisting which wasn't easy. Her hands no longer worked for her. She felt like she was parts of but not a whole body. Next day at school the prick told everyone after lunch back behind the temporary classrooms. The jokes got as mean as the boys could possibly make them probably because they knew they had no chance at getting to try to undo that bra clasp themselves. It gave them erections though just thinking about it. Some nights boys drove by her house, honking and yelling for her to come out. At times she was tempted. What worse could they say about her anyway? Maybe she should just go on and get in their car and let them have their way with her, at least with her tits. She wasn't sure why she wanted to keep what she had left of her virginity but she did so she wouldn't go out and chance losing it. She blamed it on being a Baptist. If her daddy was home he'd run out and shake his double-barreled shotgun at the boys as they burned rubber fishtailing away in disappearing red taillights. A couple of times he'd even fired at them. Anyway however much of a good reputation she might have once had was gone now. She didn't fit in with the other rich, popular girls either. Joyce and them used her but at least they acknowledged her existence. She wasn't a slut but might as well have been.

In spite of all that or maybe because of it Jolene's feelings for Candy were getting stronger. Still there wasn't any way to let the girls know about it—those feelings—or she might be kicked out of the group her-self. She couldn't even be seen talking to Candy in the hall unless she was making fun of her or pushing her around some way. She wanted to see her, to be alone with her but where could that happen?

Candy figured it out. She asked Jolene to meet her in the auditorium after lunch, on the back row in the shadow of the balcony. As the other kids rushed out of the lunchroom to the playground when the STOP sign turned to PASS Jolene and Candy went by separate routes to meet in the empty auditorium to talk and . . . Alone in the near darkness on the back row.

Just the two of them but one day Joyce Demetros wandered in. She couldn't make out for sure what was going on but as she got closer for just an instant she was pretty sure she saw Candy buttoning her blue silk blouse. And, good Lord, there was Jolene looking all innocent herself but she seemed to be quickly zipping up her skirt. Joyce didn't know whether to act like she saw nothing or run from the auditorium to tell Linda what she was pretty sure she had seen. Whatever—she was appalled. Jolene saw her and tried to say something but Joyce just turned and left as the bell rang to end lunch break. Jolene was late to her next class. For once she wasn't looking forward to the bell that ended the day. She wanted to stay in the building. She knew what was coming from Joyce and Linda so she tried to cut it off.

"I was just trying to get her to help me with some homework."

Linda laughed.

"I mean it. She's smart and . . . okay . . . I don't know what you are thinking but nothing was going on between her and me but homework."

Nearly all the kids and lots of the adults did whatever they could to stay out of their way. Looking at one of them wrong could bring the wrath of all of them down on you. That was scary enough but there was something else they did that was even more frightening. That was when they held Cat Court in study hall. Anyone could be judged by them there. Nobody was immune. Not boys. Not girls. Not teachers or janitors or kitchen help or the assistant principal. When they held court the only thing missing was long black robes, a big desk, and a gavel as they sat lined up there on the back row. Of course they were supposed to be studying so they had to keep their voices down and much of the evidence was presented in writing. Most of their decisions were easy and didn't even require the judged one to be there. A name would come up. Linda would look at Joyce would look at

Jolene and a wordless decision was made. This wasn't some temporary thing. When the verdict came down as to whether the judged one was a cat or a square that decision was final and permanent. There were lots more squares than cats. If the girls had any doubt about the catness of someone the defendant might be allowed to present his or her case to them. It could take a day or two before a verdict was rendered. There was no appeal.

When you were summoned you had to go. Even before your trial the girls had been watching you. How you dressed. How you talked. One of the first things they checked in boys was the sound they made when they walked. Metal shoe taps did more than save shoe leather. They created metal rhythms as you sauntered down the hall, through the lunchroom, or to the back of study hall. The ultimate was a thin metal horseshoe that fit around the entire heel. Smaller toe taps were used as accompaniment. You created your own rhythms. A slight scratching drag with the left foot followed by a solid tap with the right and you knew it was Bledsoe. Tap, swish, tap, swish. He could be heard all up and down the hall and into the classrooms. You had to find your own cat rhythm. This wasn't tap dancing.

A boy's clothes made a big difference. Blue jeans or black jeans or black denims for awhile (with a buckle in the back), a white T-shirt under a many-zippered motorcycle jacket got high marks. A zip-up suede jacket was permitted but not a thin red one like James Dean wore in *Rebel without a Cause*. James Dean wasn't cool. Marlon Brando in *The Wild One* was. Johnny Bledsoe got highest cool cat marks. He not only had a motor-cycle jacket but his had white leather sleeves. Nobody had ever seen a jacket like that before. He was tough? That was a given. To dress that way you had to be. But was he or was it just his jacket and slick black hair? He was the number one coolest badass cat in school. Cool he had down. It could be seen but tough? Nobody had ever seen him fight. Maybe he didn't have to. When you got a reputation like his nobody fucked with you. Problem was Johnny fell for it himself. He began to believe he was that bad but a white-sleeved motorcycle jacket and dragging horseshoe taps can get you only so far and for Bledsoe it was as far as the foot scraper outside the school's front door. He was perched there when the new boy in school found him and asked. "I heard you supposed to be bad?" And Johnny answered, "That's right. Who the fuck are . . ." was the last thing out of his mouth but blood and teeth. Johnny should have stuck with coolest cat around because one straight right from the new boy knocked him back off the scraper and out cold. The student hierarchy was reshuffled right there with Bledsoe on the ground and Otis Nolte on top on his first day in school. Otis wasn't interested in being the number one, toughest, baddest, coolest, or any of that shit. He'd heard there might be some kind of new boy initiation he might have to deal with. He just didn't want to be fucked with by anybody, initiation or not, and he got that understood right away. He wasn't looking for any friends and that made him hard to deal with. None of the kids could find a way to put any pressure on him and on top of that he was a good student. All he wanted was enough respect to go his own way without any interference. Otis grew up fighting in a homemade ring a block from his house down in

Cut 'n' Shoot in the tall pines of the Big Thicket. By the time he was twelve he'd had over a twenty fights in the ring and lots more outside it. He never thought about whether he liked fighting or not. It wasn't even a question. If you were a boy in Cut 'n' Shoot you were going to be in that ring from a very early age. It was as natural as shooting squirrels. Then his daddy got a job as a boilermaker in a shop up in Dallas and his family sure didn't want to but had no choice than to move with him. It wasn't all Otis was but he was for sure a rough country fighter who'd as soon stick your motorcycle jacket and shoe taps up your ass as have a pleasant conversation with you.

Hair mattered 'cause barbershops still mattered. A haircut every other week was as much as anything an excuse to go to the barbershop. Sometimes there could be surprises like the time the barber in the first chair at the Lakewood Barbershop got some kind of ultrasonic, infrared wand thing that he passed over your face. Not touching skin. But close. There was a sort of low sizzling sound and a burning not unpleasant smell. It was to cleanse and make your skin clear. Maybe it did. Anyway it was worth an extra dollar. Then flattops, not burrs, got to be the thing to have with ducktails if possible which were lots of trouble unless your hair was Italian thick. Butch Wax kept the hair up in front and judiciously used could keep the hair swept back on the sides. Maybe into ducktails which had to be combed all the time as if hair didn't like ducktails. Some kind of grease or oil worked best. Girls usually had better ducktails. Flattops were cool for about a year before football players started wearing them. Cats knew limitations.

This wasn't some goofy *Blackboard Jungle Rock Around the Clock* bullshit. It was *The Wild One*. Not the French existential confusion of James Dean but the motorcycle certainty of Marlon Brando. Elvis had the look to begin with before he stuffed himself into Las Vegas sequined outfits. He had the hair, everything, but when you'd been listening to Jimmy Reed and Howlin' Wolf and John Lee Hooker he was just another singer. A good white one but just another singer.

Shirt collars turned up in the back were mostly for girls. Keep it simple. A plain white T-shirt with sleeves rolled up a couple of neat times but not all the way to the shoulder was okay. A pack of Camels rolled into the sleeve. Attitude mattered. It didn't help to have good grades. The more time you spent in the principal's office and the more time you had to spend in detention hall all worked in your favor. Assistant principals were fair game. Linda and Jolene and Joyce watched the way you talked and the way you walked. Were you a cat or a square?

Girls got judged differently. It was nastier. First if you ever wore a poodle skirt and lots of petticoats under forget it. Tight long skirts and simple white starched blouses with turned up collars got you points. Angora sweaters were cool depending on the development of your tits. There also were Angora socks whose fur could be set on fire. There would be a flash but the sock would not be burned. Carla, a tenth grader, heard about that but got the material and the garment wrong. She thought she could set a sweater on fire and there would be the flash but no real damage to the sweater. Her sweater was furry but not Angora and when she put a match to it it ignited. Before she could get the fire out she had serious burns on her face and body that would take years of skin grafting to fix. Mixed furry. Angora, maybe. Short hair and ducktails, not lots of makeup except for red lipstick and black eyeliner. Some girls though were satisfied, wanted to be squares. They were the hardest to deal with.

When Candy was first judged there was no debate, just a couple of nods and she was a square but the big bottle of gin she got Linda that night got her a rare new trial. She didn't make cool kitten. They just said she wasn't a square for as long as she kept the liquor and rides coming.

Jolene was the poorest of the girls and she was the smartest like if she hadn't been born poor she might have amounted to something. With Linda and Joyce it was simpler, they were simpler. They were what they appeared to be. Jolene grew up in a shack in Oak Cliff before her family moved to Lakewood when she was ten. When she was eight her beloved Uncle Billy convinced her it was okay to have sex as long as it was with him but he wasn't around that much to keep up with her. She was easy. Boys could come over to play with her nearly anytime they wanted to. She was the one who came up with the nasty idea for Opinion Books. A spiral notebook would have a girl's name written on the cover and be set loose for everyone to write their opinions in. After Joyce had caught Jolene and Candy in the auditorium Jolene had to come up with something to regain her status. She stole a blank notebook and put Candy's name on the cover and wrote on the first page *A new car and big tits can get you so far but your fat ass keeps you from going farther.* Jolene didn't sign her name but she made sure that Joyce and Linda knew she was the one who started the thing. The books would inevitably fall into the hands of their target. It was as mean a thing as could be done to someone. After her own Opinion Book fell into Candy's hands she got her daddy to let her transfer to Hockaday, a private school for rich white girls. That was the last Jolene saw of her, except for the reunion, before she bumped into her here at The Quiet Man.

It is Tuesday a little before six in the afternoon. Jolene drives up the hill onto the slowly twisting little road through the Samuell-Grand Park golf course's green oasis and out and back down onto the Lakewood/East Dallas back streets she's known since she was a child to get to The Quiet Man. She got off her waitressing job at the Debonair Ballroom at five. She's nearly always lived in the neighborhood, never been far from home, except for a trip to Los Angeles to see Uncle Billy when she was fourteen and some trips around Texas and Oklahoma. Otherwise she'd lived in lots of places in East Dallas, mostly duplexes, some apartments, and a couple of little houses, often alone. She never had roommates. She wasn't about to share her space with some woman but she had lived with some guys. Once when she was drunk she ran away with some asshole she'd just met in a bar to Oklahoma to get married. The marriage lasted nearly six months before she got tired of the prick doing nothing but lying around her apartment drinking and watching television and kicked him out. She swore after that never to get married again and even though she dreamed about having kids and a family she couldn't figure how to do it without a man. A couple of times she'd gotten pregnant and one guy even agreed to marry her but she preferred getting an abortion to living with him.

She moved into the Tropical Arms on Gaston a year ago. It was cheap and clean and most of her neighbors were girls from East Texas who'd moved to the big city to find husbands but had mostly found low-paying jobs as secretaries or waitresses. They were all younger than her and some of them were pretty nice-looking, naive, and sweet. The Tropical Arms was one of a string of apartment houses that had been built in the 1950s especially for these girls. It was a short bus ride to downtown and jobs. There was a swimming pool and several dried out palm trees in the courtyard of each around which the girls could party after work and on the weekends have luaus. It hadn't been that many years ago that big houses lined Gaston where mid-level executives and doctors lived. The senior executives lived in mansions a block north on Swiss Avenue. A block the other way were smaller houses where those a little further down the corporate ladder lived, even farther south were rent houses where the lowest-paid, mostly Black workers lived. By the 1960s those apartments had begun to fall apart and to become less desirable and most of the big houses on Swiss and Gaston had been abandoned or divided up into apartments or bulldozed to make way for places like the Parisian, the Palm Grove, the Sun and Surf, the Sans Souci, and about a dozen others with such faux exotic names.

But after twenty years they were in real bad shape. All the hopeful small-town girls had either found husbands, moved back to East Texas, or grown old in newer, bigger versions of Gaston Avenue like The Village up north on Greenville Avenue, off Lovers Lane. Places farther out. Farther north.

The Gaston Avenue landlords realized they had to do something so by the late sixties they began to remodel the apartments. No big structural fixes but lots of new Sheetrock and paint. The Sans Souci became a retirement home, the Royal Palms a drug rehabilitation center, and another one Jolene couldn't figure out what it was. Strange, not gangster strange, but sideshow strange, people came and went from it all hours of the day and night. The rumor was that it was a home for retired circus performers. They never bothered anyone in the neighborhood so nobody bothered them. Jolene got to be friends with a midget who lived there before he lived with her for a couple of months but in that short time he taught her a lot of close-up circus tricks. Rents were cheap at the Tropical Arms and the rooms were clean and, for now, they were good enough for Jolene and her cats, Boots and Randolph, after the midget moved on. She hadn't given up on finding a husband. She'd gone with several interesting and several dull men but, other than Sonny, none of them seemed husband material. Not that he did by anybody but her standards. She'd loved Sonny Baldwin, "Stick," for so long he seemed like her real husband, her soulmate, or maybe her incestuous brother. No matter who she was going with she knew she could always call Sonny. He rode a Vincent Black Shadow. He was the only Scorpion who didn't have a Harley. He had something better. She knew he'd always be there and maybe that was best.

Not being married precluded the possibility of divorce and losing him altogether. It was best that they hadn't gotten married. They'd talked about it. They'd fantasized. They'd even lived together for a couple of years. And it wasn't hard for them to separate. No big fights or anything. He just was gone one day when she got home from work. He left a phone number for her to call but she didn't use it for a couple of months. When she did get in touch with him everything was cool, they were still best friends like they hadn't shacked up for two years. A couple of times when she was drunk she tried to get him in bed again but he'd always find a way to turn her down.

Jolene's Gaston Avenue apartment suited her. Everything she needed was close by. She couldn't imagine living anywhere else except maybe in the woody valley down under Love's Lookout just outside Jacksonville in East Texas. She sure couldn't imagine herself in the suburbs. Just seeing the cars speeding up the ramps out of town and up onto freeways spiraling into the sky on their way home to Richardson or Plano was enough to make her call Sonny.

Jolene Goforth has been drinking at The Quiet Man for a couple of years. For the last three years she has been waitressing and sometimes bartending at the Debonair. Before that she worked in the Purple Room, at the Zoo Bar, the Purple Room again, then the Casba . . . shit she couldn't even remember all the places. For awhile she worked at the Fare, a topless joint, but not as a dancer. She worked the door. She is forty-two and looks good. Her ass is nearly as hard it was when she was fourteen but she doesn't have to wear tight skirts to show it off anymore. Not often anyway. She even decided to stop getting her hair bleached a couple of weeks ago. Last time she stopped . . . well, she never had really . . . ever since she was twelve it had been blonde. The brown and blonde hair now have reached a truce and if you didn't know you might think she'd had it done to look like it did.

The Debonair Ballroom is a just a big 'ol honky-tonk at night with a country band but during the day it has a life unlike most other beer joints. The pressure cooker hours are from around noon until five or so in the afternoon. This is the time when stir-crazy married women put a roast, some onions, carrots, potatoes in a pressure cooker, add water, salt, and pepper, latch the cover on, turn on the fire, check the pressure valves, and go upstairs and get dressed. Not just dressed but dressed up. Dolled up. Too dressed up to be going to the grocery store or the doctor. The kids will not be home until after 5 and the husbands later. They take their time finding just the right tight pair of jeans and new blouses that they would never wear on a date with their husbands. Some put on boots. And they drive to the Debonair.

Men who work night shifts who get off around noon know where to go to drink and meet women. They drive to the Debonair.

Jolene works the day shift serving men who work the night shift and the women whose husbands work the day shift. She gets off as the purple afternoon darkens into night. It is not a bad gig. There is rarely any trouble. Not inside the place. Tiny, the security guard, can handle anything. There had been those car bombings in the parking lot a couple of years ago and somebody tried to burn the place down late one night after the place was closed a year ago but that did not concern her. That was just something going on between the owners and some gangsters. Something to do with money or drugs. She stayed out of it and didn't even want to hear the other waitresses' gossip. Nobody'd fuck with her. It could have something to do with her Scorpion connections.

Candy normally wouldn't be caught dead in a joint like The Quiet Man. Well she used to feel like that. A friend told her about it a year or so ago. First time she saw it she nearly didn't go in but having no place else to go did. It wasn't just the looks of the place but she just didn't see how she could fit in with the crowd that she suspected would be there. She at least didn't wear a suit that day. The place was lots friendlier than she thought it would be, but still . . . She told herself every time that she wouldn't come back again but she did. She'd even wear a suit now and again. She started going in about once a week. She liked the people she'd met there. It was surprising that she hadn't run into Jolene there so far.

Candy did not have that much to complain about. Her parents were killed in a head-on car wreck on Central Expressway. It was upsetting. She'd never lived anywhere but at home with them. She was quiet sad when they died but got over it pretty soon when she found out about the trust fund they'd set up for her. She did get lonely. She'd never have to work. She thought about college, charity work, all sorts of hobbies but never was motivated enough to do what was needed. She couldn't set goals. And why should she. She had everything. She was bored, living in the same house she'd lived in all her life. It was way too big for her living there by herself. She wished she did drugs. She ate too much. Her tits were too big now but so was the rest of her. She wasn't fat. Not that fat. She still had friends but they rarely called. She decided she needed some new ones. She would have never even gone into The Quiet Man unless Freddy the Queer had told her about it. She'd known him since high school. He drove a red convertible and had lots of girlfriends who he used to attract boys. She'd been his "girlfriend" for awhile when she was seventeen. They were still friends.

Neither Jolene nor Candy ever thought they could wind up being Quiet Man regulars but they did. Not everyday regulars but in often enough that the bartender knew their names. All the customers are misfits of some kind even the businessmen. Jolene was introduced to the place by Sonny Baldwin. He rode with the Scorpions until he was killed five years ago when he lost control of his Black Shadow on a rainy night out on Belt Line trying to balance a case of Lone Star on the gas tank going sixty. He went into a long pretty skid with his bike sliding to rest under a semi, bloody, dead. His death hit her hard.

Jolene drank with Sonny at the Little White Cloud on Henderson and at the Scorpion Den clubhouse on Hall. Hardly a week went by that she didn't see or at least talk to him on the phone. One night he told her about this new bar he'd found. She asked him if it was a biker bar. He said it wasn't but that some good bike mechanics hung out there as well as one of the best bike builders he'd ever meet. Bill Jenkins rode a very quiet BMW and was the very antithesis of a biker. If the weather was decent he sat at one of the picnic tables in front with other mechanics or anybody else who wanted to join them. Some were artists. There were also teachers, businessmen, actors, and just plain drunks. If Sonny had any mechanical problems Jenkins or somebody at that table could just about always come up with answers. Sonny never came with any other Scorpions and always behaved himself.

When Jolene first went in she'd always sit with Sonny to start with but often found herself talking with other folks who had absolutely nothing to do with motorcycles. She liked the change of pace. She'd known Sonny since high school. He was a couple of years older and hung out with Red Rock and the Litton brothers. The Littons were the most notorious fighters in East Dallas. Her boyfriend was Bobby Angel. His name was more interesting than he was. She often wore peasant blouses with stretchy tops and no bra. In civics class she sat in the front seat of a row of seven. Everyone on her row was boys. They fought to sit in the desk right behind her. When Miss Snarkle, the goofy old teacher, wasn't looking she'd let the boy behind her reach around and feel her tits. When she passed out papers it was sometimes possible to reach up her mid-calf skirt. If lucky the boy's hand would get all the way to her panties before she moved away. Melvin who sat on the next row over told Johnny Bledsoe he'd better be careful because her boyfriend was Bobby Angel. Johnny took his hand out of her dress and asked, "Who the fuck is Bobby Angel?" and put his hand right back up Jolene's dress. Melvin went back to his seat. Jolene got an A in civics.

They don't hug. Jolene says, "My goodness. Candy Metcalf. How long has it been?" Candy answers, "I don't

know. Ten years?" Jolene says, "Good to see you. We
got a lot of catching up to do. What are you doing here?
Come on let's sit in a booth?" "Okay," Candy answers.

"How you been?" Jolene asks. "Fine," Candy answers.
Jolene tell her, "It's weird but I had a dream you were
in a couple of nights ago." Candy has a new Mercedes.
In Jolene's dream Candy had a Rolls and was lonely.
Jolene would never admit it but she could use a new
friend herself. They wind up spending the night together
at Candy's house. It wasn't the first time Jolene'd been
with a woman but it was the first time it'd felt right.

"Why don't you move in with me?" Candy asks Jolene
the next morning. "I got this whole big house that I just
rattle around in by myself.

"I can't afford it," Jolene tells her.

"Yes you can because it won't cost you anything. I
got plenty of money," Candy assures her.

Jolene doesn't like the sound of it at first. She'd
always been independent had never depended on any
man or woman to support her but what the fuck? Maybe
she deserves it and after how last night was so sweet
with Candy she says "Okay." "The only thing," Candy
says, "I would ask you to do is either get rid of that
pickup or at least hide it in the garage. Oh and one
other. Tell me I'm cool."

Jolene wasn't about to give up her truck. It wasn't
that she liked the truck all that much it was just that
she wasn't going to give up everything. It wasn't rational
and she usually was except she had a totally irrational
place where no matter how good the argument was
against her that's where a stand's had to be taken. Or
maybe it's just her getting stuck there. Why stuck in

that particular place wasn't the point. There should be a name for that stuck place where no matter if the yardstick says you are five-foot-six you insist, you know, you are five-foot-eight. No use to argue. Jolene was not giving up her pickup.

She loaded all her stuff in her Chevy and moved in with Candy. She gave her two weeks' notice at the Purple Room. If/when she had to she could always get some kind of job in the service industry. Her boss said, "Why don't you just leave now," and gave her a hundred-dollar bill. He was short a bartender that night.

Jolene is forty-two. So is Candy. She pulls up at Candy's a little after noon. Before they hug Candy gets her to move her ragged pickup to the back. Then they hug and Candy shakes up a tumbler of martinis. They walk out the back door into a small woods down a stone- and moss-covered path with a little stream running alongside it to a black bamboo grove and sit in comfortable chairs near a little waterfall that flows into the goldfish pond and drink until they drown all their memories and start to make up new ones. They make love and drink exotic liquors and single-malt Scotches. And make love. After a couple of months they have drunk up all Candy's daddy's good stuff and don't make love as often. They get to drinking all day. They drink and they fall down and get bruises and go to bed and get up and drink or want to drink but are out of alcohol. Candy calls her liquor store and orders more. They ask her what she wants and are surprised when all she asks for is gin. Five big bottles of gin. Good gin.

Neither can remember when they switched to vodka, cheap vodka, threw away the lid and started drinking it straight in glasses, plastic tumblers, coffee cups, Jolene's mason fruit jars full of vodka, all day long. The only people they see are the deliverymen and a handsome young yardman who they pay too much money. Plus they give him a jar of vodka. He watches Candy fall down and leaves.

One morning before she's had a drink other than some vodka in her coffee Jolene gets depressed. She longs for the clogged beer line at the Debonair and to see Ken at The Quiet Man but they don't go out anymore. They order food and don't eat much of it or do the dishes that often. Candy is losing weight. She wears flannel now instead of silk. Ashtrays spill butts onto the mahogany furniture. Purple and yellowing bruises splotch their bodies like the peeling paint on Jolene's Chevy. One morning Jolene decides her clothes are too dirty to wear so drapes one of Candy's silk blouses over her purpling emaciated body. Her bruises covered with silk. Many days they don't get out of their flannel and silk. Jolene is depressed. Candy is anxious and depressed. She is used to the depression, has been functioning with it for as long as she can remember.

Jolene wants out. Just after the sun comes up she finds some wearable jeans, a sweater and goes out to the garage but her truck won't start. She slams the door over and over but it never will latch. Finally she gives up and goes back in the house to figure out who she might call to get the truck running. She sits out on the patio. Jewel-green hummingbirds hover in the passion flowers. Yellow finches scoot through the undergrowth. It is a still cool spring day. She gets a glass of vodka to help better enjoy the weather and to think best as she can.

Candy comes out to join her. She hasn't seen her for a couple of days. She's stayed shut up in her bedroom with her bottle. After a jar full of vodka Jolene forgets about her truck and trying to get away. She is coming apart. She finishes her vodka. Candy finishes hers and looks for another bottle but all of them are empty.

It is around noon when she calls the liquor store. She doesn't have to say anything more than her name and they know what to send. It takes nearly an hour for the deliveryman to get to them. Next time they got to remember to order before they run out. Candy softly rubs a new bruise on her hip.

One Turns to One
(Walter Cronkite's Head)

The head of Walter Cronkite should be on the screen but it isn't. Maybe the problem is with the reception. It has been a cloudy gray day. It could be with the television set, an old black-and-white Philco twelve-incher. It sits on a stainless steel shelf above the bar in The Quiet Man. I rode the bus here from work this afternoon to have a beer and watch the evening news. Mike Carr, the bar's owner, will only allow the set on for the news and baseball games. There is always electronic snow on 4, 5, and 11 (where one turns to one and asks: *What you looking at Bud?*). Channel 8 and 13, the education channel, usually come in clear after the horizontal knob has been twisted to stop the picture from jumping, It is five forty-five and instead of the expected head of the most trusted man in America speaking there is an out-of-focus big gray ball or balloon or something, something round and squishy in the bottom corner growing to fill the screen. It seems to be floating above and bouncing down to a highway. An out-of-focus pickup truck swerves to miss it. Ken, the bartender, tries all the knobs to get the thing in focus. He can't. There could be fog.

The round thing grows larger and floats higher up the screen, then slowly descends flattening out as it engulfs a Buick which it seems to gather energy from to spring back up into a breeze which it floats away on a few feet above a field of fresh bales of hay. There must be fog. There is silence then a sound of something or someone breathing.

Televisions have souls. Each is different. Especially in the early days of a model before the flaws are worked out, before standardization conceals its essence. It takes a while for the new thing to lose its newness and reveal itself. A few months, a year? Radios last forever. The changes in televisions are subtle and often hard to hear and see. Once I had an old black-and-white set—it had been my mother's—whose picture over several months became more and more squashed down. Every day the images shrank imperceptibly, flattened until they were only about an inch tall but were still twelve inches wide. I tried everything I could to fix it but couldn't. After many attempts I gave up and accepted the images as they were. Unconsciously, I filled in the missing dots to see a full screen.

One day after working in the warehouse I got home to my apartment in time for the news. I got comfortable, got a beer, flopped into my La-Z-Boy, and took the tray out from under the chair. It was mostly seeds and stems but there was enough for a couple more joints. I reclined and clicked the remote to turn on the set knowing what I would get but the sound still worked and when the pot started working I could do the rest and imagine the pictures as they should be, could get the proportions of the people and cars and tanks and generals and the head of Walter Cronkite right.

The images, as they'd shrunk, had also gotten brighter, and in the center of the screen was a tiny spotlight that seemed to originate in the picture tube. It shone more intensely right into my eyes each time I turned the set on. I tried to look around it to see the pancaked people. I watched for a few minutes, avoiding looking directly into the little intense light, but even if I did not look directly into it I could not avoid it. I couldn't get it out of my eyes. They would drift back to look like I was longing to be blinded by it. Finally I could take it no more so I turned the set off. Then I turned the set back on hoping it would be gone but it was still there. I turned the set on and off several times. Then there was something new. Horizontal bands of hot yellow outlined the top and bottom of the image which took up about an inch in the middle of the screen. I liked it. After several days my mind stopped correcting the picture. It looked like a moving squashed de Chirico. The yellow bands thickened at the rate of bamboo growing in the spring to consume more and more of the image. They seemed to be trying to crawl over and obscure the image. One night after watching I went out drinking. When I got home a little after midnight I rolled my last joint, turned on the set, and waited. A narrowed test pattern boxed in with the yellow lines came on. I changed the channel and got some dating show. I was bored. I went to the kitchen and found nothing to drink except the bottle of champagne sitting in the heat on top of the refrigerator that was not supposed to be opened until my ex-wife and I had our first child. We got a divorce instead and I moved from our beautiful home into this crummy apartment. I didn't have a proper corkscrew but was able to get the thing open with a knife and a Phillips-head screwdriver. Nearly half of the warm champagne spewed all over me. I filled a mason jar with the rest and went back to my La-Z-Boy. I took a sip of the champagne. It was terrible. Flat, tasteless. But it was all the alcohol I had so I took a bigger swallow. I switched the channel looking for something, anything (except dating shows). I watched the head of an Indian with a headdress full of feathers squashed in the middle of another test pattern for awhile. I would have just turned it off and listened to some music but my record player needed a new needle. I tried my radio but there was nothing on but easy listening, bad rock and roll, and droning news. I tried the television again and, good Lord, there it was. The screen was filled with an image as tall as it should be, life-size, and in color. It looked more like a painting than an electronic image. I looked closer. The picture's colors seemed to have been hand-tinted. It was a photograph of my ex-wife. She was holding a baby.

It freaked me out. I tried to change the channel but couldn't. I tried to turn it off and when I did the image shrank more and the yellow lines reappeared growing until they devoured the image in a flash of light leaving only a bright yellow line. I tried again and the set allowed me to turn it off. I'd had enough so went to bed. The next day the dark cloud of my depression lifted. I didn't get another set. Instead I entered a Buddhist monastery.

Up on the TV at The Quiet Man the balloon is gray.

The sky is gray. It is twilight. There is fog. Ken is fed up and says, "Let's change it. I mean you can't make out shit. This isn't any different from a blank screen with no program on it." I ask him not to, not for a while anyway. Until we at least figure out what in the world is going on and where Walter Cronkite is. Just then his head flickers onto the screen for a moment talking. "Be calm America," Walter Cronkite says and then he vanishes into the visual static out of which emerges the head of the most trusted man in the metroplex. Harold Taft was the first televised weatherman in the country. He still hand-draws his weather maps. He looks at the balloon on a monitor and using his pointer he says, "It is a weather balloon," which is somehow not reassuring, like maybe Harold Taft is not telling the truth which is impossible. He says, "There is fog. An unusual fog for this time of year and for this time of day." The balloon drifts out of the fog. Mr. Taft says, "It is nothing to worry about. It was launched a few days ago from outside Palestine in East Texas. It floated high above the clouds gathering invaluable weather information but something went a little wrong. It descended too fast and in the wrong place."

If there are reports of flying saucers in an area the first thing investigators check out is whether or not there were any weather balloons. Harold Taft will not speculate on anything but the weather. He plays it safe. He says things like, "It is possible to tell if it will be a cold winter by the thickness of the fur around a rabbit's feet." Harold Taft has a secret. He knows more about flying saucers than anybody in Texas but he keeps it to himself, will not talk about them except to a few close friends. He wants to remain the most trusted man in the metroplex. So there he is not talking about what can't be seen as the balloon vanishes again into the fog.

I ask Ken to switch the channel. "Switch the channel." On 4 is the same picture as is on all the other channels. We return to Chip Moody, the most trusted anchorman in the metroplex. He flies his own planes and never lies. He is hugely popular and handsome. It is hard to figure why he is always changing stations. It could be the money. This year he is on channel 8.

The balloon fairly bounds down the highway. Cars and trucks dodge it. Chip talks about the history of weather balloons as the camera stays on the . . . nothing. Just fog. He tells the audience everything he knows about weather balloons. Running out of things to talk about he talks about the history of weather forecasting as an image of his head flickers on the balloon.

The director switches back to the studio where Harold and Chip are talking. Chip asks Harold about extraterrestrial spacecraft. Harold asks if he would like to see how he colors the weather maps. On the screen there is a camera shot from a helicopter, then a tiny dot as the balloon breaks out of the fog. The director sees images from a remote camera truck but they are too disturbing so he does not send them out. Harold and Chip have run out of things to say so they repeat what they have already said.

I tell Ken that when my set doesn't work right I have had some luck with hitting it. He needs no more prompting, He gives the side of it a good wallop which causes the image of the balloon to jump a little but nothing more. The thing is starting to get to him like it has taken on a life of its own. I tell him I had another set that I swear could read my mind. He says he saw one once that could turn itself on and off and change channels without it being touched. I say, "Yeah. Something like that happened to me several years ago when I was over at some friend's house where one of them showed me how he could change channels by just pointing his finger at the set. I was fooled for hours before I was shown the first remote control I had ever seen."

All over Dallas people turning on the news see a snowy screen with a round thing bouncing around or just drifting over the suburbs. Down at the TV stations the producers and directors don't know what to do. People are turning their sets off or watching the education channel. Repairmen have never received so many calls. The news is in trouble. A real-time balloon threatens the whole news operation.

Ken has gotten busy serving drinks and ignores the set that has become more like an electric terrarium than a television.

The anxiety grows at the television stations. The news hour is nearly over and still the weather balloon won't stay down. It will descend and stay on the ground long enough that it looks finished but just as the camera is about to be turned off it slowly ascends and the camera must stay on it. It is big enough to be dangerous. If it were to descend on a playground it could smother any number of children playing there. It could cause automobile accidents or snuff out the lives of an entire baseball team. It must not be ignored. Perhaps it could be shot down by fighter planes. A jet is scrambled at the Carswell Air Force Base over in Fort Worth. The news comes back on. There is the head of Walter Cronkite. He should not be on at this time. It is time for the local news.

The balloon descends again. The balloon floats up from the bottom of the screen obscuring Walter Cronkite and blocking the camera so nothing can be seen but a snow-filled screen that might hold an image but may not. It could be fog. Then it clears and the head of Walter Cronkite is on the weather balloon.

The jet is in the air but it is getting dark. It dives but the pilot cannot see clearly so pulls up. The director watches it all on a monitor trying to guess if the weather balloon will go back up. As it does he switches the monitor to "On Air." It must be telecast. It could cause great damage.

The sky is gray. The balloon is gray. There is fog.

The Fastest Man in Texas

Gary Castle was a runner. He seemed out of place in The Quiet Man. The women were too smart for his lines. His stale jokes were nearly as dated as some cornball thirties Grand Ole Opry comedian's. Some of the men fell for his bullshit at first, a few saw through it but were challenged and tried to outdo him. Most just eased away. He was fast, not like when he had been a track star in high school, but still fast enough to outrun anybody in the bar. The 440 was his race, the quarter mile. Born with natural speed he convinced himself that training didn't do anything but wear him out and make him slower in races. He had this haywire theory about how he had in him a limited number of fast quarter miles before he broke down and he didn't want to leave them on the practice track but save them for official meets. He was a pain in the neck for his coach but he was funny and that helped keep his coach from riding him as much as he did the rest of the team. Girls and not training hard enough kept him from possibly winning a championship at the state meet in '58. Only three Garland Owls had qualified for the finals that year: him, a big country boy shot-putter who wore cover-alls to school, and a broad jumper who was an A student from a good family and wanted nothing to do with Gary.

At the finals in Austin they got put up in a cheap motel with a neon green cactus out front. The broad jumper and the shot-putter got a room together and Gary got one by himself. That afternoon in the prelim-inaries he had come in second to Billy Southern which got him into the finals where he would have to face him again. Nobody in the state had ever been faster than Southern. His only competition in the whole country was Bobby Morrow from Kansas who beat him by a breath in the National Schoolboy Finals the only time they had ever faced off. Gary wasn't in that league but he might have been if it hadn't been for women.

The night before the finals sank him. After a steak dinner at the OK Corral with the other Owls his coach said, "Everybody go to your rooms now and get a good night's rest." Gary intended to do just that. He didn't drink so had no need to sneak out with his teammates to look for a bootlegger or some club that would let them in. He went to his room, got in bed, and started to read Mark Twain's *Pudd'nhead Wilson*. He didn't read all that much except for Mark Twain (a lot) and Karl Marx (very little although he had a copy of *Das Kapital*).

The first real book he'd read on his own was the first he'd ever owned. It was *Tom Sawyer*. The last time he'd seen his mother was at the orphanage where she'd dropped him off when he was five with the promise that she'd be back soon to get him. A year had passed and he'd heard nothing from her. It was Christmas and he really figured she must visit him now but there was no word from her. And then a couple of days past New Year's there she was. She was crying as she hugged him and he started crying too. She told him how sorry she was that she'd missed being with him at Christmas but didn't mention where she'd been the rest of the year. She said she'd been unable to come because she had been in jail like that was some kind of good excuse. But she was lying. She hadn't been locked up at all. She'd gotten drunk with her sorryass boyfriend Merl. They'd drunk a bottle of good and several of cheap wine and then drank up everything else they could find in the house with any alcohol content. Right after they polished off the vanilla extract she managed to stumble outside for something but couldn't remember what so crawled up into the bed of Merl's old pickup to try to figure it out and passed out. Luckily the alcohol generated enough heat in her body to keep her from freezing to death. Next morning Merl woke her with a surprise, a fresh bottle of vodka, and teased her into coming into the house with it. They didn't go out again until after New Year's. Even ordered alcohol to be delivered from the package store just across the road. Until they ran out of money.

Evelyn Castle, his mother, handed him the present. It was obviously a book. It was wrapped in funny papers. He tore Dick Tracy in half as he was staring into his wristwatch, ripping into the gift trying to imagine it was anything but a book.

She told him when she was waiting for Santa Claus in the back of Merl's pickup on Christmas Eve she'd had a vision. All she could recall now was the tinkling of tiny bells and his face, Gary's face, her son's face . . . Her New Year's resolution was to sober up, take presents, and see him more often. She started with a book and ended with a book.

Inside the front cover of his *Tom Sawyer* was an inscription: *Danny Billingsly. Age 9.* Besides an old cardboard-covered Bible it was the only book Gary owned. He spent many hours wondering about Danny Billingsly. He imagined him from ink on paper into a friend and finally into a brother. A perfect big brother.

Gary really didn't read Marx until he got to college. A foster family had taken him in when he was nine but they had little control over him and by the time he got to be a teenager he pretty much did whatever he wanted to. Drifting around town and not coming home many nights. When he was first in high school his mother's brother Uncle Charley came to see him. He was a merchant marine who'd just gotten in from a year circumnavigating the globe on a freighter. He had plenty of free time at sea so he read, read anything he could get his hands on from *Sports Afield* to Shakespeare. He'd wanted to be a writer and still made some stabs at the novel he'd been working on for years. It was about an orphan boy who gets shanghaied to work on a whaling ship. He brought Gary a book with a picture of Karl Marx on the cover that Uncle Charley said looked like Gary's granddaddy who he had never seen. It was the last time he saw his uncle but now he had some idea what his granddaddy looked like and from him he could imagine his father.

He must have read *Tom Sawyer* ten times before he got to *Huckleberry Finn*. It was hard to know whether he kept reading Twain now because he liked him so much or because his mother had got him started or was it simply another way to impress girls that he was more than an athlete. More than an orphan. He was an intellectual. He even at times wore nonprescription glasses to complete the effect. He did know Mark Twain's work well enough though and had the ability when it came to bookish talk to steer the talk to what he knew. The conversation would be about, say, Allen Ginsberg and next thing you knew you were discussing Mark Twain. Gary didn't know anything about Ginsberg.

The night before the big meet he'd read for awhile in his motel room when he had to go to the bathroom and that was his downfall. After peeing he was admiring himself in the mirror on which he discovered a scratch. Looking closer he found that he could see all the way through into the adjoining bathroom. He looked and saw a naked part of a girl from the Timpson track team who he knew was next door because he'd hit on her earlier. He also knew there was another girl sharing the room so he kept looking when the first one stood up and left. It wasn't but a minute before the other girl came in. When she sat down to use the toilet she fell below his line of sight. He waited until she stood up and left but he didn't have to wait long before the first girl came in to take a shower. He watched her undress, step into the shower and pull the curtain to. He kept looking until the curtain opened back up. By eleven the girls had turned the lights out and gone to bed. His neck got stiff but he wasn't otherwise tired. One of them might get up in the night to piss. He didn't want to miss her so he went and got his book and brought it back to read while he sat on the edge of the sink where he could look through the scratch if he heard one of the girls come into the bathroom. At around four he gave up and got a few hours of sleep. He was in no shape for the meet the next day.

The 440 is one of the most difficult races in track. It takes both speed and endurance. Gary had both if he had enough sleep. Maybe handicapping himself by staying up all night was just a way of acknowledging Southern's superiority. He knew he would lose to him so he might as well enjoy the trip. He stood by the mirror all night waiting. The next day Southern beat him by a hair.

He had all sorts of routines for getting at women. He'd do anything including climbing a tree to peep into a window of the girl's dorm at East Texas State. He'd show a sitting girl an album cover, a black reflecting one, and then hold it in front of her at the right angle so he could see up her dress. He spent a lot of time at the fairgrounds trying to pick up the loose girls who drifted around there at night. He and his friend Carl Thunder worked on strategies. Carl was big. He was an all-state tackle at Garland High. Gary would find a couple of girls to hit on and after bothering them for a few minutes Carl would show up, acting like he didn't know him, and ask the girls if Gary was a problem. If they said, "Yes," Carl would run him off. The girls in appreciation might give him their address. It could be a day or two before he showed up at their apartment and, to their surprise, Gary would be with him. This mostly worked on country girls new to the city. If no girls were available Gary wasn't averse to boys.

He never seemed to go to school. Of all my friends he was the only one who my divorced mother forbade me to see. I think he must have tried to fuck her once.

I always had mixed feelings when I would run into him. I knew there would likely be an adventure. I knew there could be trouble. I hadn't seen him in several years when I ran into him in the Purple Room after work one day. I was married at the time working as a book-keeper for Ryder Truck Rental. I was bored. My wife was six months pregnant. Gary was playing pool with some suckers. He bought me a beer and tried to convince me to go with him to Villa Acuña, a border town with plenty of whores. I said, "No way." He bought me more beers and said, "I have a car," which I suspected was stolen. I knew how stupid it was to say, "Maybe," so I said, "Okay," and called my wife to tell her I'd have to be gone for a few days to return a truck to Omaha. We were only gone four days. Before leaving Mexico I bought her a big red-and-gold sombrero. Driving back to Dallas with the South Texas heat clinging to us I knew I was in more trouble than a sombrero could get me out of so, at a roadside stand on the outskirts of town, I bought a watermelon for her. Shortly after the baby was born she left me and I lost most of my friends. Mother was right.

Gary was a big influence on me. He told me about Karl Marx and communism and suggested I read Dollard's *Caste and Class in a Southern Town.* My grandfather on my father's side was in the Ku Klux Klan. My grandfather on my mother's side was a good man except when it came to n█████. I've always been mystified how a decent Southern man could go so far off track when Negroes were discussed. Like racism was some kind of genetic trait that they had no control over. Honesty, integrity, modesty, and racism seemed to go hand in hand but Dollard's book made me examine my prejudices. By the time I was eighteen I was in marches for civil rights.

Like the flaw of irrational racism in many Southern men, the flaw in Gary was women. But in his twenties he developed a new passion. He became a gambler, a poker player, a good enough one. He cheated but so did most of those he played with. He was just a little better and hadn't got caught until one night he did. Bull Stewart wasn't as dumb as he looked and when he caught Gary dealing from seconds he stuck a screwdriver through his neck. Rumor had it that he had also got shot in the head in another game. Except for the scars he looked pretty much as handsome as he always had.

He became a bail bondsman. He'd taken up drinking as a social activity and one of the places he hung out in for awhile was The Cave on Greenville Avenue. It was dark. The floors were usually wet and sticky and there were gray Styrofoam stalactites. One night at closing time he invited all the drunks he'd been drinking with out to the parking lot where he opened his car trunk and shined a flashlight on a tub of iced-down bottles of Lone Star. After everybody got one he helped his stripper girl-friend onto the roof of his car. When she began to dance he shined his flashlight on her. With his other hand he took out his .38 and as he fired it into the Dallas night sky she started taking off her blouse to the rhythm of his gun.

Then he opened his own bar in downtown Dallas and named it Walking Tall. Lots of lawyers and judges drank there who he could always get whores for. There were small rooms in the back with dimmer switches, fake velvet couches, and locks inside the doors. He hadn't lost his love for Twain although he no longer read him. He'd get the stories mixed up, sometimes in interesting ways, like talking about Huckleberry Finn in King Arthur's court.

Gary never figured he'd meet Danny Billingsly. He'd always imagined he was rich basing it on no more than what a nice copy of *Tom Sawyer* Danny had had. One night Gary was in a dive down on Industrial hustling some suckers out of their money on the pool table when he overheard a man talking about a book that he had lost, he said he thought it might have been stolen, when he was a boy. "The book was *Tom Sawyer*. It's like I have never gotten over it." The bar girl said, "I understand. I lost a locket when I was four and have been looking for it all the rest of my life." Whoever it was talking told her, "I have never been able to read another book since." Gary was rattled by what he was hearing, "Danny? Is it . . . could it be you? Danny Billingsly?" Danny answered, "You got the first name right but my name is Castle. Danny Castle. I don't know anything about any Billingsly." Gary didn't quite believe him. "Pleased to meet you. My name is Gary. Gary Castle." With that it didn't take them long to figure out they were brothers and that Danny was five years older than Gary and that they had been in the same orphanage at different times. When he was five Danny had been taken in by a foster family named Billingsly in Garland and never knew anything about his younger brother as Gary knew nothing of him. Danny told Gary that the only time he'd seen his mother since was when she visited him just before Christmas one year. She'd given him a book . . . well as he could remember it had been *Tom Sawyer* . . . as a present but when she left she'd taken it with her. He didn't know if it had been an accident or what but Gary knew even though he didn't say anything. They talked until closing time and then exchanged phone numbers. Gary had been taken so aback by meeting him that he didn't bring up Billingsly again but when he got home that night he looked in his *Tom Sawyer*. After he'd read it the first time he got another copy so as not to mess up the precious one from his mother. He kept that one on his bedside table but never opened it again. When he got home from the bar that night he went straight to the book, opened it, and there on the inside cover Danny Billingsly's name had been erased and replaced with *Danny Castle. Age 9.* The handwriting looked like his mother's but he wasn't sure. Could she have somehow snuck into his house or gotten her hands on his book and changed the name? But why? It was more than he wanted to think about but it wouldn't go away. He'd been so young and maybe his memory had twisted all this into what he wanted it to be. Had he invented Danny Billingsly but then what had been erased in the front of his book?

Danny had worked hard to build up a small roofing business. He was as straight as Gary was not. He had spent years rebuilding an old house in Garland for his wife and twin girls. He had some money in the bank and was respected in the business community. He didn't go to bars as much as he used to but he still had to get a fix so went every couple of weeks. Gary used old cons on young men and invented new ones for bar veterans. It kept him busy. That and women. He'd lived with a bunch of women for short periods in his life usually moving into their places. They often weren't quite sure how that had happened but there he was. It would take awhile to get him out. But now it was just him and his cat Shark living in a little servants' quarters house behind a big house on Beverly Drive in exclusive Highland Park. He'd expanded his reading to include John Steinbeck. He'd tell you *Tortilla Flat* was about a utopian community in California whose currency was wine.

He did everything he could to avoid a straight job and to meet as many women as possible. He was still fast for his age. He'd go to a new bar where no one knew him, have a few drinks, and take to bragging on his speed. There was a new customer at the end of the bar. Bill Jackson was brown-eyed handsome with a perfect flattop, younger than Gary. He just looked fast. He was drawn into the conversation and revealed that he had been city hundred-yard champ a couple of years ago down in Tyler. The hook was set. Bets were made. It was easy to bet against Gary. Everyone in the bar filed out to the Safeway parking lot next door. By now there was no one Gary hadn't pissed off with his bragging. He took on all the bets against him. He won in a close race. Later he and Bill met to divide up the take.

Danny was as quiet as Gary was loud. It was hard to find anyone who didn't trust him. He was good. So good that you didn't mind it when he won your money instead of Gary. You just thought Danny was lucky. Danny and Gary Castle would meet later that night at Brownies, an all-night diner on East Grand, to split up the take.

It was a Saturday afternoon after I had been drinking at home for a couple of hours that I walked to The

Quiet Man. It was quieter than usual which was fine with me. There were only a couple of bikers, Scorpions, out front, a couple of retired gangsters inside, some women sitting in a booth, and Ken the bartender. I didn't even notice him when I first came in but after ordering a beer I heard someone talking about Mark Twain to the women. It couldn't be but there he was. Hadn't seen him in years, since I'd graduated from college. My friends now were artists and writers and teachers and actors. Not the sort who could be easily conned, not that he didn't try. He couldn't see me from where I sat in one of the back dark booths but I could see that he had on eyeglasses. I couldn't tell if they were prescription or not. He put his finger through the glass to scratch his eye. The illusion worked for a second. Thank God there was a backdoor to The Quiet Man so before he spotted me I left through it. I never saw him there again or anywhere else. In the last few years though I've heard stories in neighborhood bars about him having been there the day before drunk asking about me. Like he was knowing where I hung out but that would be the extent of it. He never tried to make contact. My wife has told me she's heard enough Castle stories and is beginning to wonder if I didn't make him up. I got out the Yellow Pages and there under "Bail Bondsman" his phone number was listed. I showed it to her to prove someone named Gary Castle did exist but I never called him.

The Only Song I Know

Right after Michael Matthews wrote "Texaco Becky" he sang it for her on the patio of The Quiet Man. It was a cold November afternoon. The patio wasn't much more than some redwood picnic tables and benches in front of the small bar in the corner of a Safeway parking lot right off the public sidewalk. It was enclosed in a see-through wall of crossed cedar lattice panels attached to a three-foot tall brick wall topped with planter boxes whose flowers would start blooming in the spring but would die under July's blistering sun. It is the only song I know of that was written for or about a Quiet Man regular.

Matthews was born in Fort Worth wearing a tiny black Stetson. He was brought up not far from Panther Hall, a big old roadhouse on the outskirts of town. Panthers used to roam and sleep in the streets of Fort Worth. He could play the guitar before he was nine. He wrote his first song when he was ten. He tried college. He dropped out. He tried acting. He wasn't any good. Nothing satisfied him. He was nineteen and torn between living as long as he could for free at his parent's house or trying to make something out of himself. He finally gave up on making a decision and joined the army. It wasn't so much that he was a patriot but he'd liked fighting all his life and here was an opportunity to get paid to do it. To get off his ass and do something useful. He joined the army and became a 101st Airborne Division Screaming Eagle. In 'Nam he volunteered to be his platoon's point man. Point men had to be either a little crazy or a lot brave. Matthews was some of both. Point men went out ahead of the rest of the soldiers slipping into the jungle trying to locate the enemy from the direction of their fire. They crawled down into the grid of enemy tunnels where the chances of being shot or tripping some booby trap and getting blown up were very high. He got shot in the hip down in one of those holes. After he crawled out he couldn't stand up so was helicoptered to a field hospital tent.

In the hospital tent he was injected with enough morphine to have him floating without pain. He wasn't sure how many days passed but as he came back to the world he heard the voice of a young man talking softly to him as familiarly as if they were old friends in a bar. He asked him where he was from and, as many native Texans will do, he didn't say the name of his hometown, he just said, "Texas." The medic was a Texan too. Tim Holliday wasn't the name on his birth certificate. He was from Abilene, where his father was a prominent doctor. Rumor had it that Tim was adopted. In Vietnam they called him Doc. He had a great baritone voice and would sometimes get his guitar out after fixing a soldier's wounds and sing for him. Sing Ernest Tubb and Hank Williams songs. "I'm So Lonesome I Could Cry" went over good with about everybody. He sang Ernest Tubb's "Waltz Across Texas" for Matthews who, when he got well enough, played and sang with him before he was sent back to the states with a Purple Heart, an honorable discharge, and no place to go but home to Fort Worth. Before he left though he'd talked to Doc about maybe putting a band together when they got back to Texas. Tim said he'd like that but he thought they needed stage names. He wanted to leave Doc in 'Nam. Like Townes Van Zandt there were stories about Tim's prominent West Texas family. He didn't want those following him around either so needed a new last name. One evening a few days before Matthews was to return to the states he was smoking and trading stories with Doc/Tim when he said, "I think I'm going to keep my name but I got an idea if you want to change yours . . ." Free-associating on the opium he asked, "How about Doc something else like Doc Holliday?" "You mean the gunfighter?" Tim asked. "Yeah the gunfighting dentist killer," Matthews answered. Doc said, "I like it," and Tim Holliday was born.

They didn't see each other for a couple of years after they got back to the world. Matthews tried again to get a college degree in the daytime while he played honkytonks at night. Holliday went to Nashville and tried to sell some songs. He even played in Ernest Tubb's band for a while. Not for long though. Tubb wanted songs played the same way, note for note, his way, every time in identical outfits with the rest of the band. Tim got bored and dropped out. Then he got to drinking so heavy that one morning he woke up in the afternoon and remembered saying something out of line to some producer or record company executive in a bar near the Grand Ole Opry. He was pretty sure he hadn't killed anyone but he figured he should just get out of town. He opened a quart of Old Granddad in his cheap motel room and threw away the cap. After that things got hazier and hazier. A couple of days later he was in his little blue pickup heading home to Texas. He kicked around Abilene for awhile trying to write songs and playing low-paying gigs before he realized that the only thing he liked about Abilene was its name. Then he remembered how he and Matthews in 'Nam had talked about putting a band together. Maybe he could find him in Fort Worth so he loaded his stuff up in the back of his little blue pickup and drove to Cowtown. It wasn't hard to find him. There was his name on the marquee of Panther Hall.

Matthews said, "I know a good bass player from Mississippi we could probably recruit. I can play lead if you want to play rhythm. Maybe write some songs together." Holliday had a name for the band. "How about we call ourselves Stumpbroke? Like a stump-broke horse, you know, who has been trained to back up to you standing there on the stump to let you fuck it. In the ass like what club owners do to musicians." Matthews liked it and they became Stumpbroke. They started getting little jobs, made barely enough to buy food and dope. After a couple of years they still had some ambition so got a girl singer and the band started getting paid a little more but after they paid her they were worse off financially than before. Waiting for the big record deal to come along after a couple more years they agreed they'd take any record deal but none came. Holliday just about stopped writing songs after he wrote his suicidal "Feed the Fish." Matthews wrote "How Can I Get You Off My Mind If You Won't Get Off My Face?" which was much beloved in biker bars but they were still about to starve. They were good but going nowhere.

After a gig one night sitting in Holliday's pickup they got to thinking and talking about 'Nam. Matthews said, "I could write some songs about that," and wound up writing a whole album about the war. They got popular and made more money than either of them ever had playing for veterans' gatherings around the country. It all culminated with them singing Matthews's "The Wall" right in front of the Maya Lin granite sculpture in D.C. with the names of all those killed in Vietnam carved on it.

Holliday wore a black Stetson with a bull-rider roll.

To keep the momentum going Matthews told a group of vets, "We need to go on a remembrance march down to Austin. We could call it The Last Patrol." They liked the idea and a few months later thirty-one of them, with television cameras rolling, were off marching to the state capitol. One person from the war that they all agreed they despised was the general who they blamed for their defeat, the first for the USA, General Westmoreland, but when he joined up with them in Austin to march to the capitol Matthews hesitated for a moment then threw his arms around him. It was not a comfortable moment especially with all those cameras rolling. Lady Bird Johnson didn't march with them but did show up to give them her blessing.

Becky Sloan was a cook at the Stoneleigh P. It had for many years been an old-fashioned drug store, a pharmacy, with a soda fountain, more than just a place to get prescriptions filled. Tom Garrison bought it in the midseventies and turned it into a bar and grill. Before removing all the potions and medicines and first aid stuff from the shelves he had them photographed and the black and white pictures blown up to fit behind the sliding glass doors. A faux drug store. A real bar. After The Quiet Man went out of business a new owner bought the lease and hired a management team which named it The Ice House. It was dead as soon as it opened. Mostly fraternity boys from SMU hung out but not enough. Most of the old Quiet Man crowd moved across town to the Stoneleigh P. It soon became the hip place to drink and hang out in and Becky Sloan was one of the main attractions. She made the best cheeseburgers in town. She was from the West Texas town of Jacksboro where she'd been a high school cheerleader until she got kicked off the team for hanging out with a bunch of hot rodders. Her life became like that. Some sort of balance between success and just not giving a damn. She was a refugee from her hometown and I was one from The Quiet Man. She'd put on a little weight over the years but it was in all the right places.

I don't know all the details . . . whether it was Matthews who fucked Becky in the Texaco bathroom or he had just heard about it but either way it was a good enough story to be a song as she was too.

Ima May had a very successful cake-making business in Jacksboro. A Dallas debutante wedding just couldn't happen without an Ida May cake. When she got too old to keep up with the business she gave it to Becky who'd resigned from the Stoneleigh P. a couple of years ago to work for and learn all she could from Ida May about making cakes. She'd make them out there during the week and drive them into Dallas on Fridays. The last place she lived was in an old Airstream trailer on Possum Kingdom Lake not far from Ida May Cakes' galvanized tin building in downtown Jacksboro. Over the next few years as her business got better and better she got to drinking more and more after work every day in her Airstream. She was in love with a married doctor who loved her too but loved his wife more. Becky got left alone to quietly drink herself to death sitting in her trailer or out front overlooking the beautiful lake.

Holliday played and sang in Dallas bars for several years before he nearly died from too much drinking so he abandoned his career and moved to a big doublewide in the East Texas Piney Woods on a piece of land he'd been able to get with a government loan. He got religion there too or at least he got it from an old Sioux who lived in the Black Hills and brought it back to his woods. He had met some Sioux vets in Washington and they told him about the old medicine man. It just took one visit for Holliday to realize here was what he had been searching for in all the wrong places all his life. The old man offered him peace and gave him an eagle feather. He went to visit him as often as he could for more lessons. He stopped drinking and it was even hard to talk him into sharing a joint. He built a sweat lodge in front of his trailer and vets would come from all over to use it for its healing powers. His life had never been in better order when he got throat cancer. It took a couple of years for it to kill him. He was forty-five.

Matthews still plays bars in Dallas and Fort Worth

and at various vet gatherings. His album about Vietnam
kept him popular with 'Nam vets even after Holliday
passed. After she passed "Texaco Becky" wound up on
his third self-produced album.

·

"Holliday's Hat"

When Tim talks
now I can't
understand him.
He used to sing pretty
until passed closing time
then we'd go to his place
to finish off the whiskey
and smoke light into the darkness.

One night he gave me his black
cowboy hat whose brim
had a bull-rider's roll.
I wore it until it fit.

A couple of years
later he landed up in the mental
ward of the Dallas VA hospital.
When he got out on a weekend pass
he came down to sing at The Saloon.
He picked up Cowboy's guitar
strummed a chord then held up his arm
to show off his hospital I.D. wrist band.
He told the small crowd that if he cut it off

they wouldn't let him back in.
After we smoked in the alley
during the first break he asked me
if he could have his hat
to wear in the next set.
I gave it to him but
never got it back.

Now he lives in a trailer
in the East Texas Pines.
He talks through a voice box
since the cancer doctor cut out
his voice. I can't understand
much he says when he calls
on the phone one night years
after I'd last seen him.
But I think he said
I should come get my hat.

Is Kurt Dead?

Whither is God? I shall tell you. We have killed him—you and I.
All of us are murderers . . . God is dead. God remains dead . . .
Fredrich Nietzsche, *The Gay Science*

*I am a bad person. No doubt about it but nobody's got
any idea how sorry a man I am. I manage to keep it
hidden. Some people think I am good, no saint, but basically a good person. Some think I am a little crazy. Got
them all fooled though. I know what I am doing. Some
think I am smart. Others have their doubts. If they only
knew the crimes I have committed all the creditability
I have worked for years to earn would be gone. If they
knew my thoughts and fantasies I would probably be
shot,* thought Kurt Schumann.

With those who contend that "God is dead" I am at one in attest-
ing, the demise of a particular form of theistic belief which not
only is unreasonable to contemporary men, but has also proved
incapable of doing justice to the historic witness of the Christian
community.

"Love Unbounded: The Doctrine of God"
Schubert M. Ogden
The Perkins School of Theology
Journal XIX 3 (Spring 1966)

Kurt Schumann hasn't showed up here at The Quiet Man for several days which is unusual for him. Most weekdays he is in by four or five and rarely misses more than a couple of days. A regular. He has a gift. He can drink all afternoon and then when he is just high enough, right before he is drunk, he stops just like that with the beer and starts drinking Dr Peppers instead. Most of the time. Rarely does his self-regulating mechanism fail him but when it breaks for who knows what reasons—he's drunk too much; he's depressed; he hasn't been eating right; he is tired; or his madness can no longer be contained—he can become a problem. He can get nasty. He can get violent. Not that anyone besides himself is going to get hurt. He's a small tweedy guy. Not very strong and certainly no street- or any other kind of fighter sober but when the alcohol talks, twisting his tongue and his brain, he can become awfully brave. He has red kinky hair, not real red but like every other hair is brown.

Kurt should have started drinking Dr Peppers by now but orders another beer instead. He should have started drinking Dr Peppers so maybe he wouldn't have taken a swing at Motorcycle Al who'd pissed him off for something he can't remember. He stood up from his barstool and swung a roundhouse right at Al which didn't land but spun Kurt around. His fist revolving around his body in bar space like a lost drunk planet running down. When it found no place to land he fell. Even if he'd connected Al wouldn't have been hurt by his limp punch. It was the kind of behavior that in any real bar would have gotten his ass kicked. We suggested to him that if he really was all that interested in getting mauled he might take his act over to the Casba or out to one of those redneck bars on East Grand where he could get a mudhole stomped in him by any number of cowboys.

That isn't exactly what Kurt wants. Problem is he has no idea what he wants. He is safe among friends here in The Quiet Man. It isn't often that he gets so snot-slinging belligerent drunk. When he does we step back and dodge his punches. There have been a few times when his drunken kitten violence turned scary though. Like no one ever expected him to pick up an empty beer pitcher during an argument with D.J. and hit him with it but he did. It was just a glancing blow off his shoulder and really there were a lot of other people in the bar who had wanted to go upside D.J.'s head. After the pitcher struck D.J. Kurt spun and fell off his barstool onto the floor knocking himself out. It looked like he was done but in a minute he got up all crazy. He didn't apologize or say "kiss my ass" or anything to anyone. He stood weaving about ready to go another round. He even took a swing at Ken who was trying to calm him down. It isn't a good idea to swing at Ken. Not that he is going to bust you up or anything, but as the bar manager he has the power to banish you from the joint for a day or for life, something he rarely does but Kurt was close to being exiled when the cops showed up. Nobody was sure who called them but everybody was happy they were there. Kurt got to spend that night in jail.

When Kurt isn't hanging out in The Quiet Man usually behaving himself he is in classes or teaching at Perkins School of Theology getting his second or third PhD. It is hard to figure out when he studies. He is smart but no genius. He has just turned thirty as in "don't trust anyone over thirty." It eats at him. "All I've done my whole life is go to school and teach to make enough money to keep going to school and to keep drinking." He's like that giant older boy way too big for his desk sitting next to you in your nightmare of the third-grade class who has been in school far too long. Kurt says, "I know I should be getting on with it, making something of myself more than a professional student and drinking in this bar, but I guess I don't feel it strong enough to do anything about it. Sometimes I feel like Nancy down at the Knox Street Pub who we all love." Nancy's a youngish, intelligent barmaid who really likes being a barmaid but is not going to be youngish much longer and needs to figure out what to do with the rest of her life soon or she will be enjoying being a barmaid until she gets too old to work in a decent joint and winds up on the graveyard shift waiting tables down at some Industrial Boulevard all-night diner where we will still all love but rarely see her.

Kurt says, "But I just signed up for another semester."

It is a very exciting time to be at Perkins. It is plunked down right in the middle of Southern Methodist University which is in the middle of rich University Park. It hasn't always been so conservative but by the midsixties it has become an intellectually shabby home to right-wing thinking and thinkers. It doesn't even get racially integrated until the midsixties and some of the reason for that was so Black athletes could be recruited. By then Perkins had had African students for several years. Several rich Dallas families kept SMU afloat but barely. The endowment was very weak but the football team was getting better. The school's colors are red

(Harvard) and blue (Yale) but it has never gotten close to those places academically. The buildings are very attractive Georgian revival and the campus is spacious and gracious but the soul of the place is dead. And right in the middle of it is Perkins School of Theology. It is a wonderful island of sanity in an insane city.

One of the best things about Perkins is its library. Bridwell is a small Georgian building with a superior collection of theological manuscripts, as good as any in the country. Its Special Collection has over twenty-five thousand printed books from the fifteenth to the twentieth century. There are over seven hundred incunabula from before 1501. There are Mayan codices up on the top floor. There are most of the first-edition works of John Wesley as well as his manuscript correspondence. And it is not locked away like in most libraries but much of it is easy to take off the shelves and study. Later it gets about the most publicity it ever has because it is where a rising star, a soon-to-be bishop in the Methodist church, Reverend Walker Railey, says he was on the night his wife was strangled and left permanently comatose. He escaped for California before his trial for the crime with New Age psychologist Lucy Papillion. Then over in Fort Worth at First Methodist, the church's most progressive minister who conducted the funeral services for Stevie Ray Vaughan, Reverend Barry Bailey, has been sexually harassing the help and is kicked out of the church.

Robert Kennedy, Martin Luther King Jr., and Malcolm X are dead, assassinated. And in Dallas after President John Kennedy has been shot the city gets known all over the world as one of the most virulent cities in the country and home to more right-wing groups, many secret, than just about anywhere. Outfits like the John Birch Society. When Tailgunner Joe McCarthy wasn't conducting his House Un-American Activities Committee witch hunt for Communists he often visited Dallas to hang out with his pal millionaire Cowboy owner Clint Murchison and go cocaine-fueled to the Playboy Club to fondle bunnies.

In the middle of all this right-wing stranglehold on the city Perkins has become a leading stronghold along with the University of Chicago for the radical "God is dead" business—

> The important point just now is that recent announcements of the death of God are as widely received as they are largely because the God who is said to be dead is quite clearly the God conceived by a form of theism which has long since ceased to be reasonable to a vast number of contemporary minds.
>
> *Love Unbounded*
> Schubert Ogden

—and it mostly manages to get away with it although there is strong reaction against it from some Methodist ministers.

Kurt disappeared right after his thirtieth birthday party at The Quiet Man. Didn't show up for over a week. There was some concern after a few days but no search parties were sent out. Mary Olson was the last one to see him. He had a thing for her but she didn't for him. She liked him and they drank together and once even might have had sex. At her house they had gotten real drunk and woke up together on her couch fully dressed except for her panties which she later found in her purse. And there were still-wet stains on the front of his jeans in the morning. He hoped that they had had sex and that she was now his girlfriend but she wasn't. She hoped they had not had sex but couldn't figure how her panties had wound up in her purse. After his birthday party at The Quiet Man they had gone to her house but she wasn't drunk and rejected all his advances. Mary had a boyfriend. Not one she was particularly proud of. He was going through an unpleasant divorce from a stripper he'd been married to for a couple of years. He owned the Spotlight Lingerie and Costume Store. It was mostly oriented to strippers. He put out a catalog. Took the pictures himself of the women in crotchless panties, G-strings, pasties, and babydoll pajamas. He was taking antidepressants and speed. He always came to see Mary late, after midnight, but never stayed till morning. He parked his car a block from her house and looked both ways before going to her door. She was never sure of why he was so secretive and never asked. He wasn't a great lover but somehow the secretiveness of it appealed to her. He didn't hang out at The Quiet Man. Didn't like the people there. Thought they were a bunch of phonies but he had met Kurt at her house late one night. Kurt was about the kind of person he liked less than any other.

A little over a week after Kurt disappeared, Ken, The Quiet Man manager, was in the bar in the morning cleaning up what the night shift had left undone. He took out a black plastic bag of trash. Opening the dumpster's lid he got ready to heave the bag into it when he stopped. On top of the garbage there was something that looked like a small mannequin. He set the trash bag down and peered in for a better look. It was pretty

ROBERT TRAMMELL

dark inside and it took a minute for his pupils to open big enough for him to see. It was no mannequin. It was a man. A small naked man lying face down with black dotted lines running all over him. Good Lord. Ken shut the lid and stepped back. He felt like he was about to be sick. But he had to look again. Ken opened the lid and saw the lines looked like they were made with a Marks-A-Lot and indicated places to cut. The body had reddish hair and a small ass with the word *Rump* on it. Then he saw the other words in the black outlined spaces: *Sirloin*, *T-Bone*, *Flank,* and other cuts of beef. It appeared to be there waiting for the huge garbage collecting truck to come and empty the dumpster into its maw where its hydraulic piston would crush everything into an indistinguishable mass and haul it to the city dump. He went in to call the police but as he was talking to them he heard the big truck arrive. He heard the dumpster being lifted by the truck's forklift and violently emptied and shaken and slammed back down. He put the phone down and ran out too late. The truck was already headed down Knox toward Central Expressway.

Ken told the cops what he saw and asked if there was any way the truck could be stopped before it got to the dump. One of them said, "No." The police kept their eyes on The Quiet Man. They knew hippies hung out there. They hated hippies and knew they were all on some kind of drug or other. Ken had never taken any drugs in his life but he did drink a lot of beer. The cops asked him if he might not have been hallucinating. Ken tried to convince them that he had seen a body. One of them got out his flashlight and shined it into the now empty dumpster. Ken said, "Nothing there." The other cop picked up the cue and turned his flashlight on to look around the out-side of the dumpster even though everything was sunlit. Then they both took their lights and looked around the parking lot for awhile. "Nothing here. We'll file a report and try to get somebody at the dump to keep a watch for a small body marked up like a side of beef." Ken doubted they'd do what they said they would. He went back inside and opened the bar. He didn't tell anyone what he had seen until D.J. came in in the afternoon. Ken hesitated before telling him but when he did D.J. asked what the body looked like other than the black marks. Ken said it wasn't a big guy and he had reddish hair. Before he fin-ished it hit him. It was about the size of Kurt and had red-dish hair. D.J. said he had talked to Kurt right before he disappeared and he had told him about being depressed because of Mary. Real depressed. Maybe he had gotten himself drunk, took his clothes off, marked himself up, crawled into the dumpster, and passed out. "Yeah. Well how did he mark up his back?" Ken asked. "That's a good question," D.J. answered. Then he remembered how Mary had told him one drunk night about her secret boy-friend. She'd said how much he didn't like Kurt. Maybe he had done it. Regardless what was to be done now? Kurt was still missing or under a mountain of garbage.

A couple of days later Lloyd Scott was in The Quiet Man for the first time. He sat at the bar and ordered a beer. Ken introduced himself and got to talking to him. He asked him what he did and Lloyd told him he was fin-ishing his Doctor of Divinity degree out at Perkins. Ken asked him how he liked it there and Lloyd said he really did and that he especially liked Bridwell Library. He said, "It's been pretty upsetting lately though because somebody has been stealing books. Not just books but some of the very rare ones. There were several volumes of the Wesley books missing. But it's not just that the books are gone but that the openness of the library has been taken away. There's a security guard on duty all the time now and it's a lot harder to get to see some of the rare volumes." Ken asked him, "Are there any suspects?" Lloyd said, "I don't know what the police think but among the students there is one."

"Who is it?"

"Oh there's this guy who has been hanging around the school forever. He's not enrolled in the school. Maybe at one time he was but not anymore. Sometimes he shows up in a class with notebook and pen acting like he is a student. Some of the professors seem not to mind him sitting in. Others just run him off. He seemed harmless until recently when one of the librarians saw him hurrying from the library with something under his coat but she just wasn't sure enough to stop him. That night though she got to thinking about it and convinced herself that he did have a book under his coat. The next day she looked into the Special Collection and discovered another Wesley book gone."

Ken asked him, "How long ago was that?"

Lloyd said, "A little over a week."

Ken asked him what the suspect's name was already knowing the answer. "His name was Kurt something. I remember the last time I saw him. It was a few days before. He was in the library reading. I walked by his table to see what book he had. He was reading Professor Schubert Ogden's *Love Unbound*." Ken asked, "Isn't that about the death of God?"

A week later God was on the cover of *Time* which asked in bold red letters on a black background *Is God Dead?* The same could be asked about Kurt. He was never seen again in The Quiet Man or at Perkins or the city dump or anywhere else in Dallas. About a year later though D.J. was in Chicago doing some kind of research at the University of Chicago School of Theology. He was in the library up on the third floor. Standing by the window he looked out and saw someone who looked like Kurt walking across the campus. Shit it was Kurt. D.J. rushed down to try to find him but he was gone. He looked around and asked other students if they knew him. None said they did so after an hour or so he gave up to catch a plane back to Dallas. And that was it. We never heard anything more about Kurt. Maybe he was working on another PhD somewhere.

Ingrained

Genesis, Exodus, Leviticus, Numbers, Deuteronomy, Joshua, Judges, Ruth, 1 Samuel, 2 Samuel, 1 Kings, 2 Kings, 1 Chronicles, 2 Chronicles, Ezra, Nehemiah, Esther, Job, Psalms, Proverbs, Ecclesiastes, Song of Solomon, Isaiah, Jeremiah, Lamentations, Ezekiel, Daniel, Hosea, Joel, Amos, Obadiah, Jonah, Micah, Nahum.

He'd started reading the Bible again. Last time he'd so much as had one in his hands was when he was a kid, maybe ten, and even then he hadn't really read it. Not on his own anyway, though like every other kid he did have to memorize some verses and the names of the books of the Old Testament for Sunday school: *For God so loved the world that he gave his only begotten son . . . Do unto others as you would have them do unto you . . . This little light of mine. I'm going to let it shine . . .* He had those verses so well memorized that he didn't even have to think about what they meant as he parroted them

back to his Sunday school teacher. Gave his only begotten . . . begotten? Genesis, Exodus, Leviticus, Numbers,
Deuteronomy . . . John 3:16, and when he could recite
the names of all the books of the Old Testament to his
teacher he was given a Bible.

Soon as he was old enough not to have to, he never
went to Sunday school again. All that those Baptists
had tried to teach him about God and his only begotten
son Jesus just fell away down into some unfathomably
deep, dark place in himself. He shook it off. He forgot it.
But now and again the books of the Bible, like some irri-
tating pop song, would slip into his head, come from who
knows where: "Does Your Chewing Gum Lose Its Flavor
on the Bedpost Overnight?" Not only a goofy melody but
corny pink bubblegum words that about made him sick
but wouldn't go away. Maybe that was the point. "Doing
the Bristol Stomp." Popping like soap bubble memories
spraying everything with real glitter. Like saying something out loud over and over until it becomes meaningless. Some words and phrases lend themselves to this
more than others. Something to do with how memory
works or can work. More than mnemonic. Something
you'll never be rid of. *Genesis, Exodus, Leviticus,
Numbers, Deuteronomy, Laws?* It had been going on
forty years now since he'd opened a Bible. At least a
Christian one. In 'Nam, after the monks burned themselves in the streets, he got interested in whatever their
religion was, and he got half-serious about Buddhism
and read parts of several important books about it.
Some of them he figured could be called Bibles.

When his platoon returned to camp after surviv-
ing the hot beauty of another meaningless firefight,

he'd go to his tent, get as comfortable as he could on his cot, get out the little bronze opium pipe he bought in Saigon and the long, elegant pin with its bejeweled handle used to roll the poppy sap into a little ball to heat over a blue flame. When it was cooked just right, he'd twirl it on the end of the pin into a sticky black ball and put it into his pipe. He'd fire it up. Just before floating away he randomly opened and read some stuff from a small, stained bloody Buddhist book he'd taken off the dying body of a Viet Cong warrior. It was an English/Vietnamese edition, like maybe the dead soldier was trying to learn English from it. He'd landed on a verse from the Diamond Sutra.

> *The Lord said: here, Subhuti, someone who has set out in the vehicle of a Bodhisattva should produce a thought in this manner: "As many beings as there are in the universe of beings, comprehended under the term 'beings'—egg-born, born from a womb, moisture-born, or miraculously born; with or without form; with perception, without perception, and with neither perception nor non-perception—as far as any conceivable form of beings is conceived: all these I must lead to Nirvana, into that Realm of Nirvana which leaves nothing behind. And yet, although innumerable beings have thus been led to Nirvana, no being at all has been led to Nirvana."*

For a little while he would be in his own Nirvana, not Vietnam. For just a little while.

Oh, and he did read the Bible when he was first in

the penitentiary down in the Big Thicket's Diagnostics
Unit of the Texas Department of Corrections where he'd
been probed, examined, tested, analyzed, and had a couple of teeth pulled by an evil dentist. There was a row of
three dentist chairs and in the one next to him a convict
wouldn't open his mouth, so the dentist got some sort of
scalpel and told him he'd just cut his way in through his
cheek. That convict opened his mouth, and when he was
asked, he did too. All this to get him checked out, cleaned
up, and ready to go to whatever farm it was determined
to send him to. A panel of punishment experts would
decide what his job would be there. Otherwise he had to
sit alone in his cell with nothing to do but wait for their
decision or be given another psychological test.

Talking to the person in the next cell could get you a
few hours standing on the wall so he was quiet, mostly.
Standing on the wall looked like nothing. Put your toes
against the wall and your nose there too. Hands straight
down at your sides, just stand there for hours until your
blood slows down, about stops flowing into the parts of
your body it should be flowing into, like your legs, and
you fall into the wall maybe breaking your nose. In the
old days you used to have to stand balancing yourself on
a wood Coke case on its side so when the blood slowed
down and your legs buckled and you lost your balance
you really fell a long way onto the concrete floor, maybe
breaking a bone or two.

It was a strange solitude. An imposed one but still
monkish. He was given a toothbrush but no shaving
razor of his own. Every other day one was passed to
him through the bars by a screw. Just that—a shaving
razor, but no shaving cream and no instruction on how

the fuck he was supposed to shave, but he was and, if he wasn't cleanly shaved when the screw did his inspection he'd get to spend some time on the wall. When he started to shave he realized there was no mirror. He looked for something that reflected. The only thing he could find was small. The built-into-the-wall flush button above the toilet. It was chrome, convex, about the size of a silver dollar, and the light was bad. He straddled the toilet, sat backward on it, and bent forward to see a blurred, distorted tiny funhouse face not recognizable as his own. Sunlight drifted slowly down from the big barred windows across from the cells. Little made it to the flushing button on the back wall of his cell. He got his bar of hand soap to make a very thin lather and spread it on his face. He picked up the razor, bent down to try to see his reflection in the little chrome toilet button. When he could nearly make out his reflected face he drug the blade over his cheek and nothing. The razor was very dull. He speculated for a moment on how many other convicts had used it before it got to him. He didn't have to worry about cutting himself. He pressed the dull steel to his cheek and drug it across his flesh. After a few more deeper scrapes, he took the blade to his sink to wash it. The sink too had a shiny push button. The water would only flow when the button was pushed in, and it was so hard to push it almost took two hands. He managed to get the blade under the flowing water finally. He washed away about as much skin as hair. It took a while to shave.

Once a day a trustee pushed a book cart by his cell with mostly *Reader's Digest Condensed Books* along with a bunch of dull novels. It was either one of them or a Bible. The Bibles were better written. He got a black one with gold trim and Jesus's words in red. He made himself comfortable and read all of the New Testament. He was up to *Lamentations* in the Old in the three weeks that he was there. He felt safe in his cell but worried about what came next. He'd gone back to the fiery wheels of *Revelation* when a screw yelled out his number and his cell door violently opened. The panel had convened and was ready to make assignments. He silently prayed that they not send him to a hard-time prison farm like Beartracks's Ellis. They gave him a good job on a first-offender farm. The next day the Chain pulled in through the big iron gate in the razor-wire-covered stone walls to gather convicts who needed to be transferred. He put the Bible back on the book cart, got his toothbrush, and said goodbye to his cell; before the sun came up they called his name. The Chain would take him to the Walls, his new home. The big bus with barred windows was called the Chain because convicts used to be chained by the neck to a long bar that ran down the center of the bus. He'd heard that came to an end after the bus was in a bad head-on crash with a fully loaded concrete mixer truck that stopped it cold. When the highway patrol got to the scene they found the bodies of several decapitated inmates, and shortly after, found their heads. After that they didn't use those neck chains anymore, but the bus kept its name. It was still dark as the Chain pulled away and meandered for around an hour through the Big Thicket's ancient trees, panthers, and orchids. He didn't know where he was or what time it was other than what he could guess by where the sun was.

Clocks and maps are not allowed in prison because they could be used in escape attempts. If you don't know where you are or what time it is . . . if you don't know where you're starting from, the theory went, how could you know how to get to where you're going, if you even know where you want to go to get to where you could hide?

In prison, some turned to homemade alcohol. Some turned to drugs. Some turned to basketball. Some turned to rape. Some read the Bible, but he didn't touch another one after the one in Diagnostics. For some strange reason the library on his unit was great. He learned they had bought out all the stock from some bookstore that was closing and took all the books and put them uncensored in his library. Not legally his but it might as well have been. Hardly anybody used it but him. There were Donald Bartheleme books.

All that was years ago, but he'd recently discovered he still owned an old, black, cardboard-bound Bible. He'd forgotten he had it. Well as he could remember it was the one he'd been given for perfect attendance in Vacation Bible School when he was five or six, or maybe it was the one he'd been given in Sunday school for getting enough gold stars for knowing the names of the books of the Bible.

Vacation Bible School bored him. Most things about church did. Going to church should have been enough but his mother always tried to get him to go to Sunday school too. Like church wasn't quite going to be enough to get him straightened out. It was going to take Sunday school too, and probably Sunday night services and Wednesday Night Prayer Meetings, and maybe a few hours with the old woman in the dark house who stuck paper Jesus and his disciples along with some sheep onto a green felt board while she gave instruction on how to be like Jesus. Maybe though, his mother thought, if she could get him to Sunday school as well as church it would get him headed in the right direction.

Until he was twelve he lived with a foster family in Oak Cliff and only saw his mother on Sundays when he rode the bus across town to her little apartment to spend the day with her. He was always glad to be away from the Baptist family that was raising him. They were okay but they weren't his mother. He really didn't want to go to church anywhere. More than anything though he wanted to be with his mother, so he rode the early bus and got to her place in time for Sunday school in the refuge of a Methodist church.

When he got old enough to, he never went to church again or touched a Bible. So it surprised him when a couple of weeks ago he came across his old Baptist Sunday school Bible in a box of books that he was going to recycle. He took it out. Other than a couple of Big Little books, he'd had it longer than any other book. It was about as cheap a Bible as there could be. Covers made of cardboard. The front cover torn off and taped back to the body with yellowing Scotch tape. Not like some Willie Nelson Family Bible with ancestors' names on all the branches of the family tree in the front of the book. His had a tree with no names but his on one of the lower branches. Like he was all there was. The first and the last of his family. He'd signed it when he had just learned longhand, and looking at it took him back to that moment. It was right after his father died when he was seven. The night of his death he'd prayed. Not his usual *Now I lay me down to sleep, I pray the Lord my Soul to keep, If I should die before I wake, God bless Mother, my sister, all small dogs, Darryl and Kenny, snapdragons, tanks in the war*, and he would fall asleep *God blessing* an infinite list of people and things and animals, but after his father died he said a real prayer asking for God's help. To do what, he wasn't sure but he was sure he needed help and it wasn't coming from people on the earth. God didn't answer right away.

A few years ago he was pulling weeds from his garden when he thought he heard God say, *Get your old Bible*. He said, *Okay, I will*. Then God said, *Read it*. He trembled a bit and said, *I will*. But he didn't because he couldn't find it, and God had said *Your old Bible*, not just any old Bible, so when he couldn't find his old Bible he tried to put the whole thing out of his mind. When he finally came across his old Bible he sat down and flipped through it, reading a verse here and there. Anyway, more than just the names of the books, and as he read it, he could see that there was some good stuff, but still it wasn't long until he put it on the top of a stack of books where it soon worked its way farther and farther down the stack then to some out-of-the-way bookcase and forgotten. Before he put it down though he wrote his name in it again, but on a higher branch. He wrote John not Johnny. He didn't even worry that it was a Baptist Bible that had his name in it twice because it was the same one the Methodists used.

He'd fallen into the hands of the Baptist family when he was six. He wasn't sure why he was with them except that after his father had run away with that red-haired woman from Pleasant Grove his mother had said, *I got to live my life too.* And next thing he knew here he was with this hillbilly family in Oak Cliff and they were raising him as if he was one of their own, i.e., to be a Baptist.

Everybody on both sides of his family had always been Methodist. Since there were Methodists, his family had been Methodist. His uncle was a Methodist preacher in a little East Texas oil town, and his uncle's father had been a notorious Methodist circuit rider. Before he opened the Bible he tried to see if he could remember the books of the Old Testament: *Genesis, Exodus, Leviticus, Numbers, Deuteronomy, Laws?* There is no *Laws.*

He opened that old artifact, but again he wasn't sure if he was reading the Word of God or the word of the Baptists. But wasn't this the same *Revised Standard Edition* that Methodists used? It couldn't be. There was nothing in it about dunking and half drowning young folks in a glass water tank in front of the whole congregation and calling it baptism.

He started to put it back in the box with the paperback mysteries, yellow *National Geographics*, Beta video tapes, eight-track audio tapes, and *Reader's Digest Condensed Books*, but changed his mind and put it on the dusty Read Now section of his bookshelf instead. Maybe it was time to have another look at it. He'd read enough Tibetan, Hindu, Buddhist stuff. He decided to try it fresh. Give Jesus another chance. To open his heart. He remembered too much: Christmas, Easter/The Cross, his Baptism, his uncle's Methodist church, and those big cultural can't-avoid Christian images like the Last Supper and the Wise Men and the Star. He sat in his large, soft, padded chair in a quiet place. Got some tea.

Smoked some dope and started to read. He was getting into it when he felt his left arm go dead, and the Bible fell from his hands. He felt sort of dizzy. He started seeing things. He had a vision. A death vision. Or was he dying? Had he died? He wasn't sure, but when he came back into his body he was sitting in the same chair he'd been sitting in before. Nothing seemed to have changed but him. Even the music was the same. Yet everything was different.

Before His Funeral

Years ago he'd been drinking, and because there were no bars in the little East Texas town he went to a tent revival hoping to meet some easy small-town girl. The place was a frenzy of people rushing down the aisles to be healed of various physical maladies. There were several bodies flat out around the altar who looked more dead than healed. After he got in and got a seat at the back, he saw a couple of pretty girls who looked over at him, and when the preacher called for anyone else who hadn't been reborn to come down to the front, he went. He walked down the aisle and accepted the Lord Jesus Christ as his one and only Savior so to be born again. The preacher said, *If you have truly been born again you are saved and have a ticket to heaven.* He did feel something when the preacher touched his forehead. Who knows, maybe he really was born again. One of the girls went home with him. She was a Baptist. He wasn't sure if it was love or loneliness, but he married her anyway. It was like a Baptist curse that he couldn't escape, so he let her talk him into getting Baptized the right way, fully dunked.

At His Funeral

This came up at his funeral. Was he a Baptist? His wife said he was and asked the preacher to say that in his eulogy. The preacher did not know him and agreed to say whatever the family asked him to, but in a small back room before the services his daughter and all his Methodist family said, *You better not. Don't you dare mention that. He was a Methodist all his life and he died one no matter how much he was manipulated by Baptists. He will be buried as a Methodist.* And he was.

After His Funeral

When he got past Saint Peter and into heaven, he trembled when he met God. God said, *John you know it was a close call. You about went to Hell because of all your sins but you did one thing that saved your ass. You were baptized in the Baptist church, so we let you in.* John said, *But I'm not sure if I'm really a Baptist or a Methodist.* God said, *You are a Baptist. Like it or not. You were born again and baptized in my church.* John said, *Yes, I was baptized in the Methodist church, too.* And God said, *Yes, but lucky for you Baptist baptism trumps Methodist or any other baptism. Relax. I am a Baptist, too. Welcome to heaven.* This made John nervous. He just couldn't say anything back to God, so he shut up for a long time. God said, *There is no way out.* And John wondered if this was really heaven and if he was really God. Then God said, *And one more thing. This may not be the heaven you wanted but it is the heaven you got now.* John asked, *What do you mean "now?"* And God said, *Oh there are other, higher heavens. This is just the first one.*

And yet, although innumerable beings have thus been led to Nirvana, no being at all has been led to Nirvana.

. . . Habakkuk, Zephaniah, Haggai, Zechariah, Malachi.

Claudia and Crobar

Just after the first rays of the sun breathe pink and gold light into early morning clouds, when the fun of the night before could turn to regret, the first bird sings. The almost full moon sits on the horizon refusing to go down so the night can end. The stars join the rebellion and will not dim out. The mockingbird who has sung since midnight makes way for the morning songs. For awhile there is a promise of eternal silence. It is broken by a cardinal. Doves coo. A tree full of sparrows chatters. Grackles clatter like a river. Sudden crows at the window cry and wake her up in the arms of a stranger. The sun retreats for a moment below the horizon and withdraws its rays. The colostomy bag at her side is full of her life draining away. Crobar gets up to empty it.

It made sense to her to go home with him. At least it made sense the night before. She's been married for twice as long as she's known she has cancer. She kept it to herself. Didn't even tell her husband. Until it got to be too lonely and she finally told him. He asked her why she hadn't told him before and she answered, "Because there's nothing you can do. I'll be dead in six months." She wasn't too worried about making any mistakes now. They wouldn't matter for long, not that she wanted to make mistakes. She just wasn't going to worry about it. She was excited to see Joe when he showed up at The Quiet Man for the first time in years. She'd always liked him. Her husband Zorro was happy to see Joe too but he had to leave early because he had to be up at five to get to the job. He was a carpenter. She went home with Joe. He wasn't a stranger but close enough.

Everybody knew Joe had been in prison for possession but that didn't hurt his chances with the women in this bar. He'd slept with more than a few of them. He had a reputation as a good but difficult lover and surely nobody you wanted to get married to or expect any kind of long-term commitment from. He was infamous for some of his shenanigans with women. Like Loretta, the dumpy, country young woman who he'd been out drinking with once.

Joe told me, "We worked together as clerks at a title company downtown. I never had that much to do with her until one day after work we went drinking together at a dive around the corner from our jobs. After a few beers she said she had to make a phone call. She came back to the table and told me how upset she was. I asked why and she said, 'Because the guy who was going to fuck me tonight was hung up with his family.' I told her, 'I will,' and we caught the bus to her apartment in deep Oak Cliff. We picked up a six-pack and walked to her place. After a couple of beers she asked me to turn my head while she changed clothes and I did. When she got comfortable and we'd had a couple more beers I hadn't even put my arm around her or tried to hold her hand. She broke out some good weed.

"We smoked it and I used my usual line. 'Let's go to Mexico and get married.'

"She said, 'I'm up for one but not both. How about we'll go to Oklahoma and get married?'

"I said, 'But we have no car.' She picked up the phone in her bedroom and made a call.

"I couldn't hear what she was saying but when she was done she told me, 'I got us a car.'

"I'd had enough to drink and smoke to put my arm around her but was interrupted by her doorbell.

"She said, 'It's my boyfriend.' I was alarmed but she said, 'Don't worry. We're on track.'

"I didn't know what she was talking about so just put it out of my mind.

"She said, 'We'll give you a ride home.' Her boyfriend was perfectly nice and I was in bed by a little after two happy that Loretta and her boyfriend had got reunited. I was relieved and slept good.

"The next day at work Loretta came over to my desk and said 'After work.'

"I asked, 'After work?'

"She said, 'I got the car.'

"'Do you mean your boyfriend's car?'"

"She said, 'My ex-boyfriend now. After work we can go.'"

"I was young," Joe recalled, "and had my whole life ahead of me which I didn't really want to spend with Loretta no matter how romantic the notion of running away with her to Oklahoma and who knows where from there was. I was about to graduate from college and decided to do that instead. It was hard talking her out of it but she finally accepted it telling me, 'You don't know nothing about women.' I agreed and haven't learned that much since."

Crobar's real name is Claudia. She is small. She is real pretty, not cute, with short blond hair and brown eyes that turn gray when she is happy. She doesn't always wear coveralls but does a lot. She looks good in them. When she's wearing a long dress or anything but coveralls though she is Claudia. She is Claudia as she takes her dress off to get in bed with Joe.

Joe comes from a long line of storytellers or liars depending on your perspective. He is still trying to figure out where the line is between the two. He's made no promises to Claudia. She is too smart to fall for any of his bullshit anyway. He is relieved that he doesn't have to try.

As the crow at the morning window grows louder she says, "I got to go."

He says, "Adios then," and as she walks out he listens to the birds' chorus through the open door. It is like the first time he's really heard them and the last time he ever sees her. After she shuts the door he can still hear them singing as he falls asleep.

Fill It Up to the Brim

About the only good reasons to leave The Quiet Man are: Last Call, jail/prison, and the Knox Street Pub. Otherwise everything is here. Women. Men. Plenty of beer. Interesting people to talk to. A jukebox with "Hey Jude" sandwiched between Webb Pierce singing "There stands the glass that will ease all pain that will settle my brain. It's my first one today . . ." and Paul Desmond's sax on "Blue Rondo à la Turk." I am the only one who ever plays "There Stands the Glass" and the number for "Blue Rondo" doesn't get punched much either. "Hey Jude" and "In-A-Gadda-Da-Vida" are the most played by far. There are a couple of Mozart records. Hillbillies who will hear a song they like, buy it, and play it over and over and over amaze me. How they hear music isn't like how Gisele MacKenzie's radio songs on *Your Hit Parade* in the fifties were heard. Most were dated as soon as they were sung. Number one this week. At least there was Vaughn Monroe's "Ghost Riders in the Sky" and Johnnie Ray's "Crying."

The bartenders at The Quiet Man are men. Once there was a woman but she was the wrong kind of woman for the job. She didn't look good enough to make up for her sarcasm and rudeness. Carolyn's looks do. She is a bartender down at the Knox Street Pub. She is famously rude but there is a big difference. Carolyn is beautiful not in that standard bleachedblond highschool dropout exotic dancers way but more in an SMU sorority girl way. Her intelligence is debatable.

I am in love with Nancy, the other bartender. She looks like the woman bartender in the mirror in the Manet painting. She is Scandinavian-big and has long hair and deep, warm eyes. She reads. Books. When I am not watching her in the mirror I am waiting to talk to her. I usually sit at the big round table up front with friends or in a booth or play pool but when she is working sit at the bar or one of her tables. There have been a couple of women I loved so much I didn't want to go out with them and fuck it up. I wound up going out with them and fucked it up. I can't remember if Nancy wouldn't go out with me or I haven't asked. Her younger sister comes from Kansas City to visit. I fall in love with her too.

Marina Oswald owned the Knox Street Pub before Sonny and Mike bought it from her. Sonny and Mike have been lovers for years. There is an original pressed metal ceiling and darkwood wainscoting. Tucked in a small room back by the bathrooms is a full-sized pool table. There are ferns. It was an ur-fern bar with a flower—one daisy—in a thin vase on each white tablecloth. Lots of roadside Texas cafés have a sweet potato with toothpicks in each side to balance it half submerged in a glass of water from which great long vines grow. Vines that overgrow the shelf and flow up the wall and over the doorway and out into another room. There seems no limit to how long they can get. The size of the original sweet potato matters some. The age of the café can be told by the vines' length. Ferns in the Knox Street Pub are as utilitarian as a sweet potato vine. They don't need much light or care or water.

I don't remember her name. I think it might have been Evelyn. She tells me it is the first time her husband has been gone in over eight years. I know her husband. I think he is a journalist. I have often sat with him and others at the big round white tablecloth–covered front table for hours. The conversations there are of a higher tone than those at The Quiet Man. Pachelbel's "Canon" is on the jukebox. Everyone but the person who plays it is sick of it. There are small candles on each white table-cloth. I am attracted to her but keep it to myself. I like her husband. Her husband is out of town. Nancy's lit-tle sister has gone home. Nancy is not working tonight. Most of my friends have gone back to The Quiet Man for a last drink or to look for some grass.

She says she is not afraid to go home alone but who knows? With her husband not there who knows what might be waiting in the dark? I tell her I got a flash-light. She doesn't have to say anything. I say, "I can fol-low you home and make sure nothing lurks there." She doesn't have to say anything. She has a big black sedan of some sort. I have an old Buick Roadmaster. I am not sure how many of the lights work on it. Her house is in Highland Park. Highland Park is where the richest peo-ple in Dallas live mixed in with some nice, more modest houses. There is an aggressive, bored police department. I follow her down Lovers Lane and turn in the middle of the Miracle Mile. Eventually I hit Strait Lane and then take a right down her block. It is very quiet. Her house is bigger than I thought it would be. As she turns in her driveway I quickly turn off my headlights. I look for my flashlight. My expectation is rising. The street is dark except for her yellow porch light. I shut my door softly. There are sudden red lights turning in my side rearview mirror. Her porch lights are off. The cop says, "All your lights are working but the right tail is cracked. What are you up to in Highland Park so late at night?" She doesn't come out to say goodbye as I am handcuffed and taken to jail but she does come down in the morning to bail me out. She doesn't wait to see me after my release.

I get my Roadmaster un-impounded and drive to The Quiet Man but it is closed for another hour. I pull around back and sleep in the shadow of the building until the bar opens.

Unintended

I t is a little past noon Saturday when I am awakened by a banging on my door. Something heavy, padded is repeatedly hitting it down at the bottom. Then I hear the motor and am reassured. It is my mother vacuuming. It is how she wakes me on weekends when I have been out too late. Mother has always kept a room for me. No matter what is going on in my life I know there is always this room. This time I've been here for a little over six months. Since I got out of the joint. Last night I hung out at The Quiet Man and then continued drinking over at Greg and Elizabeth's until real late. I've got to get a job. It is a condition of my parole. I've been looking but not that hard. Every now and then they let me be a fill-in bartender at The Quiet Man. It gives me a little pocket change. My probation officer isn't pleased with my job situation but he doesn't pressure me much. He knows I don't really have a criminal mind and am not violent. I can always get food and a place to sleep at Mother's. And being a bartender gets me free drinks from other bartenders. Even part-timers like me don't have to pay as long as the owner isn't around. There are women there who can take care of most of my intellectual and other needs . . . for awhile anyway. There are lots of women.

Mother is an executive secretary at Dallas Power and Light. The "executive" part just means that she has to dress better than nonexecutive secretaries and she's got to know what all the bosses want in their coffee. Her boss, Mr. Feeley, takes sugar and a little cream.

She's been divorced for over thirty years. There have been lots of men but she's married none. Either she doesn't like them enough or me or my sister don't.

There've been times when she had to borrow money from one of her boyfriends so we would have enough to eat. Most didn't expect to be paid back at least not in currency. Years after the divorce my father still comes around, sometimes to borrow money from Mother. He had a sense for when she might have a little extra. He'd promise as he had so many times before that this time he'd pay her back. He never did. Every time he came over she asked him not to do it again but she always gave him one more chance but a chance for what wasn't clear. He never came to see me. We'd say hello passing in the hall.

For years after the divorce she didn't have enough money to have me and my sister live with her. We stayed in a nursery and at foster homes and finally with a redneck family in Oak Cliff. Her first job at Westinghouse Elevators paid her fifty cents an hour. The only future she had was if she could marry one of her bosses. She took courses to learn shorthand but she was never any good, never could remember all the symbols. She was best at filing and serving coffee at the Board of Director meetings. She was a darn good typist though she thought.

Doors that had been closed to women forever were beginning to be opened but she was a little early for that. In the 1950s rumblings could be felt but she was immune to them. It was a tough time to be a woman, especially a divorced woman with children. Divorced meant available, beddable.

By the time my sister was ten, Mother'd worked her way up to making a dollar an hour. She figured if she watched her money closely her daughter could live with her now. She got a small cheap duplex for them. She did the best she could.

She couldn't afford me though. If her ex would pay her his child support it might be possible but she feared he wouldn't. He did pay the twenty-five dollars a week to the foster parents for keeping me. He'd go to jail if he didn't.

When I was thirteen Mother moved me in with her and my sister. The money would be tight but we'd all be together. It was about six months before we moved to another new place. About once a year from then on we had to move to a new place. Not a better place. Just a different one. Moving became a way of life. Moving and settling in and moving. It was years before I figured she wasn't paying rent on time and we were getting evicted. Somehow Mother protected us from ever seeing the managers or constables or whoever was kicking us out. And somehow there always was someone who would rent her another place.

My sister got married when she was fourteen, had

a beautiful daughter six months later, and moved out leaving me and Mother behind. She continued to have boyfriends but I became her life. She'd do anything for me. I stayed in trouble, nothing dramatic but enough that she had to take many days off to come to school to try to keep me from being expelled. She'd do anything for me. She'd lie and write notes to the school excusing my absence when I'd cut school to drink and play poker all day. I could do no wrong. When I'd call from jail to get her to bail me out she was never angry at me but at the cops. It must have been humiliating and terrifying but there was nothing she wouldn't do for me. She let me and my friends gamble at our house and drink all the beer we could afford. She really didn't mind having a house full of good-looking young men. I got to be such a good poker player that I was able to pay my way through college with my earnings. I'd had to spend an extra year in high school after me and four other guys were kicked out for starting a riot at a football game. That was not really a problem. Now we could play cards all day until school was out when we'd cruise around it in Bill's '49 Mercury. When I got back in school I had some making up to do in the spring. Mother got the school to let me take an extra course. I set the school record that still stands when I made five Gs. It was not hard to make Fs. Any idiot could do that, but to make a G took work. I got to return for an extra year for that. Next year I was the oldest student in school. I managed to stay out of trouble and finally graduate. It was enough to go off by myself to a small junior college in East Texas where I knew no one. To get away from my bad influences. My second year I got a scholarship. Then it was at last on to SMU like my mother had always wanted me to do. Southern Methodist University is on a hill that overlooks the city. A sort of pinnacle that could be seen from poor Oak Cliff. A degree from there almost guaranteed success in Dallas and a possible way into Dallas society. At least that was the myth. I wanted to be a Clarence Darrow lawyer but after getting my BA I was so bored with school that I did my postgraduate work in prison.

Mother always kept a room for me until I could get a place of my own.

It was autumn. There was a football game on the little silver kitchen radio, a Southwest Conference game. Oklahoma versus Texas. It was my favorite time of the year. Not spring. Everything started fresh in autumn. The air was clean. The air was crisp. I had to get out of the apartment. It was an embarrassment to be living with—off of—my mother. I was forty. It was just a couple of miles to The Quiet Man. I had no car. It was a good day to walk.

It was about an hour and a half to the bar. There were hardly any customers when I showed up. Just a couple of old men and Jimmy Ace. Ken was running the bar. The Game of the Week was on television. Dizzy Dean was singing and mangling the language. Saying "ain't" had got him in trouble with oldmaid school teachers. Oldmaid school teachers weren't his audience. He kept saying "ain't" until it got into the dictionary.

I knew Jimmy Ace a little. Never liked him but envied him for his good looks, his black hair, and his '58 Impala which he kept in showroomfloor shiny shape. He also had a Norton motorcycle. He wasn't big but had a reputation for being a fierce fighter. Tougher than

anybody besides Chief. It wasn't clear if it was all reputation or if he was really bad. Nobody'd seen him fight.
He didn't hang out here that much. Just enough to be a
part-time regular.

I said hello to Ken. He said, "Hi Luther," and I sat at
the bar a couple of stools down from Jimmy Ace. Jimmy
said, "Let me buy you a beer." I said, "Sure."

Jimmy had a sister. I didn't know Candy was his sister. There was rarely any violence in The Quiet Man.
Peace and love ruled the barstools and all the way out
to the street. If I'd known Candy was Jimmy's sister I
might have stayed clear of her but probably wouldn't
have. My friend Ronald once told me I had more brains
in the head of my dick than in the one between my ears.
I wasn't sure if that was a compliment or not. I never
saw myself that way. Never saw myself as a cocksman
like Jimmy Ace.

"Yeah man Candy is my sister."

"I heard you."

"She said you left her for no good reason."

"Everbody's got a story."

"Well I'm about to step into yours."

"Come on in."

The phone behind the bar rang. Ken answered it and
said, "It's your mother Luther."

"Tell her I'm not here."

Jimmy Ace said, "Are you in trouble again man. You
better go and talk to your mother Luther."

I didn't mean to hurt him so bad I just reacted and
shoved him back off his barstool, didn't mean to push
him over, didn't intend anything. I just shoved him.
His head hit the floor hard enough that an ambulance

had to be called. Jimmy got a bar towel to soak up the blood pouring from his head. While George Jones sang, "Another man might not make it through the night," I started the long walk to my mother's.

Reunion

D.J. Arnett licks the grease from his fingers and reaches for another rib. He has nested four paper plates into each other so the resulting construction will be strong enough to not crumple and collapse under the weight that is about to be heaped on them. At the long red-checkered food table D.J. piles his plates high with barbecue ribs, barbecue beef, barbecue pork, and barbecue anything else from long aluminum foil–covered silver pans. He'd love some barbecue bologna but there is none. He sets that heavy plate down, makes another reinforced four-ply one, and moves on down the line to the trays of potato salad, beans, coleslaw, fried okra, and one of brownish, watery stuff with lumps of something in it that he cannot identify. His second plate is full but he scoops out a big spoonful of the mystery food and slops it on top of the coleslaw anyway. Coleslaw is one thing he will not eat so he buries it. He'd love some raw ground beef as an appetizer but knows that is not going to happen at this meal.

The breads worry him. He has no room for them on his plates. He thinks about starting a new plate but three would be too many for him to carry. He never gives a thought to who'd brought the food or that he might should have brought some himself. After all he'd driven hundreds of miles to get here. What more could be expected from him?

And there are still desserts so he walks quickly over to an empty picnic table and sets the two plates down then scurries back to the food table, relieved that no one else has gotten in line. He really doesn't think anyone would take his plates of barbecue but he keeps an eye on them just in case. He is usually talking, trying to order the world into his vision of it. About the only times he shuts up is when he is sleeping, eating, or driving alone.

Speeding across the unforgiving miles of far West Texas's vast loneliness D.J. visualized the food that would be at The Quiet Man Reunion. He knew almost certainly what would be available. He made up his perfect meal, imagined it into existence, and for hours got ready to eat.

He doesn't need all of the third plate for bread so he fits desserts on it too. Pies and cakes, peach buckle, and a big brownie all find places. Most everyone else at the reunion has already started eating but D.J. is in no rush. He'd lingered over each tray of meat, smelling and caressing each with his eyes before piercing the slabs with the big forks and transferring them to his plate. By the time his plate was loaded everyone else had found a place to sit. Nearly all the seats were occupied but he found an empty wood picnic table off to the side and spread his food out on it. Oh shit, he forgot iced tea. He's brought his own glass. A big, blue plastic insulated one which he fills with sugared tea from the tea cooler. At last he is ready to eat.

The drive from Santa Fe hadn't been bad. Long but D.J. liked driving out there where the highway and the earth merged with the sky. Where there was hardly any traffic. He'd been living in Santa Fe since his fall from politics. He runs his own tourist agency now and would do public relations work if anybody'd hire him.

He has to make one more trip to the food table to get a stack of napkins. He will need a lot to keep the grease wiped from his fingers and mouth as he devours rib after rib. D.J. is just getting warmed up. He'll take care of the stains on his shirt later.

Sheryl Dumont was chairman of the Dallas Republican party. D.J. worked for the Democratic Party as a speech-writer and publicity hack. They'd known each other for years. Both of them put in many hours on the job and had little time to meet anyone outside politics so one lonely, desperate night they slept together. Then, like a bad habit, they continued for years.

Late one night Sheryl Dumont called 911 and told the police, "I want D.J. Arnett arrested for rape." "And who is the victim?" she was asked. "Me. He did it to me." Highland Park is the richest part of Dallas and the most conservative. I hear there are more police per capita here than any place else in the state. There is little crime. The cops are bored and just to have something to do will stop cars passing through their jurisdiction that are in any way suspicious. Things like a broken taillight or being Black can get you stopped and likely thrown in jail. So when the report of a possible rape came in all the cars on duty rushed to the scene. Mrs. Dumont was embarrassed but she was intent on getting D.J. for what he had done to her even if it shredded her reputation.

The police found him in Bridwell Library at SMU and quietly arrested him. It wasn't clear if he was hiding or studying, He had a book of John Wesley's letters on the table in front of him. The cops didn't notice that.

At the police station he told the detectives, "She was all for it. She'd put together a fundraiser that evening and when she got home she called me up and asked if I would like to meet her at her house. It was well after midnight when I arrived. She was waiting for me in her robe. There was no need for formalities. We went straight to her bedroom. Problem was I didn't have a rubber so promised her I would pull out in time. I intended to but didn't quite make it. She was outraged. I had never seen her so pissed. She said she was going to call the police. I tried to reason with her. I told her she couldn't win. We'd both be the losers. She didn't have a case. I left as she was dialing the phone to call you."

The response time for the police in Highland Park is about one minute.

D.J. kept going. "I know y'all know who I am so I took off to develop my defense. Not my alibi, my defense. I drove to see my friend Stony Blake. I'd known him for years. Ever since we worked together on the underground paper the *Iconoclast*. He had a little photography studio in his house and I got him to set up his brightest lights and take pictures of my naked body. There were hickeys that in Mrs. Dumont's passion she had sucked on my neck. What better evidence could there be of her willingness to have sex with me. I have the photographs at my office."

D.J. was fat. His body was not beautiful but that was not the issue. The resulting black-and-white images recalled those of dead cowboy outlaws shot full of holes, tied to a board, stood up, and displayed in front of the barber shop for all the town to see. The grand jury was disgusted but could not deny that they were good evidence for his defense. He was not indicted but his career in politics was over and so was hers.

Several years before Congressman Bulldog Malone had asked D.J. to be his press aide when he ran for the House of Representatives. D.J. accepted. They won the election and were off to Washington. Malone had been a member of the state house and Texas attorney general. He was a liberal with a fierce reputation for taking on big business. He was on the side of the people. D.J. and him made a hell of a team in spite of some screwups like when D.J. wrote a speech for a Fourth of July campaign event in a little Dallas suburb that compared Malone's opponent to Hitler. But they won the election and hit Washington like a sixteen-pound sledgehammer ready to reform the place. Malone was a rising star. He worked hard and was given important committee assignments. It would be the political pinnacle for both of them.

After his exile from serious politics he was back in Dallas drinking, violent, and dangerous. He had no place to go so Luther let him stay with him and his wife for a few days. The second night he was there he got drunk on cheap wine, spouting all sorts of revenge on those responsible for his fall. He finished off another bottle, opened a drawer in the kitchen, and took out a big butcher knife and a meat cleaver and waved them around in crooked circles like a fat drunk ninja. Luther kicked him out the next day.

After college D.J. got a job as a reporter at the *Houston Chronicle* and became a stringer for *Newsweek* but he wasn't satisfied. He wanted to get in politics so when Malone called he was ready. He'd wanted to write a novel, to be like Hemingway, but he put that aside.

After his acquittal he hung around Dallas for awhile before moving to Santa Fe. He'd saved enough money to live on for a year or so. Now he had time to write. He had stories to tell. He had to get them told but he wasn't another Billy Brammer yet. He was just jobless and desperate. He rented a small, neat adobe. He got an Underwood manual typewriter and set it up on an Navajo blanket–covered table in front of a window that faced the rising sun. He'd forgotten to get typewriter ribbons so tried to use the worn-out red and black one that was on the machine. Just the red worked and even it was nearly used up. The typed letters were so faint they were almost impossible to read but that wouldn't stop him. He put on a big pot of coffee. He'd bought a long roll of teletype paper like Kerouac and some bennies in Dallas before he left. He poured himself a cup of coffee, popped a handful of bennies, sat down, and rolled the paper into his typewriter. He sat there flexing his fingers waiting for his muse but he was too wound up, speeding too fast so he opened his last bottle of good wine to mellow himself out. He got too mellow so decided to stop for the day. He'd got a start he thought. All he had to do now was write his book.

The next day he went into town to try to find type-writer ribbons but nobody had the kind he needed so he bought a case of red wine instead. A good Beaujolais. And a case of red Gallo for when he was drunk enough that it didn't matter what he drank so long as it had alcohol in it. He'd drive down to Albuquerque in a day or two for the ribbons. Days turned into empty wine bottles and just before he ran out of money he set up his tourist-slash-political consultant business. The roll of paper yellowed and he hadn't been able to find any more ribbons. He probably could have found some in Albuquerque but he never made it there.

D.J. takes the plate of desserts to his table to join the rest of the food. He sits alone, quietly, at a redwood picnic table on top of Flag Pole Hill at The Quiet Man reunion. He digs in. Later, he visits with some of The Quiet Man veterans. That out of the way, he goes back for one last piece of cherry pie and eats it. He is ready to drive back to Santa Fe now. The only person he says goodbye to is Ken.

D.J. gets in his car and heads west out of the city. On the long drive back from Dallas it comes to him. His novel. But it will be more than a novel. It will be nonfiction to begin with. He'll tell the truth as only he can about how politics look from the inside. He is not sure if he will include in it his troubles. The book will be nonfiction but more. It will be more creative than some old civics book. It will blur the line between nonfiction and the truth. It will be as important as gonzo journalism. It will be set in The Quiet Man in 1966. It will open with him debating a Nazi. There will be Birchers and left-wing radicals and artists and regular people and each will be listened to by the others no matter how outrageous what is being said is. The world will be funneled into The Quiet Man. There will be little action other than words. The jukebox won't be playing. One of the characters will take his shoes off and get into a big argument with the owner about it. The owner will tell him he is in violation of the health code and demand that he put his shoes back on or be banned. He will make a stand and say, "No man. This is the sixties. Fuck the health code."

A couple of weeks pass and D.J. is still a little cranked up to get his book written although his enthusiasm has faded as the days have and the bottles of wine have been emptied. He is just drinking the cheap stuff now and he still hasn't gotten a new ribbon. He can wait no longer though so he sits again at his typewriter one morning after a month has gone by. He will get it done now regardless of any excuses or worn-out typewriter ribbons. He takes the old one out, turns it over, and rewinds it. It should be good enough but isn't. He types and the keys strike the paper but leave only random lines like faded memories of letters. He'll not be defeated though so he hits the keys so hard that they will leave impressions on the paper deep enough he believes will be legible if held sideways up to a light. He hammers an "A" as hard as he can which tears a hole in the paper. He turns the roller to feed the paper through to get to some that is not so brittle. He types another sentence and turns it into a brilliant paragraph. He is not worried about the ribbon now he is just writing but as the paper feeds through the rollers they grind it all to dust even before he can get the story told.

Juan Acosta's Hearts

Juan Acosta is lost, walking in a city he doesn't know. He just got out of the Dallas city jail where he's been laying out a fine for the last eight days for fighting in one of the Mexican blood buckets that line a four-block stretch of lower Grand Avenue. On his release he heads in the direction of his cousin's house in Little Mexico where he's been staying since he got to town a couple of weeks ago but he is lost before he starts so he does what he always does: he just keeps walking. After awhile he comes to some railroad tracks. They are always a refuge for him as there are hardly ever any cops and they give him some direction to go in.

He'd heard there are parts of Dallas that he could be arrested in for simply being a Mexican and he doesn't want to go back to jail. As he wanders down the tracks he passes the backyards of bigger and fancier houses.

A couple of weeks ago he'd hopped a train and ridden in a box car up from his ancestral home on the Rio Grande in Starr County. When he got to Dallas he jumped out in the switching yards behind the School Book Depository at the edge of downtown not far from where Oswald gunned down Kennedy. He wasn't exactly lost when he hit the ground he just wasn't sure which way to walk. Not that being lost was something Juan was unfamiliar with. He was so used to being lost that he kind of figured he was an expert at it. It didn't bother him at all.

He got out of jail a little past noon and has been walking down the tracks for a couple of hours when he comes to a little abandoned train station near where Knox Street crosses the tracks. He looks down the street one way and sees the mansions of Highland Park. He looks the other and sees businesses, shops, furniture stores, a drugstore, bars. He really wants a beer so he heads toward the bars passing a couple of fancy ones until he comes to The Quiet Man, a small, simple brick building in the front corner of a Safeway parking lot. There is a patio out front right off the sidewalk. He sits at one of the picnic tables there but isn't sure if he will be served. Regardless he will sit and rest for awhile until he gets a beer or gets run off. After a few minutes Ken, the bartender, comes out and asks him what he wants. Juan isn't sure how to take that question but answers, "Una cervaza, a beer. Por favor." Ken is back with it in a few minutes.

Juan is the only one sitting outside. There is no roof or awning or anything just a hot blue Texas summer sky but the sun is near the back edge of the building and soon will go down behind the dumpster. His frosty beer arrives with a cool breeze. Cars and pickups pass slowly by on Knox as he drinks another. He must drink them pretty fast as they get hot soon in the sun. Customers, regulars, start drifting in and filling up the other tables. He has a couple more beers and as the first stars blink on to awaken the night he heads back to the tracks hoping they will take him to his cousin who has agreed to let him stay on the couch until he finds a job as long as he doesn't cause any trouble. If he can't find his way back there maybe he can get back to the switching yards where he might just jump another box car for the Valley, for home.

He gets to neither. He walks deep into the night. Right before he passes out he climbs up an embankment into some trees. He finds a big old cardboard box up there which he opens and spreads on the ground to sleep on.

The heat wakes him sometimes after noon. He gets up, brushes himself off, and slides down to the tracks to walk back in the direction he came from. He knows he must smell like a mangy bordertown dog. When he comes to a road he looks down it and sees a Gulf gas station. The bathroom is not locked so he goes in to wash up. He takes his shirt off. It is not easy using green squirts of handwashing soap and drying off with rough brown paper towels but he manages. After splashing water on his face Juan opens the door and heads back to the tracks.

Before he gets to Knox Street he stops at a backyard with a clothesline full of clean clothes. He gets over the fence. There are many shirts. He picks a white one with a Neiman Marcus label. It nearly fits. It makes no sense to just get a white one as he would soon have it too dirty to wear so he gets a dark blue one to replace it when that happens. Juan puts on the white one and hides the blue one under a bush. He is ready to return to The Quiet Man. It is about the same time he was here yesterday. He is real glad he laid out his fine instead of paying it because that left him most of the cash he came to town with. He still has plenty for beer. Ken brings him a cold one.

He is not sure what attracts him to the place other than they serve him and it is not some low Mexican dive where he must keep his hand on his knife but he keeps coming back for over a week, sitting alone in the same place. He doesn't want to get too drunk and do something stupid like get into a fight and get himself kicked out or arrested. There are only a couple of other Mexicans who drink here. Both are stained-glass artists. He watches them go inside but ignores them.

The patio begins to fill up.

Juan Acosta looks very much like a working-class man who hasn't worked for years. He must be in his forties. His clothes are usually the same khaki brown as his skin but now he has a fancy white shirt which doesn't go with his khaki pants but as long as he is sitting at the table who can see his entire outfit. His hair is fading black preparing to be gray. His eyes are cloudy black. He is small and seems to get smaller the longer he sits and drinks. His only distinguishing feature is a thin, nearly faded pink scar that runs down from his hairline, cuts across his left eyelid, slices through his lips, and jaggedly ends under his chin. It is an old scar.

He doesn't fit in with this crowd but who does.

Little attention is paid to him as no one expects he'll come back but he does, showing up each afternoon for the next few days just before the regulars arrive. He sits at the same table each time. He soon begins to arouse some of the regulars' curiosity. The Quiet Man is a little place and it would seem everyone would know everyone else but they don't. There are several groups that are independent of one another: Oak Cliff Benny in the morning, businessmen at lunch, old men in the afternoon, and at night there is the bunch from Texas Instruments, a few bikers who drink with the English mechanics, actors from the Theater Center, alcoholic professors from SMU, rugby players, some writers who will drink with anyone, some fringe customers who would like to drink with anyone but are usually excluded, and a few who are happy to drink alone. Some of the groups interact. Some don't. The amazing thing is that they all manage to fit peacefully into the small space. There is hardly ever any trouble. Like the diversity prevents it.

Finally after having seen Juan sitting there alone for days now Zorro Spradling's curiosity gets the best of him. Zorro is a big, likable, twenty-two-year-old carpenter who drinks after work with his friends several times a week at The Quiet Man. They are sitting on the patio this evening. Crobar, Zorro's wife, asks if anyone knows the Mexican who has been drinking alone for the last week. No one does. Zorro takes matters into his own hands. He picks up his pitcher of beer, walks over, fills Juan's mug, introduces himself, and invites him to join them at his table. Other than not being Mexicans they are not unlike Juan. They are carpenters, plumbers, craftsmen, a few untrained laborers, artists. Juan says, "Thanks but no thanks. I like to drink by myself," but if that is so why then is he in a bar when he could be drinking at home except for the fact that he has no home, at least not in Dallas. He does have his cousin's where he can crash as long as he hasn't gotten drunk. His cousin isn't all that happy he is there. He told him he could stay until he found a job but he could do no drinking in the house and if he's been drinking when he gets in he has to sleep in the back along the railroad tracks that run behind the house.

Juan is drinking alone on The Quiet Man patio again.

After he has a few beers he sees a couple of pretty women join Zorro and his pals so he gets up his nerve, goes over, and asks if he still may join them. Zorro says, "Sure." For a while Juan is silent. Everyone at the table is drinking from pitchers of beer and someone is always keeping his glass full. Around ten he is drunk enough to start talking even though he doesn't have much to say which is no problem as everyone else is drunk enough not to notice. He is not a good storyteller at least not in English. It isn't that his stories are not so good but his telling is the problem. Being a good storyteller matters in most bars but in The Quiet Man it is essential. It doesn't matter what you do, if you can tell a good tale you have instant status. Juan realizes this so starts stories a couple of more times but before he completes them no one is listening. It is not until the talk turns to drugs that Juan really comes to life.

Zorro is talking about how Martha Anderson got busted a couple of days ago. He says, "The cops surrounded her little house like she was John Dillinger before they broke in her front door. After totally searching the place they came up with a penny matchbox of weed. She told them it wasn't hers and it might not have been. There was a good chance they had brought it with them. Anyway it was enough to haul her off to jail for possession." Some of the regulars had put up her bail and she bonded out and Zorro said she was coming down to The Quiet Man tonight.

Johnny asks, "Do you know what the average sentence for possession in Dallas is?"

Zorro answers, "I've heard but can't remember."

"It is twenty years."

Martha isn't some hippie chick. She's got a good job as a tech out at Texas Instruments.

Johnny says, "You know the cops watch us down here all the time. They know who we are. It don't make a fuck to them how good a job somebody has. As a matter of fact the better the job the better the bust."

Zorro says, "Let's not get all paranoid now. That's just what they want."

Johnny reacts, "It isn't paranoia when it is really happening and we all know it is."

Now the paranoid stories of dope busts gets started. One generates more. Nobody here is into hard drugs just LSD and Mexican pot.

Juan listens for awhile then contributes, "I don't have to worry about any of that. I can't be busted."

Zorro asks, "What are you talking about?"

Juan answers, "I got permission to legally smoke."

"Yeah. From who?"

"From the government of the United States."

Crobar asks, "What? How is that? I've heard if you have glaucoma you can legally smoke and that the government will even give you the dope because weed lessens the pressure on the eyeballs?"

Zorro says, "You know the government grows acres of pot over in Mississippi but I've never heard what they do with it. Do you get it from there?"

"No," Juan answers, "I got to get it on my own although I have heard about Mississippi too and I'm trying to get some of it but haven't been able to figure out how."

"Okay," Johnny LaRue asks, "What's the deal? How do you have permission from the government?"

"I got it because I have two Purple Hearts."

Even though everyone figures he is bullshitting they still want to hear his explanation. Danny the plumber figures it might have something to do with Juan being a Mexican. He knows nothing about Mexicans but somehow thinks maybe there are different laws for them.

Zorro doesn't believe him at all. "Okay Juan. I've never heard that you can get permission to smoke weed if you have two Purple Hearts. Don't you get a Purple Heart for being wounded?"

Stan Mikilas has been sitting at the end of the table listening to all this. He is considerably older than the others. He fought in Korea in '51. "I'll tell you what it is," he tells them. "It is something you don't want but are proud of if you get. It is the only medal you are awarded for what happens to you not for something you do. It is also the oldest military award in the world that is still given."

"So how were you wounded?" Zorro asks him.

"I was wounded at the Battle of Pork Chop Hill."

"But how?"

"I was shot."

"Where were you shot?"

"I was shot in the foot."

"In the foot? How did that happen?"

"It was the worst battle of the war," Stan says. "We were under attack from all sides. Thousands of Chinese soldiers coming in wave after wave. For five days they came. Pork Chop Hill was blown to pieces. We had only a few trenches to get in for protection. Finally our withdrawal in armored personnel carriers made the Chinese think we were bringing in fresh troops and once all the Americans were off the hill we blasted it with a massive artillery attack killing hundreds of those slant-eyed bastards."

Zorro asks, "So the Americans won the battle?"

"Son there was no winner there. We had over a thousand killed."

"And you got shot?"

"Yeah."

"In the foot? How did that happen?"

"Okay. I shot myself when I was reloading my rifle on the fourth day of the assault and I didn't even know it. In the steady noise I couldn't hear my own rifle. I don't know what kept me from feeling it but I didn't. It wasn't until we were being evacuated that I looked down and saw the blood and realized I'd been shot. It took me awhile to realize what had happened."

"You mean you can get a medal for wounding yourself?"

"Not exactly. It has to be a battle wound. I was loading my rifle when it accidentally went off."

"And that counts?"

"Yes. I got a Purple Heart."

Johnny asks, "What does it look like?"

"It is a purple heart on a gold heart with a silhouette of George Washington in the middle hung from a purple ribbon."

"Why is George Washington on it? Because he was the first president?" asks Danny.

Stan answers, "Because he was the one who came up with the medal. It wasn't a medal to begin with it was just a purple cloth heart with the word 'merit' embroidered on it. Washington only gave out three. Some say they were given out because he didn't have the money to pay those three soldiers. Anyway that was it for a long time until Franklin Roosevelt revived it during World War II to be given to any soldier injured in battle."

Zorro asks, "So you just got one?"

"Yeah. That's all you can get. I don't know what Juan is talking about getting two. I mean you can be given the award each time you are wounded but you don't get another actual Purple Heart. After the first you get a bronze Oak Leaf Cluster for each injury. If you get five bronze Oak Leaf Clusters then you are given a silver Oak Leaf Cluster."

So there is something screwy about Juan's story. Maybe he just got tangled up in his explanation. His English is okay but he does get confused sometimes. In a way a bronze Oak Leaf Cluster is another Purple Heart. Maybe that's what he meant.

"Una momento," Juan says. "I'm still here. I'm not sure we are talking about the same thing. My Purple Heart has flames coming from it."

"Maybe that is some kind of Mexican version," Johnny says. "What else does it have?"

"On my two?"

"Yeah."

"Now just a minute yourself Juan. Why don't you tell us how you got your two Purple Hearts. Where were you anyway when you earned them?" asks Stan.

"In Vietnam."

"And when was that?"

"In 1958."

"I don't think so. The US was there but not in any official way. I really doubt any Purple Hearts were given out then."

"Yeah well I was there."

"Where?"

"All over."

Stan calls his bluff. "Do you have the papers you got from the government that says you can legally smoke dope for getting those Purple Hearts."

"Of course I do," and Juan pulls out his billfold and takes from it a piece of old, yellowed, crumbling paper. The print is faded to the point that it can hardly be read at all. From what can be made out it looks like an official document with some kind of official seal on it. Juan says, "Here. Go on and read it," handing it to Stan who takes it and tries but can hardly make out any words at all. There seems to be a salutation at the top to Juan or is it to John? In the text the word "permission" is fairly legible and maybe the word "marijuana" but it is right on a fold so only "mar . . . na" can be read. Maybe it says "marina."

Stan asks, "Were you ever in the Merchant Marines?"

Juan is insulted. "I don't even know what the Merchant Marines is. I got this 'permission' from the president for being injured in battle whether you want to believe it or not."

"President of what?" Zorro asks.

Juan has heard enough, has been questioned, insulted, disbelieved. He will just show them. He reaches into his shirt pocket and takes out a cigarette. "The president who can make it legal for me to smoke marijuana." he says. And he lights his cigarette but it takes just a second for everyone to realize what he has lit is not tobacco.

"Put that shit out," Zorro commands.

"Why man? I got permission."

"Even if you do, we don't. You are going to get us all in trouble man."

Juan says some Mexican word that they figure is a cuss word, snuffs his joint out, gets up, and leaves but before he goes he says, "I'm not going to come back but one more time. I'm going to bring my hearts tomorrow and then you won't see me no more." And he is gone. Crobar says, "I think we have seen the last of Juan Acosta." Everyone agrees and that's it. He doesn't come back the next day or the next. After a month or so the memory of him is no more than the faded scent of his smoke. For awhile the story of the Mexican who claimed he could smoke dope because he had two Purple Hearts gets retold every now and then. Maybe he couldn't tell such a good story but he left one that lingered.

Several months later the group is sitting outside on a cool fall day just before the patio will shut down for the winter when Crobar says, "Look. Across the street. That guy over there. Doesn't he remind you of Juan Acosta?"

Stan says, "Not me."

Johnny agrees but Crobar insists, "No. Come on it's him."

Zorro says, "Just because it is a Mexican that kinda looks like him . . ."

But when the Mexican glances over at The Quiet Man he does look a lot like Juan Acosta.

Then he is crossing the street and they all see he is back. He nearly gets hit by a station wagon, dodges it, and walks slowly toward The Quiet Man. He's wearing his khaki pants and shirt and carrying a brown, crumpled paper sack. He says nothing but walks right up to the table, stands there for a long moment, then sets down the sack. Zorro says, "Hello." Juan says, "Buenos dia," and stands silently for awhile longer before reaching into the sack and taking out a cardboard box that costume jewelry might have come in. He hands it to Zorro and says, "Open it." There is something a little scary about it but Zorro smiles and does as he is told. Its cheap hinges make a low creaking sound as it is opened to reveal its contents. Laying on tin foil is a red construction paper heart with a picture of Pancho Villa on horseback glued on it. Flames surround him. On each side of the heart is a dried-out, mummified joint. Zorro laughs and the rest of the table joins him. Juan Acosta does not even smile. He puts it back in the sack and takes out another box, a fine one covered in purple velvet, and hands it to Crobar. He doesn't tell her to but she holds it for a moment, feeling the weight of it before she unlatches a beautiful gold latch and opens the box. Its latches are finely made and filigreed and makes no sound as she opens it. Inside resting on velvet is a red heart with the silhouette of George Washington on it hanging from a purple ribbon. It has everything that a real Purple Heart like Stan described should have but it is red.

Juan says without being asked, "It is the light. Just wait until the sun is down a little so its rays are not direct and you will see something different."

Zorro asks, "Can I look at it?"

Juan says, "Yes," and Crobar hands him the box. He takes the medal out, holds it, and turns it over to see where the name of the person to whom it was awarded should be engraved but the name has been filed away. The file marks are still there. The color is wrong. The name is gone. Zorro puts it back in the box. Maybe Juan got it in a pawn shop or stole it. Who knows?

"Go on Juan," Stan says. "You can't fool me." But as he speaks the sun has nearly sunk behind The Quiet Man and right before the long shadow of the place moves over the table the color of the heart is no longer red but has become subtly purple.

Juan says to Zorro, "Pick it up," and Zorro does. "Turn it over and look at the back now."

In the fading light for just a moment beneath the file marks what looks like a name can be made out. The name is JUAN ACOSTA which can no longer be read after the sun is gone.

Juan closes the box. Picks it up and walks away. He leaves the sack on the table.

Nobody says anything for a few minutes until Johnny asks, "But that don't prove that he can legally smoke marijuana, does it?"

As Johnny is speaking Zorro opens the sack to have another look at the paper heart. As soon as it is opened the familiar smell of marijuana comes out but the heart is gone. Instead it is full of some of the prettiest little tight gold and red marijuana flowers that anyone has ever seen. Zorro closes it fast and in the same motion he and everyone at the table look down the street to see where Juan has gone and they see him one last time far away walking toward Highland Park. But just before he gets there he reaches the railroad tracks, turns down them, and is gone heading south.

Bob Goes to Live Under
Mary Kay's Pink Cadillac

In the early seventies, as the arcs of our postgraduate expectations seemed to be losing loft and conviction and the music seemed to be playing somewhat slower and the need to find a seat before it stopped had occurred to most, although not all, and everyone had already lived with everyone else for a time, it seemed, and the whole idea of domicile and self-reliance made for reluctant conversation—in this sad, departing summer of our lives, my friend the poet Robert Trammell lived for a while with me and my mom. My mom, an old freethinker herself, enjoyed my arty, pseudobohemian friends, and Bob, perhaps the artiest and most deeply pseudobohemian of us all, fit in quite happily, picking through her rather strange selection of books and watching bad TV in the evenings, though *Kung Fu* was pretty good. We really got into that *Kung Fu* test of enlightenment and reaction time, sometimes well into the night out on the patio, drinking our way toward the true way, snatching pebbles from each other's open hand. It was during this time that Bob—responding, perhaps, to these simple domesticities—conceived that it would be a most amazing and important and poetic thing were he to go and make his home beneath the big pink Cadillac we'd noticed always parked in the drive of the house, not far away, of a wealthy cosmetics manufacturer.

He sort of basked in this idea for a while. We'd joke about it. Marvel at the justice of it—his becoming something like a moral visitation, like gout, the painful consequence of opulence and excess. Or, a little more dramatically, the Phantom of the Opera or the Hunchback of Notre-Dame, the dark imponderable at the center of our loftiest affections. He began to imagine what he'd actually need: a few small tools, the means to siphon from the gas tank (for the camp stove) and the radiator (should there be some workable filtration system—failing that, a means for gathering rainwater or an expansion of the protocol to allow an occasional visit to the faucet or the pool while on those requisite excursions undertaken in the small despairing hours when the world is fast asleep and there is none to watch the slow, precise detaching of himself, the separation of the shadow from the mechanism, something like the soul released to drift across the lawn into the plantings for a while and maybe even into the dreams of she who sleeps above in splendor under fragrant moonlight-colored layers of anti-aging cream).

He would need lightweight, dark-colored, water-repellent clothing. Maybe a jacket for the colder months.

A flashlight and a radio. A picture of his Scandinavian girlfriend—in a little oval frame perhaps, with a magnet on the back. A pen, a notebook. Bungee cords and marijuana. He would probably need to consult one of those Chilton automotive guides devoted to that particular year and model. He would have to make a study, as would anyone preparing for an extended stay in some exotic country. As did Dracula, of course, before embarking on his fearful journey west. As did Thoreau, don't you imagine. Take your time and figure it out, devote yourself to the idea, and then, when it's right— you might want to wait for a storm, a terrible night with lightning scattering all across the city, rushing, twisting wind and bending trees and window-rattling thunder all night long—then you go in, in the middle of that, insert yourself as if the moment had developed from within the actual process of the storm.

And there you are. It seems impossible at first. But then you feel around and touch the blackened surfaces, inhale the dark eternity of this, the mix of fluids spilled and burned. The lightning flashing off wet concrete gives you glimpses of the structure so obscure in its reality, like the history of the underclass, ungraspable except by slow, assimilating stages. Not till dawn do things let up. The tattered clouds withdraw before the pink-and-golden light that, from an upstairs window, shows it's all okay—blown leaves and twigs and a branch or two in the drive but all is well. The pink of the Cadillac has never shown so purely pink before, as if there could be any purity in pink, as if it could be understood as fundamental, even primary, in some way—the blush of passion as experienced or as skillfully applied.

Bob felt there ought to be a point at which his instincts should turn inward. All his cunning with regard to stealth, concealment of the evidence—the smoke, the smells, the residue, the groanings in his sleep, those soft, unbidden little noises that emerge on contemplation of the photograph, whose bright, clean, snowy Scandinavian distance stretches out behind her fading smile forever—when all that has fallen away and he no longer needs to care, it is because he's come to inhabit the Cadillac truly and completely. He has come to understand his place within it. Found the yoga-like positions corresponding to the circumstances, sensed the pallid color of desire as emanating from himself, as percolating from these elemental regions where he rides along, essential to it now, adept at snatching raw materials from the street. Half-eaten meals and bits of clothing if he's lucky. All of life in its disintegrated forms comes back around to him. He's at that deep, regenerative level. At the level of the barnacle, the saint perhaps, the Cadillac infused with him at this point. They reduce toward one another, and inevitably there are compromises—subtle at first but gradually more detectable. Gas mileage suffers—hardly an issue ordinarily, of course, in such a vehicle. But noticeable after a while. A sort of lassitude or something about the steering, about the functioning in general—you can tell when something's changed, a general change, you know. Before you know it, even. An alteration in the basic terms of things. A Cadillac—well, that's a thing to be relied upon to carry certain assumptions. There's a mass and a momentum to appearances—that's one. Conviction overpowers error is another. Doubt is weakness. Life

is sweet. And so on. There are smells that come and go.
And dreams. And so at last it's taken in and hoisted up.
And there is quiet in the bay. Pneumatic power tools
fall silent. From within the glass-walled waiting room
she watches with her driver till she's summoned. Eyes
of four or five blue-uniformed mechanics fix upon her.
They withdraw at her approach, then stand around
not saying anything. Not getting back to work. A radio
somewhere across the shop plays Mexican songs of love
and loss. Her own mechanic stands by quietly with a
work light and a look of vast apology, as if to say there's
nothing he can do. As if, were she not dressed in such
a delicate print, her presentation of herself so near
the fragile verge of passion, pink and saffron shad-
ing into frail translucencies of age, all love and loss as
it turns out, he might reach out to take her shoulder,
guide her under. But she follows, gazes up with him.
A short, soft phrase in Spanish is repeated over and
over right behind—they've gathered in. The light's too
bright and there is nothing for a while. What should it
look like anyway? What should she be expected to find
in any case? She's never looked beneath her Cadillac
before. She's never listened to Mexican music on the
radio. She knows, of course, those mariachi bands that
play in restaurants—so exuberant and colorful and fes-
tive. Not like this. What is he saying over and over just
behind her? Like a prayer. She looks and looks until it
strains and starts to darken at the edges. Light draws
into a sort of halo, which surrounds a sort of face. Is
that a face? What sort of face is that—so battered and
composed? Is this what she's supposed to see? What is
he doing under her Cadillac? A couple of the mechanics

and a woman from the office have knelt down. Can she emerge from this somehow? She must look awful in this light. Is this a miracle? Is there another car that she can take? Can she be beautiful again?

—David Searcy

Thank you all
for your support.
We do this for you,
and could not do
it without you.

DEEP
VELLUM

PARTNERS

pixel ||| texel

ADDITIONAL DONORS, CONT'D

Mark Haber

Mary Cline

Maynard Thomson

Michael Reklis

Mike Soto

Mokhtar Ramadan

Nikki & Dennis Gibson

Patrick Kukucka

Patrick Kutcher

Rev. Elizabeth & Neil Moseley

Richard Meyer

Scott & Katy Nimmons

Sherry Perry

Sydneyann Binion

Stephen Harding

Stephen Williamson

Susan Carp

Susan Ernst

Theater Jones

Tim Perttula

Tony Thomson

SUBSCRIBERS

Joseph Rebella

Michael Lighty

Shelby Vincent

Margaret Terwey

Ben Fountain

Ryan Todd

Gina Rios

Elena Rush

Courtney Sheedy

Caroline West

Ned Russin

Laura Gee

Valerie Boyd

Brian Bell

Charles Dee Mitchell

Cullen Schaar

Harvey Hix

Jeff Lierly

Elizabeth Simpson

Michael Schneiderman

Nicole Yurcaba

Sam Soule

Jennifer Owen

Melanie Nicholls

Alan Glazer

Michael Doss

Matt Bucher

Katarzyna Bartoszynska

Anthony Brown

Elif Ağanoğlu

AVAILABLE NOW FROM DEEP VELLUM

MICHÈLE AUDIN · *One Hundred Twenty-One Days* · translated by Christiana Hills · FRANCE

BAE SUAH · *Recitation* · translated by Deborah Smith · SOUTH KOREA

MARIO BELLATIN · *Mrs. Murakami's Garden* · translated by Heather Cleary · MEXICO

EDUARDO BERTI · *The Imagined Land* · translated by Charlotte Coombe · ARGENTINA

CARMEN BOULLOSA · *Texas: The Great Theft* · *Before* · *Heavens on Earth*
translated by Samantha Schnee · Peter Bush · Shelby Vincent · MEXICO

MAGDA CARNECI · *FEM* · translated by Sean Cotter · ROMANIA

LEILA S. CHUDORI · *Home* · translated by John H. McGlynn · INDONESIA

MATHILDE CLARK · *Lone Star* · translated by Martin Aitken · DENMARK

SARAH CLEAVE, ed. · *Banthology: Stories from Banned Nations* ·
IRAN, IRAQ, LIBYA, SOMALIA, SUDAN, SYRIA & YEMEN

LOGEN CURE · *Welcome to Midland: Poems* · USA

ANANDA DEVI · *Eve Out of Her Ruins* · translated by Jeffrey Zuckerman · MAURITIUS

PETER DIMOCK · *Daybook from Sheep Meadow* · USA

CLAUDIA ULLOA DONOSO · *Little Bird,* translated by Lily Meyer · PERU/NORWAY

ROSS FARRAR · *Ross Sings Cheree & the Animated Dark: Poems* · USA

ALISA GANIEVA · *Bride and Groom* · *The Mountain and the Wall*
translated by Carol Apollonio · RUSSIA

FERNANDA GARCIA LAU · *Out of the Cage* · translated by Will Vanderhyden · ARGENTINA

ANNE GARRÉTA · *Sphinx* · *Not One Day* · *In/concrete* · translated by Emma Ramadan · FRANCE

JÓN GNARR · *The Indian* · *The Pirate* · *The Outlaw* · translated by Lytton Smith · ICELAND

GOETHE · *The Golden Goblet: Selected Poems* · *Faust, Part One*
translated by Zsuzsanna Ozsváth and Frederick Turner · GERMANY

NOEMI JAFFE · *What are the Blind Men Dreaming?* · translated by Julia Sanches & Ellen Elias-Bursac · BRAZIL

CLAUDIA SALAZAR JIMÉNEZ · *Blood of the Dawn* · translated by Elizabeth Bryer · PERU

PERGENTINO JOSÉ · *Red Ants* · MEXICO

TAISIA KITAISKAIA · *The Nightgown & Other Poems* · USA

JUNG YOUNG MOON · *Seven Samurai Swept Away in a River* · *Vaseline Buddha*
translated by Yewon Jung · SOUTH KOREA

KIM YIDEUM · *Blood Sisters* · translated by Ji yoon Lee · SOUTH KOREA

JOSEFINE KLOUGART · *Of Darkness* · translated by Martin Aitken · DENMARK

YANICK LAHENS · *Moonbath* · translated by Emily Gogolak · HAITI

FOUAD LAROUI · *The Curious Case of Dassoukine's Trousers* · translated by Emma Ramadan · MOROCCO

MARIA GABRIELA LLANSOL · *The Geography of Rebels Trilogy: The Book of Communities; The Remaining Life; In the House of July & August* translated by Audrey Young · PORTUGAL

PABLO MARTÍN SÁNCHEZ · *The Anarchist Who Shared My Name* · translated by Jeff Diteman · SPAIN

DOROTA MASŁOWSKA · *Honey, I Killed the Cats* · translated by Benjamin Paloff · POLAND

BRICE MATTHIEUSSENT· *Revenge of the Translator* · translated by Emma Ramadan · FRANCE

LINA MERUANE · *Seeing Red* · translated by Megan McDowell · CHILE

VALÉRIE MRÉJEN · *Black Forest* · translated by Katie Shireen Assef · FRANCE

FISTON MWANZA MUJILA · *Tram 83* · translated by Roland Glasser · DEMOCRATIC REPUBLIC OF CONGO

GORAN PETROVIĆ · *At the Lucky Hand, aka The Sixty-Nine Drawers* · translated by Peter Agnone · SERBIA

ILJA LEONARD PFEIJFFER · *La Superba* · translated by Michele Hutchison · NETHERLANDS

RICARDO PIGLIA · *Target in the Night* · translated by Sergio Waisman · ARGENTINA

SERGIO PITOL · *The Art of Flight* · *The Journey* · *The Magician of Vienna* · *Mephisto's Waltz: Selected Short Stories* translated by George Henson · MEXICO

JULIE POOLE · *Bright Specimen: Poems from the Texas Herbarium* · USA

EDUARDO RABASA · *A Zero-Sum Game* · translated by Christina MacSweeney · MEXICO

ZAHIA RAHMANI · *"Muslim": A Novel* · translated by Matthew Reeck · FRANCE/ALGERIA

JUAN RULFO · *The Golden Cockerel & Other Writings* · translated by Douglas J. Weatherford · MEXICO

ETHAN RUTHERFORD · *Farthest South & Other Stories* · USA

TATIANA RYCKMAN · *Ancestry of Objects* · USA

OLEG SENTSOV · *Life Went On Anyway* · translated by Uilleam Blacker · UKRAINE

MIKHAIL SHISHKIN · *Calligraphy Lesson: The Collected Stories* translated by Marian Schwartz, Leo Shtutin, Mariya Bashkatova, Sylvia Maizell · RUSSIA

ÓFEIGUR SIGURÐSSON · *Öræfi: The Wasteland* · translated by Lytton Smith · ICELAND

DANIEL SIMON, ED. · *Dispatches from the Republic of Letters* · USA

MUSTAFA STITOU · *Two Half Faces* · translated by David Colmer · NETHERLANDS

MÄRTA TIKKANEN · *The Love Story of the Century* · translated by Stina Katchadourian · SWEDEN

SERHIY ZHADAN · *Voroshilovgrad* · translated by Reilly Costigan-Humes & Isaac Wheeler · UKRAINE

FORTHCOMING FROM DEEP VELLUM

SHANE ANDERSON · *After the Oracle* · USA

MARIO BELLATIN · *Beauty Salon* · translated by David Shook · MEXICO

MIRCEA CĂRTĂRESCU · *Solenoid*
translated by Sean Cotter · ROMANIA

LEYLÂ ERBIL · *A Strange Woman*
translated by Nermin Menemencioğlu & Amy Marie Spangler· TURKEY

RADNA FABIAS · *Habitus* · translated by David Colmer · CURAÇAO/NETHERLANDS

SARA GOUDARZI · *The Almond in the Apricot* · USA

GYULA JENEI · *Always Different* · translated by Diana Senechal · HUNGARY

UZMA ASLAM KHAN • *The Miraculous True History of Nomi Ali* • PAKISTAN

SONG LIN · *The Gleaner Song: Selected Poems* · translated by Dong Li · CHINA

TEDI LÓPEZ MILLS · *The Book of Explanations* · translated by Robin Myers · MEXICO

JUNG YOUNG MOON · *Arriving in a Thick Fog*
translated by Mah Eunji and Jeffrey Karvonen · SOUTH KOREA

FISTON MWANZA MUJILA · *The Villain's Dance,* translated by Roland Glasser · *The River in the Belly: Selected Poems,* translated by Bret Maney · DEMOCRATIC REPUBLIC OF CONGO

LUDMILLA PETRUSHEVSKAYA · *Kidnapped: A Crime Story,* translated by Marian Schwartz · *The New Adventures of Helen: Magical Tales,* translated by Jane Bugaeva · RUSSIA

SERGIO PITOL · *The Love Parade* · translated by G. B. Henson · MEXICO

MANON STEFAN ROS · *The Blue Book of Nebo* · WALES

JIM SCHUTZE · *The Accommodation* · USA

SOPHIA TERAZAWA · *Winter Phoenix: Testimonies in Verse* · POLAND

BOB TRAMMELL · *Jack Ruby & the Origins of the Avant-Garde in Dallas & Other Stories* · USA

BENJAMIN VILLEGAS · *ELPASO: A Punk Story* · translated by Jay Noden · MEXICO